ORCHIDS TO
MURDER

AN AMOS LEE MAPPIN MYSTERY

ORCHIDS TO
MURDER

AN AMOS LEE MAPPIN MYSTERY

HULBERT FOOTNER

COACHWHIP PUBLICATIONS

Greenville, Ohio

CONTENTS

HULBERT FOOTNER (1879-1944)

HE WAS ALWAYS KNOWN as Bill; his chrism name was William Hulbert Footner; he was amused when sometimes at a party someone in a hurry to be intimate would hail him "Hulbert." Lots of things amused him; and he kept his wide grin under cover until there was someone he could split it with. (I always thought it characteristic how many times in his stories someone rubs his lips "to conceal a grin.")

I think Bill was pleased by the many times I told him that no living writer had given me such a total of innocent opiate and refuge. One reason why his detective tales have always been for me the perfect laxative is that I usually read them when I should be doing something else. I used to pride myself on having the most complete collection of Footners anywhere; but then I got the bad habit of parcelling them round in different hiding places (so that wherever I might be, there'd be a Footner available for bedtime or the after-lunch siesta). So now I'm not sure which are missing on loan, or which are simply cached in one of my five earth-boxes. But only yesterday, turning through some old papers, I found a letter from Woodrow Wilson, early 1921, thanking me for sending him *The Fugitive Sleuth*. So that's what happened to it! I remember Mr. Wilson, after leaving the White House, telling me he couldn't find enough really readable detective stories. So I sent him my precious *Fugitive Sleuth*. I think (I'm relying only on memory) it was Bill's first detective yarn. I read it in MS, way back about 1916, when I was contact man for Bill at his publishers. He

was the first author professionally assigned to me when I started
work at Doubleday's, in 1913. We hadn't been doing too well with
his early novels of the Canadian Northwest, and Bill wanted to
develop a new vein. He wrote *The Fugitive Sleuth* (first a serial in
one of the soft-paper magazines) as an experiment. I haven't read
it since Woodrow Wilson got my copy, but I think it dealt with Bill's
first detective, that delightful young enquiry agent B. Enderby, who
had an office somewhere on 34th Street. Thirty-fourth Street was
the great street of glamour in those days; right across from the
Hotel Madagascar as Bill always pseudoed the old Waldorf. And a
block away was the Vandermeer, which we would recognize as the
Vanderbilt. Bill had studied their exits and their entrances, and
many a lively chase took place through their lobbies and service
stairways. There followed *The Substitute Millionaire*, which I still
think a perfect plot for a movie; and many others.

For a good many years I knew Bill's books better than he did
himself. (In the list of titles he set down for *Who's Who in America*
he forgot quite a number of them.) I used to embarrass him by
pointing out unconscious mannerisms that he repeated from time
to time; or certain stock characters who took part, e.g. the stout
man walking up Fifth Avenue with a slapping archfallen behavior
of the feet, making more movement than progress. This, I sometimes had a horrid suspicion, was me. I reproached him, he denied
it, but retaliated by actually putting me and other friends (by name
and in person) in a crime story laid in Hoboken, *The Mystery of
the Folded Paper*, 1930. I think that was the first of the Amos Lee
Mappin series, which supplanted his superb creation Madame
Storey—the "psychological expert, specializing in the feminine." I
got very fond of pickwickian little Mr. Mappin after awhile, but for
my taste there never was any substitution for Mme. Storey. The
greatest mystery of all was the vanished and never explained Mon-
sieur Storey. Bill used to promise me he would some day Come
Clean about that, but he never did. My own suspicion was that Mr.
Mappin was really M. Storey.

What fun Bill had in describing the luxurious living-quarters
of Mme. Storey in her maisonette in the East 60's, and Lee

Mappin's costly apartment overhanging the East River somewhere in the 50's. When Bill's own budget was a little austere, as a writer's often is, he had special amusement in giving Rosika Storey or Lee Mappin the best of everything. Verandah-suites in Atlantic liners, blue-ribbon chefs, the most humorously attractive secretaries or faithful impassive butlers were all in the day's work; and among the clients would frequently appear an actress of dazzling beauty at the top of her renown.

Footner's first love was the stage. If I remember truly, this may have been because when he came to New York as a boy in his teens (he was Canadian by birth) he lived in a lodging which looked out on the stage-door alley of a famous old theatre on 23rd Street. Then later, when he was doing clerical work in a financial office downtown (I think it was the unforgotten Sterling Debenture Corporation) he lived in a room above a midtown chophouse. When the weather was fine he spent his off-time in a canoe on the North River. I think he remains one of the few who ever amused themselves paddling zig-and-zag across the bows of Atlantic liners and Jersey City ferries. It was symbolic of much in his life; he always deftly steered across and between and among all kinds of heavy craft; smiling his intrepid grin, and having much more fun than they. I think that was in his period as actor, when a vaudeville skit he had written (with quite serious purpose) proved to be a comedy hit because either he, or his Ingenue Lead, stumbled over the sill of the stage door and fell flat on her face at her first entrance. This was at the tryout opening somewhere in Connecticut; it got a big hand, and they shrewdly switched it to farce, and toured it profitably. Then, I don't know how, Bill got a small part—as a matter of fact he doubled as Bassick and Sir Edward Leighton—in the road company of Gillette's dramatization of *Sherlock Holmes*. I think I remember his telling me that at first he was the Cabman in Act Four, whose only line was "I've got 'er, sir"; which he must have delivered with such power that he was promoted. Bill wrote a number of plays, some produced and some not, but I'm sure his high moment in the theatre was Christmas night, 1916, when Elsie Ferguson opened (at the Hudson) in his *Shirley Kaye* and he and

Mrs. Footner left at the fall of the final curtain for a maternity hospital. Their first child and the critics' notices were published almost simultaneously.

With unfaltering courage and conscience Uncle Bill (so we always called him in my family) wrote thirty or so detective novels because by some odd chance that proved to be a way of earning a living. It was a market increasingly overcrowded; his own vein, which underplayed rather than overpushed his effects, could not possibly become fashionable, and his own sly deliberately casual social comments were often lost on the Whodunit trade. In midstream of this hard work he wrote a couple of novels of entirely different mood; I still think if they had been issued over a pseudonym they might have had more attentive reception. They are sombre, sardonic, blunt with knowledge of human trouble. I mean *Antennae*, 1926, and *More Than Bread*, 1938. They were of great importance to their author, for they gave him a chance to express certain stoic observations on the human comedy he had watched unflinchingly. And then, by happy chance, he gave himself liberty to do something in more personal vein—which was what all who knew him well most relished. He had done it beautifully in early days, an account of his explorations in the untrodden space of northern Canada (*New Rivers of the North*, 1912). Now, so long later, he wrote a testament of his love of New York City (*New York, City of Cities*, 1937) and then his most moving and heart-opening book about *Charles' Gift*, 1939, the love story of his thirty-year devotion to an old house on the Western Shore of the Chesapeake. There, in the mood of intimate confidence that never says too much, he wrote pages that are perfect and permanent. At Charles' Gift, one of the most ancient manor houses of Maryland, he had found what he needed and what needed him. How delightful it was, when he came to New York for a few days of skirmish among old friends or publishers, to see him retire again to his Chesapeake solitude; where he had his own deep and meditating pleasure thinking it over. And I don't think he ever quite realized the competition among his overworked New York friends to have him with them for an evening of his own candid understanding talk. How expert he always was in evading what was merely fashionable and getting into a corner with what was true. He had had a full and complete life: his own eras of bohemianism, of adventure, of family devotion, of nose to the grindstone. Artists in all fields had learned to respect his comments. I remember with gratitude Max Beerbohm's comment, that Footner was the most civilized American he had ever met.

The day I heard of his death I had just brought back, from a cabin on Long Island Sound which Footner himself had often visited, a large weathered Christmas Log I intended to burn for festival. I heard that Bill had gone (suddenly, without long misery, as he would most have wished) and I carried onto the hearth the great oak stump I had chosen. All day and night it glowed, clear and steady and kind, like his own seasoned affection. I kept thinking of it as his memorial.

Christopher Morley
December 19, 1944

CHAPTER ONE

JERMYN, AMOS LEE MAPPIN's lean, leathery man-servant, entered his master's bedroom and coughed discreetly. Though it was nearly nine o'clock on Monday morning, Mr. Mappin, making a little rounded hill of the bedclothes, was still slumbering peacefully. There had been a late party on Sunday night. He awoke and looked at Jermyn with a not altogether friendly eye. That stolen hour of sleep in the morning was so delicious!

"What is it, Jermyn?"

"Sorry to disturb you, sir. Major Dunphy is here."

Mr. Mappin scowled. "Good God! that crashing bore!" He glanced at the clock on the dresser. "Nine o'clock! What on earth does he want?"

"He didn't care to tell me, sir. He apologized for coming so early. He appears to be extremely agitated, sir."

"He's easily agitated. Why did you let him in?"

"How could I avoid it, sir? He mentioned the name of his granddaughter, Miss Stannard. She seems to be lost, sir."

Lee stared at Jermyn with a changed expression. After a moment he swung his legs out of the bed. "Miss Stannard? What the devil! He didn't expect to find her here, did he? It's some absurd notion that he's got in his head. I'll get rid of him as fast as I can."

"He's waiting in the living room, sir."

"All right. Make me some coffee. I'll have breakfast after he goes."

Jermyn retired and Lee got out of bed. He thrust his feet into a pair of morocco slippers, wound a white silk muffler around his

12

neck, and shouldered himself into one of the gaudy dressing gowns he affected at home—this one was crimson in color. He didn't have to brush his hair because he didn't have any, except a fringe around the base of his skull.

In the living room, a huge chamber with a balcony high above the East River, he found Major Dunphy sitting stiffly on the edge of a sofa, impatiently slapping his thigh with a pair of chamois gloves. Early as it was, the Major's toilet had been performed with his usual care. Beside him on a table lay the hard-shell derby hat that he continued to wear after everybody else had left them off. The only thing missing was the customary carnation in his button-hole. This denoted a considerable state of perturbation.

The Major was over seventy, and had the look of having been preserved under a thin film of paraffin. His still plentiful hair was unnaturally black, but his heavy eyebrows were genuinely black, and under them his eyes still burned with a kind of irascible fire. He wriggled forward on the sofa and pushed himself up with his hands. His bodily movements were somewhat restricted owing to the fact that when he was dressed to go out, he had too much chest and too little belly for his age. He commenced a perfunctory apology to Lee, but it was clear he didn't mean a word of it, being far too full of his own grievances.

Lee waved the apology aside. "I knew it must be important," he said, "or you would have telephoned. Sit down, Major."

The Major performed that somewhat complicated evolution. "My granddaughter has disappeared!" he said, more in anger than sorrow.

"How do you mean, disappeared?" asked Lee patiently. "I talked with her yesterday on the telephone."

"Mary left the house sometime before nine o'clock last night," said the Major. "Without a word of good-by," he added bitterly.

Lee, glancing at the old face twisted with self-pity and resentment, could not feel surprised. "Well, she's a free agent," he said mildly.

"But the circumstances were so suspicious; so many lies were told, I don't know what to think!"

Lee's eyeglasses glittered. They afforded a certain cover for his eyes; otherwise the old man must have seen that he was thinking: Well, if Mary has finally walked out on the old leech, I for one wouldn't be surprised.

Jermyn entered to tell his master that the coffee was ready.

"Will you join me?" Lee asked the Major.

The old man's voice quavered. "I don't mind if I do, Mr. Mappin. I wasn't able to eat any breakfast."

Lee felt a momentary compassion for him. He was a horrible old man and everybody disliked him; still he *was* old.

The coffee was poured. Jermyn retired from the room. The Major, holding his cup in a hand that trembled a little, sipped the contents gratefully.

"And so I come to you for help," he went on. "You have had so much experience in such matters and I believe that you are Mary's true friend—perhaps the only one she has."

"Indeed I wish to be her friend," said Lee heartily. "I seem to renew my youth when I am in her company. She has that effect on one. I am very, very fond of her."

"Oh, everybody falls for Mary!" sneered the Major.

Lee looked at his cup and let that pass. "Better tell me the whole circumstances," he said. "I don't understand your references to lies. Mary has such a candid character."

"Not with me!" said the Major. "I'm the old nuisance that has to be lied to and shut up."

Lee said nothing.

"As you know," resumed the Major, acid and garrulous as an old woman, "the play closed unexpectedly on Saturday night though it was a sellout at every performance. It was given out that the star, Lily Sartoris, has had a nervous breakdown. That's a fake. Everybody knows that the Sartoris woman is furious because my Mary stole the play. I happen to know that Wilson Carsley wished to give Mary the star part and continue, but Mary refused because she said she wanted a vacation. Mary herself didn't tell me anything—she never does, but I had that on the best authority . . ."

Lee interrupted. "Well, never mind about Lily Sartoris; let's stick to Mary."

"After the performance on Saturday night she went to a late party, as usual," the Major continued bitterly. "Nobody cares if I spend my nights alone. All day yesterday she and Lottie Vickers, her maid, were busy in her room over some mysterious preparations. When I went to the door I was shooed away with scant ceremony. I didn't see Mary to talk to her until dinnertime, and then she was absent-minded all through the meal. I addressed my remarks to the empty air. At the end of the meal she merely said she had decided to go up to the inn at Greencliffe Manor in Dutchess County to stay until Lily Sartoris recovered. She'd be leaving shortly before nine o'clock, she said. She was tired, she claimed, of late parties and empty gabble and drinking, and wanted a complete rest in the country in spring. And all the time her eyes were sparkling with anticipation. Anybody could have seen that she was lying."

The Major paused and took a swallow of coffee with a very wry face. "When I naturally remonstrated with her at having this sprung on me," he resumed, "and pointed out that I would be left alone in the house every night—our two servants sleep out, as you may know—she said she had arranged to have Lottie Vickers sleep in while she was away—small comfort Lottie would be to me! I confess that such a total disregard for my comfort made me a little angry. When I continued to question her about this sudden desire for the country, she merely looked at me without speaking and went up to her room and closed the door. This was something new, because in the past, when I ventured to remonstrate with her, she at least condescended to hear me out. So to rebuke her, I went to my room."

Lee's level look at the Major suggested that he was asking himself: What can one do with such a selfish old ass?

"I did not see her again," the Major went on. "She did indeed leave somewhere around nine o'clock. It was not until I heard the telephone ringing downstairs at quarter past nine that I realized I was alone in the house."

"Who called up?" asked Lee.

"Nina Gannon," said the Major sourly, "Mary's special and particular pal."

"What did Mrs. Gannon want?"

"Wanted to know where Mary was. Said she had a date to meet her at nine o'clock and she hadn't turned up."

"'Well, she's gone,' I said. 'Where was she to meet you?' Nina hesitated before answering and then said: 'At my place.' So I guessed she was lying. I said: 'Mary told me she was going up to Greencliffe Manor tonight.' 'Oh, that would be later tonight,' said Nina. When I attempted to question her further, she hung up. . . . Nina Gannon does not like me," the Major concluded resentfully, "and I must say that her sentiments are heartily reciprocated. I have always considered her to be an unfortunate influence on Mary."

This communication made Lee look vaguely anxious, because he knew that Nina Gannon was honestly Mary's friend.

"So I went to bed," the Major continued. "I spent a miserable night, tossing and turning; never closed my eyes. At eight this morning the telephone rang again. In the meantime I had switched the connection to the phone in my study on the third floor. It was Nina Gannon again. Wanted to know if I had heard from Mary. Sounded anxious. I said no. I couldn't get anything out of her. She made believe to pass it off as of no account. I then called up the inn at Greencliffe Manor and was told that Miss Stannard was not stopping there, and that no reservation had been made for her."

"If she wanted quiet and seclusion she would have registered under another name," suggested Lee.

"I thought of that," answered the Major. "I asked and was told that no new guests registered after dinner last night. No reservations have been made for any single young lady. That very seriously disturbed me so I came to consult you."

"Well, I'm sure everything is all right," said Lee with more confidence than he felt. "You can't apply ordinary standards to our brilliant and famous Mary. Very likely there is a message from her waiting for you at home now."

The Major shook his head. "The cook and housemaid came at the usual hour this morning. I left word with them that I was coming to your apartment, and told them to relay any message that might arrive. Nothing has come."

Lee made an effort to conquer his dislike of the old man. "I'll dress and have a spot of breakfast," he said heartily. "Then I'll go back to your house with you, and we'll see what is to be done, if anything. Or perhaps you'd prefer to go right back and let me follow?"

"I'll wait for you," said the Major.

LEE AND THE MAJOR made their way on foot to Mary Stannard's house. After a series of parts in unsuccessful plays, when Mary finally found herself in the money she had rented this little furnished house far east on Fifty-second Street, around two corners from Lee's apartment house. Once a low-class neighborhood, it had become one of the most fashionable addresses in town. The old-fashioned little brownstone front, one of a long row, had been altered into a smart English basement dwelling with all the modern gadgets. The former basement entrance was now the front door.

A smiling housemaid admitted them. Clearly she had no suspicion that there was anything wrong. No messages had come during the Major's absence, she said.

The kitchen lay to the right of the entrance hall and the back part of the former basement now constituted a charming dining room with the whole rear wall of glass, looking out on a garden gay, at this season, with narcissi, jonquils and early tulips.

While they were in the dining room, the Major suddenly said: "I forgot to mention that Mary received a male visitor last night shortly before she disappeared."

"So?" said Lee. "Who was it?"

"I don't know. At a few minutes past eight I heard the front doorbell ring. The servants had just gone home. I went out in the hall and leaned over the stair rail to listen. I heard Mary go down to the door, and I heard the rumble of a man's voice, but I couldn't hear anything that was said. She brought him up to the living room and went in and closed the door. I don't know how long he stayed. She must have let him out very softly, because I heard nothing though I left my door open. Or perhaps she went with him."

This sounded a little fishy to Lee. "Didn't you look out of the front window?" he asked.

"Yes. There was a red convertible coupe standing in front of our house. It had a khaki top which was up. When I looked again later, the car was gone, but of course I can't be sure that Mary's caller came in it. It was a fine car, bigger than a Ford or a Chevvy; at that distance I couldn't tell the make or read the license number."

"So," said Lee. "Let's take a look at the garden."

"Why?" asked the old man in surprise.

"No particular reason. While I'm here I want to see everything."

Outside the dining room there was a narrow, stone-paved terrace where one could breakfast in warm weather. A tiny fountain played near by. Back of the terrace a rock garden with some winding steps ascended to the level of the original back yard. Both the rock garden and the flat beds above were bright with spring flowers. Against the back fence rose an ailanthus tree.

Lee strolled between the flower beds. All had been freshly dug and cultivated. "How beautifully kept it is," he murmured.

"Mary spent a ridiculous amount of money on it," said the Major peevishly.

The thought flitted through Lee's head: A body could have been buried under one of the flower beds and the whole raked over neatly afterwards. He glanced speculatively at the Major. He's old, thought Lee, but he seems able. I suppose he would be Mary's legal heir. But she couldn't have left much, she was so extravagant.

Lee examined all the flower beds with renewed care, but could find no evidence that the subsoil had been thrown to the surface in any place. Looking around, he noted that the back windows of the house on either side commanded a view of the yard. In the next street there were apartment houses with scores of windows looking down on Mary's flowers. There was a tiny shed leaning against the back fence, masked with privet. It was not locked and Lee, glancing inside, saw the usual array of garden tools, spade, shovel, rake, hoes, clippers, etc.,—nothing else. None of the tools betrayed signs of having been used within the past twelve hours.

"What's in your mind?" asked the Major nervously.

"Nothing as yet," said Lee.

CHAPTER TWO

RETURNING INDOORS, Lee and the Major ascended to what had been the parlor floor of the original house. It had now, saving the stair well, been thrown into one long living room with windows looking on the street at one end and looking out on the garden at the other. Among the sameness of most New York rooms, it had an original and attractive aspect, and that was why Mary had taken the house.

The housemaid was cleaning the room. On top of a basket of trash lay a white cardboard box about ten inches long, and Lee picked it up. It bore the business card of Schracht, a florist on Lexington Avenue. Also in the basket lay a sheet of oiled paper and the outer wrapping of the box.

"When did this come?" asked Lee.

"Don't know," grumbled the Major.

"Must have been sometime yesterday, sir," said the maid. "I tidied the room yesterday morning."

Lee examined the wrapping paper. "No address on it," he said. "The giver must have brought the flowers. We may suppose that it was a man. Did Miss Mary have any gentlemen visitors yesterday?"

"No, sir. Not up until the time I went home at eight o'clock." She curtsied and edged out of the room.

"There was one came after eight, as I told you," put in the Major.

"Surely," said Lee. "Then he must have brought the flowers. And since no flowers were found, she must have worn them when she went out."

20

Lee kept the box. "I may need it later," he said. Nothing else of special interest was found in the living room, and they proceeded to Mary's own suite on the floor above. It consisted of two large rooms with bathroom and wardrobes between; in front lay Mary's sitting room with a south exposure, in the rear her bedroom. Both rooms were gay with chintz upholstery and hangings. In the boudoir, Mary's desk was open and it had the look of having recently been cleaned out. A little heap of charred paper lay in the fireplace.

"Looks as if she was clearing out for good!" said the Major with excessive bitterness. "Leaving me with this house on my hands! I have no money to keep it going!"

"Nonsense!" said Lee sharply. "It would be totally unlike Mary to leave anybody in the lurch like that. Some explanation will be forthcoming before long."

Meanwhile Lee knelt before the fireplace. On the edge of the charred papers lay two scraps only partly burned through. One bore the name of a place, Elkton, Maryland; the other showed part of a person's name in the same writing; it looked like McCallum. Lee examined the quality of the paper closely and held each piece to the light. They were clearly parts of the same sheet. He showed them to the Major.

The old man shook his head sullenly. "Means nothing to me," he said.

Lee transferred the scraps to an envelope from Mary's desk and thence to his pocket. "They may provide clues," he said, "if we find that we are going to need clues."

All the other papers in the fireplace had been completely destroyed.

In the middle of Mary's bedroom lay a suitcase large enough to hold dresses, and a matching case, both very smart and expensive. It was evident from the weight that they had been packed. Yet the wardrobes were still full of other clothes.

"You see, she has not gone for good," said Lee.

"We'd better see what's inside those cases," said the Major.

Lee shook his head. "I don't like to search among her things until I feel that it is necessary. In an hour we may be laughing at our fears."

Nevertheless, the Major proceeded to try the locks. "They're locked," he said. "We'll have to break them open."

"Let them alone for the present," said Lee.

They heard a ring at the front door and eagerly looked up.

"Now we'll learn something," said Lee.

Somebody came up the stairs. Lee looked out through the door and his anxious face lightened at the sight of Lottie Vickers, Mary's maid at the theater; middle-aged, portly, comely and good-natured. She carried a satchel containing her night things.

"Come in here, Lottie," said Lee. "We're anxious about Miss Mary. She went away last night without leaving any word. Do you know where she's gone?"

Lottie betrayed no alarm, but her reply was guarded. "She told me she was going to the country for a rest, Mr. Mappin. I am to sleep in her room until we hear from her further."

"But where did she go?"

Lottie hesitated before answering. "She didn't tell me, sir," she said, glancing at the old man.

Lee observed the glance. "Major," he said cajolingly, "will you excuse me for a few moments? I want to have a little talk with Lottie."

The old man flared up irascibly. "What have you got to say to her servant that *I* shouldn't hear?" he demanded. "Am I nobody in my own house? Sent out of the room like a child!"

Lee took his arm and eased him toward the door. "You get me wrong, Major," he murmured soothingly. "I don't want to keep anything from you. It was only because I thought I could persuade this woman to talk more freely if you were out of the way. She's probably scared to death of you."

The Major refused to be mollified. "Secrets! Secrets! Secrets!" he grumbled. "I'm fed up with secrets!" However, he allowed Lee to lead him out of the door and to close it after him.

After waiting a moment, Lee opened the door again. The Major was still lingering outside. Lee said nothing. The Major started stumping downstairs, puffing out his cheeks and looking very angry in an effort to save his face.

Lee returned to Lottie. "Miss Mary told her grandfather that she was going up to Greencliffe Manor last night," he said.

"That's what she told me," said Lottie. "I didn't like to let on. She generally has to keep things from him because he carries on so hateful."

"Quite," said Lee. "But Miss Mary didn't go to Greencliffe Manor. She made no reservations there. She isn't there now."

They looked at each other with a growing anxiety. The woman's hand stole to her breast.

"There is no reason that I can see why she should lie to you," said Lee.

"No, sir . . . Oh, my poor young lady!"

Lee began pacing the room. "Good Lord, don't carry on!" he said irritably. "There may be nothing in it. But I can't just sit still and do nothing. You must help me, Lottie. You were in her confidence."

"Only just so far, Mr. Mappin. She's the kindest and friendliest mistress I ever had and I love her like my daughter. But she never talked about her personal affairs. I didn't expect it of her. I only served her in the theater, you know. She said she didn't need a maid at home."

"You were here yesterday, helping her pack?"

"Yes, sir."

"And she gave you no clue then as to what was passing in her mind?"

"Well, sir, it did come to me that she was plotting something."

"Plotting!" said Lee, coming to a stand.

"Oh, in a perfectly nice way, sir. As if something very nice was before her. I could tell it from the lift in her voice and from her eyes."

"Her eyes?"

"They looked starry, Mr. Mappin. That means only one thing."

"Who is the man?"

She hesitated. "You won't tell him?" she said, pointing downstairs. "He hates him."

"I shall not tell him."

Lottie hung her head. "I'm afraid," she stammered; "I'm afraid it's Mr. Jack Fentress."

"Oh God!" groaned Lee. "He's not fit to tie her shoe!"

"That's what I say, sir."

Lee paced the room savagely. "My beautiful, clever Mary! There seems to be a sort of electrical quality in that young man that no woman can resist. It's only physical. I never thought Mary would fall for it."

"She's a woman, too, sir," said Lottie softly.

"Are you sure you're right about Fentress, Lottie?"

"Pretty sure, sir. She's been going with him since before I started to work for her. He never came around the theater much, but she saw him outside. She had his photograph in the drawer of her dressing table at the theater, and looked at it often."

"I never suspected such a thing!" groaned Lee.

"If you'll excuse me, sir, Miss Mary was a deep one, meaning it in a perfectly nice way. She never talked about her personal affairs. I've heard her say with a laugh that it was the only way she could avoid lying. She never lied. But she could keep her mouth shut."

"You're right. And you think Fentress has something to do with her peculiar actions yesterday?"

"Pretty sure of it, sir."

"When did she see him last?"

"At the theater after the show on Saturday night. Miss Mary gave a little party and asked Mr. Fentress and Mrs. Gannon and Ewart Blanding. . . ."

"Blanding!" said Lee, staring. "You mean her chauffeur?"

"Her former chauffeur. There's a fine fellow, sir. Much above his station. He's a law student and supports himself by driving a car. Handsome, too. You've seen him, sir."

Lee shook his head. "No. I have been to Mary's house and to her dressing room at the theater, but, so far as I know, I never laid eyes on her chauffeur."

"Well, she made a friend of him while he was working for her," Lottie went on. "The poor young fellow was absolutely gone on her. The real thing. You hear a lot of talk about love, but the real thing is not so common. Blanding was absolutely a goner. He couldn't hide it. I believe that's the reason she sold her car and let him go. She *said* that the car was too great an extravagance for her to keep in town. So she let him go and work for Miss Amy Dordress, the one the newspapers call the poor little rich girl."

"But she continued to see Blanding?"

"Oh yes, sir. She wouldn't cut him off all at once. She was too kindhearted. She wanted to ease him out of it."

"And she asked him to supper Saturday night?"

"Yes, sir. He came to the theater. He and Mr. Fentress didn't like each other. Started making nasty remarks right off the bat. They went to La Perouse restaurant. Yesterday I asked Miss Mary if they had a good time and she shook her head. Said she was a fool to ask Fentress and Blanding on the same night. So I suppose they quarreled. . . . There was another gentleman asked to the supper party," Lottie went on, "but he refused to come. Miss Mary was sorry. That was Mr. George Restorick."

"The real estate millionaire," said Lee.

"Yes, sir. He's been in love with Miss Mary, too, for a long time past, but he's an older man; he had his feelings under better control—though he looks as if he might be a terror, once he got going. Miss Mary depended on him a lot because he had more sense than any of the young men. They were real good friends. Startled me sometimes, they were so outspoken with each other. . . ."

"That was Mary's way," murmured Lee.

"Once Mrs. Gannon asked Miss Mary in my hearing why the hell she didn't take George Restorick and have done with it. Excuse me, sir, but that's the way Mrs. Gannon put it. And Miss Mary said George was a grand man and any girl would be lucky if she got him. But he was too rich for her, she said; such a life would suffocate her. I heard Miss Mary tell Mrs. Gannon that George Restorick had said he'd be damned if he'd come to her party. They both laughed."

Lee found Jack Fentress' number in the telephone book and asked for it at the phone. Lottie started signaling to him, and he put a hand over the transmitter.

"Be careful what you say, sir," said Lottie. "The old man can cut in on the line from the ground floor."

"I have that in mind," said Lee.

At the switchboard of an apartment house, a boy rang Fentress' apartment, and presently reported that there was no answer. Lee hung up. With Nina Gannon he had better luck. She answered promptly.

"This is Amos Lee Mappin," he said, "Mary Stannard's friend. Perhaps you know who I am."

"Everybody knows Mr. Mappin," answered Nina's gratified voice.

"Can I come around and see you for a few moments? I am a little anxious about Mary."

"Oh, *do* come, Mr. Mappin! I am anxious, too!"

CHAPTER THREE

MRS. GANNON OCCUPIED a small but very smart apartment just off Fifth Avenue in the thick of things. She was a dark, thin little woman with a passion for keeping what she called her figure. She enjoyed a moderate income as a result of some former marital association—the circumstances were obscure—and she had nothing in the world to do but amuse herself. Her dresses and hats were always a little ahead of the most advanced fashions; she had been nominated as one of the ten best-dressed women. In her sleekness and perfect grooming, she always reminded Lee of a toy black and tan terrier; her sharp, quick voice was like the yapping of such a little dog, too. Lee did not care much for her, but she had one great merit in his eyes; she was devoted to Mary Stannard.

The moment Lee entered her pretty living room, she exploded a bombshell. "Mary and Jack Fentress were to have been married last night."

"What?" cried Lee.

"It's quite true. In the chantry of St. Michael's and All Angels'. Jim Rutledge and I were on hand to stand up with them. But Mary never showed up."

"Good God!" cried Lee. "Why was she so secretive about it?"

"That was because she knew her friends didn't think much of Jack. . . . Oh, there's nothing specially wrong with Jack," she hurried on, "he doesn't drink too much—at least no more than anybody else these drinking days—and I never heard anything very discreditable about him. But he has no brains, he has no money,

27

he isn't even particularly handsome. There's nothing to him but that curious magnetic attraction that he has for women—and that sort of thing doesn't last."

"You have felt it?" murmured Lee.

"Of course I have! The worst of it is, I have felt sometimes that Mary was secretly aware she was backing the wrong horse. But she couldn't help herself. This has been going on for a long time. She was determined to marry him."

"I take it you opposed it," suggested Lee.

"I did not," said Nina sharply. "I was too much afraid of losing Mary. When a girl is in that state, to oppose her is like throwing gasoline on the fire. She knew I didn't approve of what she was doing but I never *said* a word." Nina put her handkerchief to her eyes. "Ah! my poor Mary was too innocent! A more experienced woman would have known that such a feeling, however powerful, quickly burns itself out."

"But you said the marriage did not take place," said Lee. "Perhaps Mary's better self got the upper hand at the last moment."

"Not much chance! She was too far gone in love for that. I cannot help but feel that she was *prevented* from coming. Other men were in love with her. I fear that something terrible has happened." Nina broke down and wept into her handkerchief.

In such a brisk and self-confident little woman, Lee found it very affecting. "Please, *please*," he said in distress. "Don't imagine the worst until we have something to go on! . . . Mary told her grandfather that she was going up to Greencliffe Manor Inn."

Nina nodded. "Yes. That's what she told me. For the honeymoon."

"In that case it seems strange that no reservations were made for them."

"Very strange indeed!" Nina wept afresh.

"Please try to pull yourself together!" begged Lee. "I need your help. Tell me exactly what took place last night."

Nina called in her sobs. "Well, you know St. Michael's and All Angels' Church on lower Fifth Avenue. It has a little chapel that they call the chantry, very popular for marriages. And Reverend Damien Stair, the sporting parson, he's well liked by the people we know. The wedding was set for nine o'clock. Jim Rutledge and I were on hand in good time. We waited in the vestry off the chapel, chatting with the minister. Jack was late, but only a minute or two. He breezed in with a policeman."

"A policeman!"

"He explained that he had run through a red light on Broadway in his excitement, and was stopped. He tried to talk himself out of it by saying he was on his way to be married, and since the church was only a block away the policeman came with him to check his story. When he found it was true, he shook hands with everybody and went away."

"Go on," said Lee.

"Jack was in the customary state of a prospective bridegroom; dithering with excitement and scared as hell. Kept pulling the ring out of his pocket to make sure he had it. He was carrying a little box . . ."

"What was in it?" interrupted Lee.

"I don't know. It was never opened. Orchids for the bride, I suppose."

"You didn't happen to notice what florist it was from?"

"The box was wrapped in plain white paper. There was nothing written or printed on it."

"How big a box?"

Nina measured with her hands. "About ten inches long, four inches wide and four inches deep."

"You don't know what became of it?"

"No. It was lost sight of in the excitement."

"Well, go on."

"As the minutes passed without bringing Mary, Jack became wild with anxiety. Jim asked him why the devil he hadn't made sure of her by bringing her down himself, and he said he wanted to, but Mary wouldn't allow it because of the old superstition that a bride and groom mustn't see each other before the ceremony on the wedding day. At quarter past nine I called up Mary's house and the old man said she had left some time before, he couldn't say exactly how long."

"Wait a minute," put in Lee. "Had the old man been told of the wedding?"

"Certainly he had *not* been told," said Nina. "But he might have guessed what was up. Selfish old brute! The mere suggestion that Mary might marry and leave him put him in a rage. He hated every young man who seemed to have serious intentions, but he had a special and poisonous hatred for Jack Fentress. Just for the sake of peace, Jack kept away from the house."

"What happened after you telephoned?"

"Nothing. We waited nearly an hour. The parson was very patient. Jack was in a pitiable state. He assumed that he'd been jilted. He made up his mind that Mary had finally fallen for her millionaire admirer."

"George Restorick?"

"Yes. We finally left the church, after Jack had made the parson promise to say nothing of what had happened. We walked up and down in the street for fifteen or twenty minutes longer. There seemed to be nothing we could do. I must say I wasn't altogether displeased with what had happened. I thought then, as you did, that perhaps Mary had seen the light at the last moment. It wasn't until you called me up this morning that I became really frightened. The boys drove me home in Jack's car and went away together. I have heard nothing from them. Very likely Jack got drunk. You could scarcely blame him."

There was a silence while Lee considered what he had been told. He said: "You spoke a while ago of other men who were in love with Mary. Whom had you in mind?"

"You must not think that I suspect anybody," Nina said quickly. "Neither of the two men who loomed biggest in the picture would be capable of harming Mary."

"One was George Restorick," suggested Lee. "The other? . . ."

"Ewart Blanding."

"Yes. Lottie Vickers told me something about him."

"A man in a thousand," said Nina. "The sort of young fellow who could take the job of chauffeur without apologizing for it, without losing a bit of his independence and self-respect. And how he loved Mary! He never had the slightest hope of winning her, poor fellow. Jack was ahead of him. Ewart did his best to hide his feelings, but of course he couldn't—not from me, anyhow. It was the real thing, Mr. Mappin."

"Lottie's words," murmured Lee.

"It was the sort of love," Nina went on, "that every woman dreams of arousing in a man, but it seldom happens. If any man had ever loved me like that I'd be a better woman."

"What about Restorick?"

"A fine man!" said Nina. "Of course he's forty years old; that's the best age for a man, really, but I suppose he was too old for our Mary. She's only twenty-four."

"What's Restorick's history as regards women?"

"Oh, he's no Galahad, if that's what you mean. Such a vigorous man, how could you expect it? He has never married; too leery of the gals who were always chucking their caps at his millions. It's disgusting the way girls make up to an eligible multimillionaire. Like street-walkers. It was Mary's utter independence that got George Restorick going in the first place."

"You don't think that he could have . . ."

"How do I know?" was Nina's unexpected reply. "What do any of us know about anybody else? We live on the surface. George has the reputation of being a violently passionate man. That's because he looks the part. I never heard of anything specific. He has himself under iron control."

"But when that type of man *does* break out . . ." suggested Lee.

Nina shivered. "Don't speak of such a thing! It's horrible!"

Lee took a new line. "Lottie spoke of a party after the theater on Saturday night that wasn't altogether successful."

"Anything but," said Nina grimly. "It was to be Mary's farewell to spinsterhood, but nobody was supposed to know that except me—and of course Jack. She asked George Restorick and Ewart Blanding to come because, as she told me, they were the two who loved her best. I told her it was a fool idea, but she would have it so. She loved them both, she said, simply because they loved her."

Lee shook his head at the folly of girls.

"George, naturally, refused to come," Nina went on. "He had too much sense. But Ewart turned up. I should explain that Jack Fentress hates Ewart, though since Jack himself was copping the girl they were all after, I don't know why he should. It may be that he knows in his heart Ewart is the better man, and that is unbearable."

"Well, Ewart can't exactly love Jack, either," suggested Lee.

"I suppose not. But Ewart is a natural-born gentleman. He wanted the party to be a success for Mary's sake. He hid his feelings. Ewart has beautiful eyes for a man. His expression . . ."

"Go on about the party," prompted Lee.

"We had a private room at La Perouse. The party was doomed from the start because of Jack's hateful sniping at Ewart. I couldn't believe that a man who was to be married the next day could be so hateful to his unsuccessful rival."

"What sort of sniping?" asked Lee.

"Oh, you can imagine it; sly boasting about his success; just to rub salt in Ewart's wound."

"A pretty short sport!" murmured Lee.

"For a long time Ewart took it like an angel," Nina went on. "Making a joke of it, laughing, trying to change the subject. But Jack seemed determined to provoke a quarrel. He kept hinting about the coming marriage, though Mary had expressly forbidden him to refer to it. Toward the end I could see the muscles of Ewart's jaw stiffening. Finally Jack suggested that Ewart would have to console himself with the riches of his present employer. That was too much. Ewart jumped up, knocking his chair over backwards. Jack was up, too, and Ewart gave him a smashing blow in the face that stretched him flat on the floor. I didn't mention, did I, that Jack turned up for the wedding with a ghastly black eye? It had been skillfully painted out, but you could tell."

"How did Mary take all this?" asked Lee.

"She was angry with Ewart. She took Jack's part. How could you expect an infatuated girl to be fair?"

"What happened then?"

"That was the end. Mary was kneeling beside Jack on the floor. Ewart gave Mary a sort of desperate look and ran out of the place. We all went home."

"Good Lord!" said Lee. "Imagine the feelings of that poor young wretch when he ran out of the restaurant. That's dangerous . . . dangerous!"

Nina wept again. "I wouldn't have been surprised to hear that Ewart had killed Jack Fentress!" she sobbed. "I wouldn't have blamed him. But how could he hurt Mary?"

Lee jumped up. "We don't know anything yet," he said. "Jack may have had some communication from Mary since I tried to get him on the phone earlier, but there was no answer."

Nina nodded toward the telephone. "Try Jim Rutledge's place. They may still be together."

Lee looked up the number and asked for it at the phone. Jim Rutledge answered. "Can you tell me where Jack Fentress is?" asked Lee.

"He's here," said Rutledge.

"Let me speak to him, please."

Presently Lee heard Jack's surly voice over the wire. "Who is it?"

"Lee Mappin," said Lee. "A friend of Mary Stannard's. Perhaps you have heard her speak of me."

Jack's voice became more friendly. "Sure, I know you, Mr. Mappin. What can I do for you?"

"Have you heard anything from Mary today?"

The voice hardened again. "What's that to you, sir?"

"Well, all her friends are wondering where she is. We're anxious."

The voice was electrified. "What? What?" cried Jack. "Do you mean she's disappeared? Nobody knows where she is?"

"That's right."

"That changes the picture! I haven't heard anything from her. This is terrible! I . . . I can't talk to you over the phone, sir. Where are you? Can I come to you?"

"I was about to suggest that I come to you."

"Yes! Yes! that would be better, if you can come. I'll wait for you here at Rutledge's, sir. . . . But can you give me half an hour or a little more?" he added deprecatingly. "I'm . . . I'm not in very good shape, sir."

"I'll be there in an hour from now," said Lee.

He hung up and looked around for his hat. "Be of good heart," he said to the weeping Nina. "We mustn't give way to imaginary horrors. I'll keep in touch with you. . . . First I'm going to drive down to St. Michael's and All Angels'. Would you be kind enough to call up the Reverend Mr. Stair and tell him I'm a friend of all the parties, so he won't refuse to talk?"

Nina nodded.

LEE WAS SHOWN into the parson's study. The first thing his eyes fell upon was a spray of six blossoms of an exquisite rare green and black orchid standing in a slender vase on Mr. Stair's desk. This, Lee knew, was Mary Stannard's favorite flower—perhaps because it was the most expensive.

Mr. Stair entered the room, saying: "Mrs. Gannon telephoned that you were on the way, Mr. Mappin. Of course you are well known to me by reputation, sir." The fashionable preacher was a handsome, full-bodied man with a high color, evidently one who enjoyed life. His manner was gracious.

"Good!" said Lee. "That saves explanations." He pointed to the orchids. "One of the questions I came to ask you has already been answered. Those, I take it, were intended for the bridal bouquet."

"I assume so," said Mr. Stair. "I found the box on the floor after they had gone. It seemed indelicate to try to return them to the disappointed bridegroom, so I just put them in water. Lovely, aren't they? And scandalously expensive, I have no doubt."

"Quite," said Lee dryly. "Did you happen to notice what florist they were from?"

"Unfortunately, no," said Mr. Stair. "The box was wrapped in plain white paper without any markings. I dropped the wrappings in my wastepaper basket and it has been emptied. Excuse me for a moment, and I will find out if the contents are still in the house."

He returned to the study in a moment or two with the box in his hand. It was the same size box as that Lee had found in Mary's living room earlier. "From Lamarr at Madison Avenue and Eighty-sixth Street," said Mr. Stair.

"One more question," said Lee. "Did you happen to notice the time at which the bridegroom got to the vestry?"

"Yes. He was a little late and I had just looked at my watch. It was nine-five."

Lee arose. "Thank you very much, sir."

"Excuse me," said Mr. Stair. "Your questions make me anxious. May I ask? . . ."

Lee shook hands with him. "In your profession you must have learned to cultivate discretion," he said. "The young lady has disappeared. That is to say, none of her friends know where she is."

"How dreadful!"

"If anything has happened to her, of course it must be published, but until we have something to go on, we wish to keep the matter private."

"Naturally," said Mr. Stair. "You can rely on me, Mr. Mappin. I am so sorry. I have seen the young lady in her play. So pretty! so charmingly natural!"

"That is her character, Mr. Stair."

On his way uptown, Lee stopped at Forty-second Street to consult Stan Oberry. Stan's office door bore no lettering. He conducted a quiet and efficient private agency that Lee had employed with success in former investigations. Stan himself was a big man with a small head; he had the great professional advantage of looking like a fool without being one. He was the type of man who is difficult to remember or to describe.

After he had laid his present problem before Stan in full particular, Lee said: "To hide is so completely foreign to this girl's character that I fear something has happened to her. It is possible that she never left her house last night. After eight o'clock she and the old man were alone there together. That old man hates everybody including the granddaughter to whom he owes everything. I asked Mary once why she put up with his intolerable exactions and she said: 'Well, he's the only creature in the world who belongs to me. A woman must have *somebody* who belongs to her, Lee.'"

Stan was making brief shorthand notes.

"The flower beds in the back yard of Mary's house would make a convenient hiding place," Lee continued, "though God forbid they were so used! The rear windows of the house on either side over-look the flower beds; also the rear windows of the apartment house in the next street. Make inquiries without showing your hand. Did anybody see the old man working in the flower beds, or did a light shine there last night?"

"I'll do that," said Stan. "But if the old man had it on his con-science, would he have come to you?"

"That would be the cleverest move he could make."

"That's a fact, Mr. Mappin."

Lee went on: "The old man claims that Mary had a male caller shortly after eight o'clock. I thought this might be an invention, but it was partly corroborated by finding a florist's box in the liv-ing room. It came from Schracht on Lexington Avenue. If there was such a visitor, perhaps Mary left the house with him. The old man said there was a big red convertible coupe with a khaki top standing in front of the door while the man was there. Please make discreet inquiries among the neighbors. Did anybody else see such a car?"

"Right," said Stan.

"Here's another angle," said Lee. "I am informed that Ewart Blanding, who formerly worked for Mary as her chauffeur, is des-perately in love with her. He is now working for Miss Amy Dordress, the girl who has so much money. I have very good reports on his character from two sources; on the other hand, I am told that he and Jack Fentress quarreled in a restaurant on Saturday night and that Blanding knocked Fentress down. You should investigate Blanding's subsequent movements."

"Why not start now?" suggested Stan. He pulled the telephone book toward him and searched for Miss Dordress' number. Find-ing it, he said: "She lives on Park Avenue. I know that house; most expensive in town; triplex apartments. The girl is an orphan; has complete control over her money, they say. Every young fellow about town is after her, but she can't make up her mind."

"How is she for looks?" asked Lee idly.

"Not so hot," said Stan. "Well, you can't expect everything."

Meanwhile Stan was calling the number. A man-servant answered, and when Stan asked for Blanding, he was promptly switched to the mistress. A shrill, angry voice came over the wire and Stan held the receiver away from his ear so Lee could hear what she was saying.

"No, I don't know where he is! I'd be glad if you would tell *me*! He took one of my cars last night without permission and I've seen neither hide nor hair of him since, nor the car either. If I don't hear from him within an hour I shall report it to the police!"

"Which car was it, miss?"

"The Packard. It's a red convertible with a khaki top. . . . Who are you, anyway? Do you know where he is?"

"No ma'am. Just a personal friend."

She hung up.

"Well, I'll be damned!" murmured Lee.

"I'll follow it up," said Stan.

CHAPTER FOUR

LEE HAD SEEN JACK FENTRESS on several occasions before—Jack was
a familiar figure in the gaudier spots around town, but now in his
friend's apartment Lee regarded him with a new interest. What
constituted his extraordinary attraction for women? Lee saw a man
in his late twenties, of average height and good figure; sufficiently
good-looking, not remarkably so. Fentress had uncommonly thick
and lustrous black hair and apparently a heavy beard; the notable
thing about him was the quick turn of his dark eyes, the swiftness
of all his movements. He was always on wires, as the saying is; he
seemed to give off a kind of electricity. He was an actor, but he
had never won distinction on the stage.

At the moment he was a sorry sight. His clothes were in order;
he was still wearing the fashionable suit he had put on for his wedding; but the skillful painting had partly worn off his black eye;
both his eyes were bloodshot; his face was gray and haggard; he
had not shaved.

"I told you I wasn't in very good shape," he said deprecatingly;
"I couldn't shave, my hand trembled so. Jim and I got stinking
drunk last night."

"Hardly surprising," said Lee.

"What do you know about Mary?" asked Jack imploringly.

"Nothing," said Lee, spreading out his hands.

"This is not like Mary!" cried Jack. "It's not like her!"

"It is not," said Lee.

Rutledge spoke up: "If you and Mr. Mappin want to talk privately, I'll go out." He was a nice-looking young fellow with a weak face; the kind who is always somebody's best friend or best man, but who rarely occupies the center of the stage himself.

"No!" said Jack. "There's no reason you shouldn't hear everything. You've been a good friend to me through this, Jim."

"She told her grandfather she was going up to Greencliffe Manor," said Lee. "But of course she's not there."

"That's right," said Jack. "We had planned to go to Greencliffe; but not until today."

"No reservation had been made."

"My fault, I forgot it in my excitement. The whole thing was got up in such a hurry. It was only when Mary learned that the show was closing Saturday night that we decided on it. She wanted to spend last night at my place because we have had such happy hours there."

"Then I take it," said Lee dryly, "that you had not waited for the wedding?"

Jack spread out his hands appealingly. "You know how it is, sir! We were so crazy about each other, but we had nothing to marry on. When Mary made her big hit, I still wanted to wait because I had nothing, but when the play closed she insisted that that would give us the opportunity for a real honeymoon that might not come again for years!"

"I'm not judging Mary," said Lee quickly. "She's the mistress of her own actions."

"So I gave in. How could I stand out against Mary?"

"I'm not blaming you. . . . Perhaps she has telephoned to your flat."

"No, I called there. The hallboy told me there had been only one call for me and that was a man. I told them where I could be found."

"It was I who called," said Lee.

"Oh God! what could have happened?" cried Jack, clutching his head. "Last night I thought she had stood me up and I was wild. I couldn't bear the thought of that being noised around town. That's why I got drunk. It looks different now. I don't think she stood me up. I think she was prevented from coming."

"When did you see her last?" asked Lee.

"Saturday night. I wanted to pick her up and drive her to the church last night. That would have been the natural thing to do. But she wouldn't have it because . . ."

"Mrs. Gannon explained that to me."

"Then you've seen Mrs. Gannon."

"I phoned you from there."

"Mary wouldn't even let me see her during the day yesterday, but she couldn't keep me from calling her up. I talked to her several times. I was so afraid something might happen. You see, there were other men in the running."

"She didn't appear to have anything on her mind then?"

"Oh no, sir! On the contrary, she was as happy and excited as I was."

"You speak of other men. Mrs. Gannon told me about the trouble on Saturday night."

"She would," said Jack with a curling lip.

"Blanding? . . ." suggested Lee.

Jack turned on his heel. "The hell with Blanding," he said contemptuously. "Mary never took him seriously. A mere chauffeur! Blanding followed her around like a sick cat, but he hadn't the guts to *do* anything about it."

Lee was not altogether convinced.

"There's another man," said Jack darkly; "a man who constitutes a real threat!"

"Who?"

"George Restorick. I've always feared him."

"Why?"

"Because he's so goddamned rich. He's been after her for years. And look what he can offer her. Security; a lifetime of luxury; a famous name. Any ordinary girl would have jumped at it long ago. I've always been afraid that Mary might fall for Restorick in the end. . . . Besides . . ."

"Besides what?"

"Well, I don't suppose there's anything in it, but it's a thing I can't forget. Restorick was continually asking Mary to marry him. Once when she turned him down he flew into a rage and told her that if he couldn't have her, no other man should. Mary herself told me. She laughed it off, but I couldn't."

"We'll investigate that," said Lee. "First tell me what happened last night."

Jack didn't like to recall that humiliating scene. "I bet Nina Gannon gave you an earful on that," he said, scowling.

"Never mind what she told me," said Lee. "Let me have the straight dope."

"There's nothing to tell. Mary didn't show up, that's all."

"Describe your movements before you went to the church."

Jack dropped on the sofa and lit a cigarette. He passed a hand over his face. "Let me think," he murmured. "My brain's in a muddle! . . . I started to dress about five o'clock, I guess. Jim can tell you; he was with me."

"A man always acts like an idiot before his wedding," put in Jim.

"At six-thirty we went out to eat," Jack went on, "but the food choked me. At seven-thirty I phoned to the garage for my car, and soon after I sent Jim downtown to pick up Nina, though he protested that it was half an hour too soon."

"Seven forty-five," corroborated the grinning Jim. "Nina gave me hell for showing up so early."

"Soon after Jim left, I couldn't stand it any longer," Jack resumed, "and I started out in my car."

"Where is your apartment?" put in Lee.

"Madison Avenue between Eighty-seventh and Eighty-eighth. My first stop was to pick up flowers at Lamarr's down the street. Orchids. It's a special kind that Mary likes; green and black. They were to go with a black suit and green hat she was wearing. The florists don't stock them; too expensive. I had ordered them in advance on Friday. Ninety dollars for a spray of six blossoms. I suppose you think that was foolish, poor as I am. Don't you see, it's because I'm broke that I had to make a splurge like that."

"Very natural," said Lee.

"By the way, what became of the box, Jack?" asked Jim.

"You can search me!"

"The flowers are now sitting on the parson's desk," put in Lee blandly.

"The hell with them!" said Jack. "So you've been to the parson's, too?"

"Go on with your story."

"I was looking at my watch every minute," said Jack, "so I can give you an exact timetable of my movements. It was eight-five when I left the florist's. I cut through to Third Avenue and filled my tank at the Yorkville Garage. Eight-twelve when I pulled away from there. There was little traffic and when I got to Madison Square I saw by the clock in the Metropolitan tower that I still had half an hour to spare.

"I just drove around. Made a circuit of Gramercy Square and down Irving Place. Parked my car for a few minutes and went into Lüchow's to get a drink. I needed it. When I came out, there was another big clock across the road; gas company, isn't it? It said three minutes to nine. I got in a hell of a rush then, hustled down Fourth Avenue and west through Ninth Street.

"I was in such a sweat that I ran through a red light at the corner of University Place, there by the Cafe Lafayette. A cop stopped me and I lost some minutes more arguing with him. Told him I was on my way to be married. The church was just around the corner. So he came with me, saying if my story checked he wouldn't give me a ticket. It did check and I got rid of him. It was nine-five when I arrived at the church."

"You can skip what happened at the church," said Lee. "Nina told me. Where did you and Jim go afterwards?"

"We hung around waiting for Mary until after ten. Then we took Nina home and proceeded to tank up. I didn't want to be seen anywhere, so we bought a couple of bottles and brought them up here. I left Jim for a few minutes and went over home to see if there was any message. There wasn't. So I came back here. Jim went to sleep, but sleep was impossible for me. Toward morning I went over to my place again. No message. It was impossible for me to stay alone, so I came back and woke Jim up. That's all."

"I see."

"Why don't you call up George Restorick?" asked Jack. "I can't do it because we're not friends. When he's in town he lives in that goddamn palace on Sutton Place overlooking the river. It's not far from Mary's house."

"I know it," said Lee. "It's near my place, too."

Jack gave him the number and Lee called it. There was a long wait. Lee could hear the phone ringing at the other end. No answer. Just as Lee was about to hang up, a woman's voice came over the wire.

"This is Mr. Restorick's house. He's not here. The house is closed. I'm the caretaker. No, I don't know where he is or when he'll be back. The house is closed until further notice."

"Try the Restorick Estate office in East Thirty-sixth Street," suggested Jack. "George doesn't trouble it much. They bank his rents and all he has to do in the world is write checks. But they may know where he's to be found."

This call was answered by a courteous male voice. "Mr. Restorick is out of town. Is there anything I can do for you, sir?"

"No, thank you. It's a personal matter. Where is Mr. Restorick?"

"He took a plane at La Guardia Field for Mexico City an hour ago, sir. As a matter of fact, I saw him off."

"Have you a forwarding address?"

"Not yet, sir. Presumably that will come later."

"This was an unexpected trip, then?"

"Yes, sir. Mr. Restorick had to buy out another passenger in order to secure a place on the plane."

"Did he go alone?"

The voice sounded surprised. "Why yes, sir."

"I thought he might have taken a servant."

"No, sir, the servants have been paid off and the cars put in dead storage."

"He'll be away for some time, then."

"No date has been set for his return, sir."

Lee considered for a moment. "I was negotiating with Mr. Restorick for the purchase of one of his cars," he ventured.

"In that case, you should communicate with the garage where they are stored, sir. It's the Atlas in East Fifty-first Street."

"Thank you very much," said Lee, hanging up. He and Jack exchanged a glance. "What did I tell you? What did I tell you?" cried the latter excitedly. "Restorick is the man!"

Lee shrugged dubiously.

"Restorick is so damned rich he could hire somebody to do his dirty work!"

"Well, I shouldn't think he would advertise his departure among his employees if he had a crime on his conscience," said Lee mildly. "He could have slipped away secretly."

"But to Mexico!"

"Mexico wouldn't do him much good if he's guilty. We have an extradition treaty."

"But how easy to reach Guatemala or one of those other Central American countries!"

"Wait a minute," said Lee. He called up Stan Oberry's office. "Stan," he said, "first, have you turned up anything about Ewart Blanding or the red convertible?"

"No, Mr. Mappin. He seems to have disappeared into thin air."

"Well, here's another item for you. George Restorick boarded the eleven o'clock plane for Mexico City at La Guardia Field. Have you a good agent down there?"

"One of the best, sir."

"Telegraph him to watch for the arrival of that plane and to notify us if Restorick gets off. If so, he is to keep Restorick under constant surveillance and report daily."

"Very good, Mr. Mappin. You can make your mind easy about Restorick. A man so well known couldn't possibly lose himself."

"I hope you're right. As yet, I don't know if he'll be wanted."

Lee hung up. "Jack," he said, "we have now reached the point where we must let it be known that Mary has disappeared."

Jack groaned. "It will cause a sensation! God! How I dread the publicity!"

"I also. But you can see that it is ridiculous to proceed on the assumption that harm has come to Mary while there is still a possibility she may be resting in seclusion in some country hotel."

"I suppose you're right, sir."

"I will go to my friend, Inspector Loasby, and ask him to send out a general alarm. Loasby will be goggle-eyed, but we don't have to tell him the whole story yet. As for the press, we will simply say that Miss Stannard's present whereabouts are unknown to her friends and they are anxious. Nothing about the interrupted marriage. If Mary is still alive and conscious, such an item will instantly bring word from her."

"The reporters will hound us for further particulars," groaned Jack.

"Just refer them to me. I'm accustomed to dealing with those boys."

"Just as you say, sir. Can I drive you down to police headquarters? My car is at the door downstairs."

"Glad to accept a ride," said Lee.

WHEN LEE ISSUED out of police headquarters after a brief interview with Inspector Loasby, the head of the detective force, he found Jack looking much better. "I had myself shaved while I was waiting for you," he said, "and the barber touched up my eye."

"In this neighborhood, painting out black eyes is quite an industry," remarked Lee.

"What's our next move, sir?"

"Let us drive up to the Atlas Garage and take a look at Restorick's cars."

"Good!"

Lee glanced at the young man's drawn face. "First we must eat," he said. "We'll stop at the old Brevoort on our way uptown."

"Oh, let's don't waste time eating," pleaded Jack. "The thought of food is horrible to me!"

"When did you eat last?"

"I don't remember."

"Then we'll eat now," said Lee firmly. "I don't want you to collapse on my hands. Find a place to park near the Brevoort."

When the food was actually put before him, Jack made a good meal. "I suppose I needed it," he said, "though I had no feeling of hunger."

Continuing uptown, they stopped at Schracht's, the florist, on Lexington Avenue. Jack went into the shop with Lee.

"Are you open on Sunday evenings?" Lee asked the salesman.

"From five until eight-thirty, yes, sir. There's so much entertaining on Sunday nights nowadays that we do a brisk trade between those hours."

"Last evening," Lee went on, "I have reason to believe that a young man bought flowers here near your closing time, and carried them with him. They were in a box of that size." He pointed.

"Those are used for orchids, sir. Can you describe the young man?"

"I was hoping you could do that for me."

"Oh, sir, there were eight or ten sales of orchids last evening. That is what is mostly called for."

"How about the Investia orchid?" put in Jack. "That green and black kind, very expensive."

The salesman's face lighted up. "Why yes, sir. There was such a sale. I wouldn't forget that. The flowers are so rare."

"Who bought them?" asked Lee.

"He is a stranger to me, sir. A cash customer. Nobody stocks Investias. They're not enough of them. They're grown by a nurseryman in Madison, New Jersey, and must be ordered in advance. This young fellow ordered them last week and paid cash for a spray of six, ninety dollars."

"Describe the man."

"A handsome, well-built young fellow, sir. Blond. I happened to notice his car standing at the door. A big red convertible with a khaki top."

"That's description enough. Thank you very much. Come on, Jack."

When they had left the shop, Lee said: "What made you think of Investias?"

"Just a guess in the dark," said Jack. "Blanding knew as well as I that Mary was crazy about them. . . . Damned cheek," he growled. "A chauffeur! Spending ninety dollars for flowers to give my girl!"

Lee murmured softly: "Mary must have been wearing those lovely blossoms when she . . ."

"Don't say it, sir!" cried Jack sharply.

". . . When she went away from us," amended Lee.

CHAPTER FIVE

IN THE ATLAS GARAGE on East Fifty-first Street, Lee said to the manager: "Can I see Mr. George Restorick's cars?"

The manager looked him over. "Did you bring an authorization, sir?"

"Why no. When I called up Mr. Restorick's office this morning, I was told he had gone out of town. His agent referred me to you."

"That's right. I was ordered to put the two cars in dead storage, but I haven't got around to it yet. Which car was you interested in, sir? I didn't know he was thinking of selling. That's the coupé back of you. It's waiting to be washed."

"That's the one," said Lee. "Let's look it over."

"Beautiful custom-made job," said the manager. "Mr. Restorick don't employ a chauffeur while he's living in town and his cars ain't taken out much. He says taxis are cheaper. Even a millionaire looks after the pennies."

"They always do," said Lee.

"The limousine hasn't been out since God knows when," the manager went on, "but this job was called for at eight-thirty last night, unexpected. I took it up to Mr. Restorick's house myself."

"Did you see him?"

"No, sir. I just left it standing under the porte-cochère and dropped the keys through the letter slot. That's our custom. Mr. Restorick returned it himself about two o'clock. I offered to drive him home, but he said it was only a block or two and he wanted the walk. Nice man, Mr. Restorick; easy as an old shoe."

"Right!" said Lee. "A fine fellow!"

"When he come in last night I noticed he'd picked up some mud under the fenders, and I says: 'Been for a drive in the country, Mr. Restorick?' And he says: 'Just up to my place in Fairfield County, Connecticut. I'm going away tomorrow and I had to get some papers.'"

"Was he alone?"

"Yes, sir."

While the man was talking, Lee made a close and attentive examination of the car's interior. Afterwards he said: "Will you open up the luggage compartment, please? I want to see how much space there is."

When the cover was lifted, Lee, producing a pocket flashlight and a magnifying glass, searched the interior inch by inch. The manager stared, thinking this a strange procedure on the part of a prospective buyer. Jack could guess what Lee was looking for, and an involuntary shiver passed through his body.

"Just as I feared," said Lee. "They design a fine, spacious compartment for luggage and then fill it with a couple of spare wheels. Close it up."

"You could have it rigged to carry the spares on the running-boards without much expense," suggested the manager. "Let me give you a run in it, sir. If you're thinking of buying, I won't have the battery taken out."

"No," said Lee. "After all, it's not exactly what I want. Many thanks for your trouble."

"No trouble to show a car, sir."

"Look," said Lee, "tell me something as man to man. When Mr. Restorick came back with the car last night, how did he look?"

The manager's eyes widened. "Police?" he asked.

"Associated with the police," said Lee. "I can see you're a wise guy, and can keep your mouth shut."

"Sure! But Mr. Restorick! A man of his sort . . . Good Lord! Well, since you ask me, mister, he looked decidedly upset. He looked like a man who had lately stopped a haymaker."

"Much obliged," said Lee. "Let's go, Jack."

"But . . . my God, mister! They say Restorick's got half the money in the country. A man like him . . . absconding!"

"Oh, nothing like that," said Lee. "Say nothing about my visit today. If there's anything in it, it will all come out in the end."

Back in their own car, Jack said: "Well, that's pretty conclusive!"

"Hardly that," said Lee. "Just another suspicious circumstance. If Restorick drove up to his country place last night for an evil purpose, he would hardly tell the garage-man where he had gone. He didn't have to tell him."

"They always make one mistake," insisted Jack. "What's our next move, sir?"

"How much gas have you got?"

"I filled up last night. It's still registering three-quarters."

"Do you want to drive me up to Connecticut?"

"Sure! I was hoping you'd say that."

"I don't expect anything to come of it. But it's something we should not neglect."

They left town by the Hutchinson Parkway. Jack's car was a small convertible but it was too cold to drive with the top down. Indeed, there had been a light frost the previous night; but the spring flowers in the parkway were blooming bravely. They paused in Stamford to make inquiries and had no difficulty in learning that the Restorick country place lay eighteen miles north of Bridgeport on the road to Danbury.

Jack drove as fast as the law allowed. It was half past four when they arrived. There was nothing grand about the place; a characteristic, ancient Connecticut farmhouse with an immense central chimney, it had been improved and extended to suit a modern taste. Like all farmhouses, it stood close to the road, but was partly shielded from view by recent planting. The grounds spread wide on either side and at the back to the edge of a hill. A gigantic tree partly shaded the house, and Restorick had called the place after this tree: Black Maple. As Lee knew, the millionaire was a man of simple tastes. He had inherited the over-ornate city house, but this place was of his own choice.

A freshly painted FOR SALE sign had been planted beside the entrance gate. A car stood in the private drive in front of the porch, and the house door was open. There was a young man in working clothes on the porch.

As they got out, Lee warned Jack with a glance to let him do the talking, and said: "This is Mr. Restorick's place, isn't it?"

"Yes, sir."

"Is he here?"

"No, sir. Mr. Restorick is traveling, sir."

"Whose car is that?"

"That's the real estate agent's, sir. Mr. Restorick has put the house up for sale."

"Dear! Dear!" said Lee. "That's a surprise."

"It was a surprise to me, sir, I can tell you," said the young man ruefully.

"What is your job here?" asked Lee.

"I'm the farmer, sir. Barmby is my name. Yonder is my house on a side road beyond the grounds. Last night after eleven o'clock I was wakened in my bed by a horn blowing under my window. It was Mr. Restorick, who had driven up unexpectedly. He drove on to the big house and I dressed and followed him."

"Was he alone?"

"Yes, sir. He told me he would be traveling out of the country for an indefinite period, so he had made up his mind to sell Black Maple. Under my contract, of course, I can't be put off the place without six months' notice, but I hate to change masters, sir. Mr. Restorick is one in a thousand. Are you interested in buying the place, sir?"

"Possibly," said Lee. "I just saw the sign in passing."

"I'll call the agent, sir."

In response to the summons, a smart little gentleman came out of the house, the typical "realtor."

"My name is Mappin," said Lee. "I spoke to Mr. Restorick once about buying this place, but he said it wasn't in the market. Now I see he has changed his mind."

The realtor lost no time in beginning his snappy sales talk. "Yes, sir. The sign hasn't been up an hour and you are our first prospect. We won't have this place on our hands long. It's in absolutely apple-pie order and at a very reasonable price. Everybody wants to buy in the spring. Mr. Restorick would like to sell the contents with it. You could move in tonight if you wished. Will you go over the house while we're here, sir?"

"All right," said Lee.

"I'll stay here and talk to this man," said Jack.

Lee entered a broad, low living room. A clerk was engaged in taking inventory. "There's a front door facing the road," explained the agent, "but this door from the porch is the natural entrance since the driveway passes outside. Two of the original rooms were thrown together to make this living room. Beautiful, isn't it? The furniture and pictures are veritable museum pieces. Back of it lies the dining room. This was the kitchen of the original house with an extension. The original fireplace, you see; said to be the largest in Connecticut. With all the original utensils. A unique feature! The present kitchen wing is modern with every known laborsaving device. Servants' bedrooms above. On the other side of the house is a charming little den or library—look at that Chinese rug, sir! And the entrance hall in front with the original quaint stair! You'll find the date of the house over the front door; 1790." And so on. And so on.

Lee took his own time in following the little man from room to room, using his eyes to the fullest advantage. "That's right, sir," said the agent. "Anybody could see that you are a connoisseur of beautiful things!"

The magnifying glass came out more than once, but Lee was not rewarded by finding even so much as a fingerprint. "The place is extremely well kept," he remarked.

"When Mr. Restorick is not living here, Mrs. Barmby, the farmer's wife, does the sweeping and dusting," explained the agent.

They proceeded to the upper floor. "Four bedrooms and three baths," said the agent. "The wallpapers, you will notice, are all printed from hand blocks. The large bedroom to the north is the master's bedroom. There is room for two more rooms and baths on the attic floor, but as Mr. Restorick did not require the accommodation, he never had them finished."

In the big bedroom, one of the pictures had been taken down and left standing against the baseboard. Behind its place was revealed a little wall safe. Lee tried the door and it came open in his hand. The safe was empty except for a scrap of paper on which was written: "Combination may be obtained from the agent of my estate." Lee's glass revealed male fingerprints on the door, which Lee took to be Restorick's. He had found similar prints in the car.

"Mr. Restorick thought of everything," murmured the agent.

By the time they got downstairs, Lee was thoroughly bored with the brisk little man. "I interrupted you at your work," he said politely. "My friend and I will stroll about the grounds now. There is no need for you to accompany us."

"Just as you please, Mr. Mappin. I'll see you before you go."

In the graveled drive, Lee found the marks of a car which had come and gone before their arrival. Without calling attention to what he was doing, he traced the tracks back to the garage, where the car had turned and gone back. It had not left the drive at any point.

The broad and beautifully kept lawn to the north of the house could not have been disturbed without leaving traces, so Lee kept to the planted borders, giving special attention to an old well, now completely hidden within a circle of cedars. Jack accompanied him, and the young farmer, Barmby, followed a few paces behind.

"Did you get anything out of him?" Lee asked.

"Nothing of any account," murmured Jack.

"Did he stay with Restorick all the time he was here?"

"No, indeed. God knows what Restorick had been up to before he turned on a light in his bedroom. Moreover, he sent the farmer back to bed before he left."

"He couldn't have stayed very long," said Lee, "if he was back in town by two o'clock. It's more than seventy miles."

"Long enough to do his dirty work, I reckon," growled Jack. "Probably drove like a bat out of hell."

Behind flowering shrubs to the west of the lawn stretched cutting beds, a vegetable garden, including grapevines and rows of berry bushes, an orchard. Back of all, within a screen of cedar trees, lay a swimming pool, empty of water.

"The place has everything," said Lee.

To the south and nearer the house, rose the former stable now transformed into an inviting game room with broad windows filling the west end and a terrace outside commanding a lovely view of the valley and its distant hills. There was a suite of guest rooms above, and next door, the garage, empty now. A small, all-service truck was standing in the garage. Lee examined it with particular care. It told him nothing.

To the south of the house stretched another lawn of equal size, rising gradually in the middle to a picturesque, round, rustic summerhouse, completely covered with a vine of white wistaria now in flower. Surrounding the little pavilion was a bed of hyacinths, white, pink and purple, freshly planted out, the whole making a charming springtime bower. Lee walked all around it, gazing at the beauty of the blossoms—and incidentally searching to see if the flower bed had been freshly disturbed anywhere. Apparently it had not. The floor of the summerhouse was about a foot higher than the surrounding ground. This space had been filled in with a lattice of thin wooden strips. Chains had been stretched across the entrance to the little house.

"What are these chains for?" asked Lee.

"To keep anybody from going in," said Barmby. "Mr. Restorick had them put up before I came. He said he suspected that the floor was rotten, and he didn't want anybody to go through and break a leg. He called this hut the gazebo. That was just his fun. It was never used for anything, but he wouldn't have it pulled down because the vine was so beautiful."

Lee leaned over the chain to look inside. In truth, the floor was covered with a scum of earth and the remains of rotting leaves that obviously had not been disturbed in years.

Barmby glanced at his watch. "It's my milking time, sir. I'll be leaving you, if there's nothing more I can do."

Lee gave him a generous tip.

"Do you think you'll be buying the place, sir?" he asked. "I'd kind of like to have you for my boss."

Lee, smiling, shook his head. "I'm afraid it's too big for me to swing."

Lee and Jack went on together. They had now made a circuit of the grounds, and were coming back to the house from the south side. Passing through a screen of pink dogwood in full flower, the finest Lee had ever seen, they entered a rectangular flower garden. The spring flowers were at their best.

"More neatly raked flower beds," murmured Lee.

"What's that, sir?" asked Jack.

"Nothing. Just talking to myself."

Under the open fronds of a peony bush gleamed a scrap of white. Lee picked it up. A lady's little folded handkerchief of the sheerest linen. On the visible corner, a spray of flowers was exquisitely embroidered, in colored threads, odd green and black blossoms.

Jack, looking over Lee's shoulder, gave an agonized cry and clutched his head. "That's one of Mary's wedding handkerchiefs! See! the Investia orchid! She ordered them embroidered specially! Oh God!"

Lee gently smoothed the folded square of linen and put it in his breast pocket. "Come," he said. "Don't let these people see that you are upset. We'll have to come back here again."

CHAPTER SIX

JACK FENTRESS DROPPED LEE at the railway station in Bridgeport. By taking an express to Grand Central, he could save an hour. He ate his dinner in the dining car. The saddened Lee had little desire for food, but he made it a practice always to take nourishment at the proper hours. Upon buying a New York evening paper, he found that even the bare announcement of Mary Stannard's disappearance was big front-page stuff.

In town, his first act was to call up Inspector Loasby. In any criminal investigation, Lee made it a rule to take the police into his confidence, though sometimes he found it rather a handicap. Loasby was at home, and he made a date to go up there.

He found the handsome police officer at his ease in velvet smoking jacket and slippers. Loasby, though somewhat vain of his middle-aged good looks and cleverness, was an excellent fellow, and they were old friends. Lee now told him the whole story of the disappearance of Mary Stannard so far as he knew it.

"What a sensation!" said Loasby. "Multimillionaire, beautiful actress. It has everything! This will set the whole nation agog!"

"Well, let's not give it to the press until we're a little surer of where we stand," urged Lee.

Loasby agreed. "I will take immediate steps to have Restorick arrested," he said.

Lee shook his head. "Better not! The evidence is not sufficient, Inspector. I'm not satisfied that Restorick is the man we want."

Loasby stared. "But his surprise visit at night to his country house! The handkerchief!"

"Quite so. But Mary Stannard had been a frequent visitor to Black Maple."

Loasby looked at the handkerchief. "It is clear this was dropped on the flower bed since the last rain."

"Surely." A momentary spasm of pain crossed Lee's face. "Her body may be there some place. I searched as well as I could to see if the ground had been disturbed, but of course it was not a thorough search. Send a couple of men up there tomorrow to look further. Let them be men of good appearance who can make out that they are thinking of buying the place. There's a trash pit alongside the garage that has been partly filled in. That should be looked into."

"I'll do that. In the meantime, Restorick ought to be detained."

Lee still shook his head. "That's up to you. I'm against it. We'll know in the morning if he went to Mexico City. A man like that cannot disappear easily."

Loasby grinned a little ruefully. "Well, sometimes I've been sorry in the past when I didn't listen to your hunches. I'll wait."

"Heard anything further about the other suspect, Ewart Blanding?" asked Lee.

"Not a word."

Lee called up Stan Oberry at his home. Stan had news for him. He said: "Ewart Blanding called up his employer, Miss Dordress, at one o'clock today. I couldn't get hold of you. Blanding informed her with regret that he had smashed up her car last night on Pelham Bay Parkway. The accident happened shortly after nine o'clock. A passing motorist carried him to Pelham Manor, where Blanding reported the accident to a garage and engaged them to tow the wreck in. Miss Dordress ordered him to come to her and report in person, but he declined with apologies. Said such an interview could only be painful to both. He promised her he would pay for the car just as soon as he could earn the money, and hung up. Boy! was she sore!

"She telephoned the Packard repair shop to send up to Pelham Manor and get the car and send her an estimate of repairs. Blanding lodged in a room in the neighborhood of the Dordress garage. She went around there, but found that he had already been to fetch his things and was gone. She said she was going to lay a complaint with the police, but I don't think she meant it.

"Upon hearing this," Oberry continued, "I hustled right up to Pelham Manor. Had a look at the smashed car in the garage and found out precisely where the accident occurred. Went to the scene. There was no other car involved. Blanding, traveling north at great speed, simply left the road on a curve and wrapped his car around a tree. Found a householder who witnessed the accident. Another car had stopped, he said, and the driver of the wrecked car carried a woman, who appeared to be unconscious or dead, to the car which had stopped. They got in and were driven away. Blanding was alone when he turned up at the garage a few minutes later, and of course the garage people knew nothing about any woman."

"Could the witness describe the woman?" asked Lee anxiously.

"He wasn't close enough to give me a detailed description. Young and slender, he said; had medium blonde hair and was wearing a black tailored suit. If she had a hat, it had fallen off."

Lee groaned. "Sounds like her. Was Blanding hurt?"

"He was limping when he turned up at the garage; said it was nothing serious. While I was in Pelham, I inquired at the hospital and at the offices of the four doctors. Results negative; no injured woman had been brought to any of them."

That was all.

"Well, I'll be goddamned!" said Loasby when this was repeated to him.

"We're suffering from an embarrassment of evidence," said Lee without smiling. "Better spread a net for Blanding at once. As far as I know, he has no money and he must start looking for a job. Let us put a personal ad in all the newspapers asking the motorist who picked him up to come forward and testify."

Inspector Loasby reached for the telephone.

LEE SPENT THE GREATER PART of the night pacing the floor of his living room, smoking innumerable pipes of tobacco while he endeavored to reach a conclusion. No inspiration came to him. It was sadly clear to him that he would never see Mary Stannard again, but what had happened to her? Here were two perfectly good lines of investigation, each seemingly pointing to an inevitable conclusion. There was no connection between them; yet *both* men couldn't have made away with Mary.

He got little sleep and he was still lying blinking in his bed next morning when Jermyn came in with an odd expression on his leathery countenance. Clearly, he didn't like the message he was bringing.

"If you please, sir, there's a lady calling. Very peculiar! Wouldn't tell me what her business is. Her name is Miss Dordress."

Lee almost leapt out of bed. "Good! the very person I wanted to see!"

Jermyn was considerably taken aback. "Yes, sir?"

"Tell her I'll be with her directly," said Lee, "and make some coffee."

"Yes, sir."

Not stopping to dress completely, Lee went in to his visitor in dressing gown and slippers. He found a meager little woman pacing the floor of his living room. Wealth enabled her to present a smart appearance, but beyond that one was aware of a small, sharp-featured face with an ingrained expression of ill-nature.

"Good morning," said Lee politely.

This early visitor did not apologize for interrupting his rest. She instantly burst out: "What's this I read in the papers about the disappearance of Mary Stannard and the fact that the police are looking for my chauffeur, Blanding? What's the connection between the two items?"

"I wish I knew," said Lee.

She stamped her foot. "I won't be put off like that! I came here to learn the truth and I won't leave until I do!"

Lee's eyebrows ran up. Until now, his name had not been mentioned in the press. "What makes you think that I can help you?" he asked mildly.

"I telephoned to the police," she said, "and after being referred from one official to another, I finally got hold of an Inspector Loasby. He advised me to call you up. By this time I was fed up with being passed on, so I came myself to learn what is going on. I'm sure I don't know what your connection with the matter is; I'm waiting for you to tell me."

Lee's glasses glittered. "Do sit down," he said with silky politeness.

"I prefer to stand."

"My interest in this case," Lee went on, "is that of a friend of Miss Stannard's. We don't know where she is and we are very anxious."

"Probably run off with some man," sneered Miss Dordress. "If so, this publicity will be rather embarrassing to her. . . . It might even be Blanding. I wouldn't put it past her."

Lee ignored the sneer. Fishing for information, he said: "I'm told Blanding's a fine young fellow."

"Fine!" she echoed with a hard stare. "Oh, a fine animal, I suppose." She laughed disagreeably. "A chauffeur! Of course, if your young lady's tastes run to servants, she might have fallen for him."

There was a pause while Lee struggled with his temper. One could never have guessed it from his bland smile. "Have you any evidence to suggest that they have gone away together?" he asked at length.

"Mercy, no!" she said. "I'm not interested in such people!"

"Can you suggest any other explanation of Miss Stannard's disappearance?"

"I told you I wasn't interested."

Lee had her there. "Then what *is* your interest?" he asked softly.

She bit her lip. "It's simply that I resent having my name dragged into it. It's bad enough to have an expensive car destroyed without having my name dragged into such a disgusting affair."

"Your name?" said Lee with an innocent air. "What have you got to do with it?"

"Nothing!" she almost screamed at him. "But the mere fact that I employed this creature Blanding is excuse enough for the newspapers to rehash all the lying gossip about me of years past."

"Dear! Dear! How distressing!" murmured Lee. "I wish I could do something to keep all this stuff out of the newspapers."

"Never mind that now," said Miss Dordress. "I didn't come here to answer questions, but to find out the real situation. Suppose the Stannard girl *has* been made away with, whom do you suspect?"

Lee had learned long ago that the best way to obtain information is to give it—or appear to give it. "Well, there's Blanding."

"Of course!" she said, with obvious satisfaction. "Have you got a strong case against him?"

"Strong by inference," said Lee. "Everything waits on the discovery of the body."

"You can count on any help that I can give you," she said viciously. "That — Blanding" (Miss Dordress used a very unladylike word) "has cost me several thousand dollars. I'd like to see him punished. . . . Do you suspect anybody else?"

"There are certain suspicions . . ." said Lee with a guarded air.

"Who? Who?" she demanded excitedly.

"I'm not sure that I ought to mention any names at this juncture."

She burst out in an extraordinary fashion, damning Lee up and down, there in his own living room, stamping her foot, screaming. A perfect example of the spoiled brat who had never been denied. Jermyn, entering the room at that moment, almost dropped the coffee tray. Lee, turning his back to the girl, winked at Jermyn gravely. The latter, covering his mouth, hastened out of the room.

All Lee said to the girl was: "Coffee?"

"No!" she flung at him rudely.

"Pardon me if I indulge," said Lee, pouring.

Like all such people, when she saw that her tantrum wasn't having any effect, she abruptly turned it off and went to the window. Looking out on the river, she said in a changed voice: "What a lovely view you have!" She came back with her face all smoothed out, but her little gray eyes were still glittering. "I'm sure I don't know why I live on Park Avenue. There's nothing interesting to be seen from *my* windows."

"Do have some coffee," urged Lee. "It's something rather special. Mountain coffee from the Island of Jamaica."

"Well, I don't mind if I do," she said.

A moment later they were sitting amicably toe to toe, sipping from their cups. It was not the first time that Lee had had to tame an ill-conditioned brat.

She said: "I'm sorry I lost my temper, Mr. Mappin. It was so dreadfully annoying this morning to find myself spread all over the papers, just when I was beginning to hope they had forgotten me."

"I sympathize with you deeply," said Lee.

"Now you'll tell me, won't you," she went on cajolingly, "just what is behind this horrible affair?"

"As far as I can," said Lee, who had intended telling her from the first. "Just what is it you want to know?"

"Whom do you suspect besides Blanding?"

"You mustn't repeat this to anybody."

"I will be silent as the grave!"

"There are two men the police are investigating; George Restorick . . ."

"Surely," she said, with the sneer that was habitual to her. "He's been keeping her for years, hasn't he? Maybe he got sick of it at last . . . Oh, I'm sorry! I forgot she was a friend of yours. Have they got strong evidence against Restorick?"

"About as strong as against Blanding."

"Who's the other man?"

"The old grandfather—but that's no more than a suspicion."

"Nasty old man! . . . Anybody else?"

"Nobody."

"Are you *sure*?" she demanded.

"Quite sure. . . . Can't you throw some light on the subject?"

"Oh, no! I don't move in the same circles."

"But you do go out a great deal. Sometimes a word dropped at random will open up a whole vista."

She continued to shake her head. "If I repeated all the odd things I have heard about Mary Stannard it would only make you angry."

Lee put other sly questions to her without result. She soon went away. When Jermyn came back for the coffee cups, after having seen her out, he shook his head portentously.

"That young lady is a caution, sir! I never saw the like!"

Lee was gloomy. "A bad-tempered wench, Jermyn. That sort is usually easy to handle. Temper gives them away. But this one was too much for me."

"Too much for you, sir! Why you smoothed her down beautifully!"

"Easy to smooth her down! But with all my experience I did not find out *what she was after!*"

"Wouldn't it just be female curiosity, sir?"

"That, of course. But it was that *and something else*, Jermyn."

Lee was called to the telephone by Stan Oberry. Stan reported:

(a) That George Restorick had landed from a plane in Mexico City and was registered at the Reforma.

(b) Ewart Blanding had not been found.

(c) Several months earlier, Mary Stannard had insured her life for fifty thousand dollars in favor of her grandfather. The Major had already demanded settlement, but the insurance companies, naturally, were holding out for proof of death. Inquiries among the neighbors had not brought out any evidence of suspicious activities on the part of the Major in Mary's garden.

Soon afterwards, Lee was much surprised to receive a telegram from George Restorick himself, dated Mexico City.

GREATLY DISTRESSED TO READ PRESS REPORTS OF MARY STANNARD'S DISAPPEARANCE. AM WIRING CERTAIN INSTRUCTIONS TO MY ESTATE AGENTS IN NEW YORK. PLEASE GET IN TOUCH WITH THEM.

Lee lost no time in calling up the office of the Restorick Estate. The call was answered by the same man he had talked to on the day before. Lee said: "This is Amos Lee Mappin speaking. I have had a telegram from Mr. Restorick." He read it over the wire.

"Yes, Mr. Mappin," said the agent. "I have just received the communication that Mr. Restorick speaks of in his wire to you. This message is really intended for you, but was sent to me because we have a code for wiring each other." The voice hesitated. "I hardly like to read it over the wire, sir. Can I bring it to you?"

Lee's aroused curiosity could not brook the delay. "I'm on a direct wire," he said. "There can be no leakage at this end."

"Very well, sir, I'll read it.

> . . . INFORM MR. AMOS LEE MAPPIN IT IS MY EARNEST DESIRE THAT AS A FRIEND OF MISS MARY STANNARD'S HE SHOULD CONDUCT THE FULLEST POSSIBLE INVESTIGATION INTO THE CIRCUMSTANCES SURROUNDING HER DISAP-PEARANCE. TELL HIM HE IS TO STOP AT NO EX-PENSE. TELL HIM HE MAY DRAW ON ME FOR ANY AMOUNT IN CONNECTION WITH SUCH AN INVESTIGATION UP TO THE SUM OF ONE HUN-DRED THOUSAND DOLLARS, AND LET THIS BE YOUR AUTHORITY TO HONOR ANY DRAFTS HE MAY MAKE ON YOU WITHOUT ASKING FOR AN ACCOUNTING. THERE IS ONLY ONE STIPULA-TION ATTACHED TO THIS OFFER. IT WILL BE WITHDRAWN IF IT IS REVEALED TO THE PRESS.
> GEORGE RESTORICK

Lee felt a little breathless. "Well!" he said. . . . "This is somewhat astonishing!"

"It is quite characteristic of Mr. Restorick, sir," said the voice. "I shall hold myself at your disposal."

"First," said Lee, "send a telegram to Mr. Restorick in your code but as from me. Say that I am already devoting my entire time to the investigation that he proposes. Say that I deeply appreciate his generous offer and shall not hesitate to take advantage of it, should it become necessary. So far, no great expenditures have been called for."

"Very good, sir!"

Lee hung up and passed a hand over his face. "Well, I'll be tee-totally and everlastingly damned!" he murmured.

CHAPTER SEVEN

LEE SPENT THE BALANCE of Tuesday in the routine work of investigation. Upon telephoning to the garage in Pelham Manor where Miss Dordress' wrecked car had been taken, he was told that the Packard agency had already sent up for it and were towing it down to their own shop in the city. After lunch, Lee went over to examine the wreck. He had been provided with police credentials by Inspector Loasby that smoothed his way on such expeditions.

The car had been hoisted to an upper floor of the big machine shop, where it lay in a corner. The foreman showed it. "The owner has been over to have a look at it," he said. "She wanted to junk it, but as the company wasn't able to let her have a new car of the same type immediately, she ordered it repaired. We haven't started to take it down yet."

The red coupé exhibited a sad travesty of its former smartness. The left front wheel was crumpled up and driven back; windshield smashed, top torn and collapsed, the whole side mashed in. Literally, it looked, in Stan Oberry's words, as if it had been wrapped around a tree.

"What a marvel that the driver escaped injury!" said Lee.

"Well, sir, you can see she didn't hit square, or he would have been killed, certain," said the foreman. "She caught the tree between the wheel and the engine block and made hay of the whole front axle and steering assemblies. The car would then swing around—maybe she swung in two or three circles before stopping.

65

I didn't see it when it was picked up, of course. That swing took up its momentum, see? There was no dead shock of stoppage."

"Still, I say the driver was lucky," said Lee. . . . Perhaps his passenger was already dead, he added to himself.

The car had been through so many hands since the accident, there was little chance that it would reveal any new evidence, but Lee made a patient examination of the wreck. It exhibited a mess of fingerprints that helped him not at all. He failed to find any that suggested a woman's hand. Mary Stannard had a small and delicately formed hand.

The rear of the car was uninjured. At Lee's request, the foreman threw up the top of the luggage compartment. The interior gave Lee nothing. Well, according to his information, the body of the woman passenger had not been carried there.

When the tangle of the top and the broken windshield was lifted out of the way and the leather-covered seat removed, Lee discovered a piece of tragic evidence. A small, faded blossom was lodged in the crack between the seat and the upholstered back. There was still some color in the petals, and when he had carefully smoothed them out, he could make out the green and black markings of the Investia orchid. With a somber face, he deposited it in an envelope and put it in his pocket. The foreman looked on wonderingly, but he was a discreet man and asked no questions.

"That's all," said Lee, "and thank you very much for your assistance."

One of the most baffling features of the situation was the failure both of Stan Oberry's operative and of the police, working independently, to discover any trace of the unconscious (or dead) woman who had been lifted out of the wrecked car. Lee made a trip up to Pelham to pursue some inquiries of his own, but they were without result. No such woman had been seen after she was picked up. Was it possible that the car which rescued Blanding and the woman after the accident was driven by a friend of Blanding's? It did not seem likely.

BACK IN TOWN at the end of the afternoon, Lee went to call on Major Dunphy. He was surprised to find the sidewalk in front of the house blocked by a knot of gaping people. They had even overflowed into the area-way in front of Mary Stannard's little house, where some of them were trying to peer through the kitchen windows. The maids had pulled the blinds down inside. Not for the first time in his life, Lee wondered at the number of people there are in the city who seem to have nothing to do but stand and stare.

As he went down the steps, a young press photographer took his picture. "Let me have another, sir, without the hat," he said cheerfully.

"I'm damned if I will," muttered Lee.

The photographer, quite unabashed, took out his notebook. "Name, please?"

Lee looked at him balefully and pushed on. It was not his usual method of dealing with the press, but his feelings were so exacerbated he couldn't take any more. A reporter who knew him was standing beside the house door.

"Good afternoon, Mr. Mappin," he said affably.

Lee was too sore to answer.

"What's your connection with this case, sir?"

"I am merely a friend of Miss Stannard's."

"Aren't you going to direct the investigation, sir?"

"Nothing to say."

"What are the latest developments?"

"You heard me."

The young man was still asking questions when the door was opened by the red-eyed housemaid. This was a house of death where there were no preparations for a funeral. When Lee asked for Major Dunphy, she mutely nodded and held the door wide.

"I'll find him," said Lee. "You needn't come."

Up in the living room, Lee found the old man dressed in his usual elaborate fashion to go out; derby hat, chamois gloves, gray spats, malacca stick, complete even to the carnation in his buttonhole. With his belly girdled in and his chest pushed out, he planted the hat rakishly askew and preened himself before the mirror, turning his head this way and that to observe the effect. Strange old being! At an age when other men were preparing to face their

Maker, he still strutted down the Avenue allowing himself to be admired.

"I cannot go out of the house without having to run the gantlet!" he complained. "Infernal bore! I suppose they will take my photograph!"

"That would be very distasteful!" said Lee dryly.

"I don't mind the photographers so much, but I scarcely know how to deal with the reporters. They ask such personal questions!"

"You can refuse to talk."

"I don't like to do that. One should never antagonize the press. It's dangerous."

"Then talk."

The Major shot his cuffs and thumped his stick on the rug. "I'm going down to my club, and that will be just as bad, with all the members crowding around to ask questions!"

Lee looked at him blandly. "I shall have to detain you for a moment or two."

"My days have become one long annoyance," grumbled the Major. "There is no such thing as privacy left. . . . Look! Look!" he cried, pointing through one of the back windows with his stick. "You see those men in the garden? Police. They didn't ask permission. They came right in. Acting as if they owned the place. Positively insulting! Do you see what they are doing? Prodding in the flower beds with pointed sticks, as if they expected to find my granddaughter's body buried there! Did you ever hear of such an outrage? I told them she left this house before nine o'clock on Sunday night and was never seen again, but they paid no attention to me. Pushed past me as if I hadn't been there!"

"I'll speak to the inspector," said Lee.

"What did you want to see me about?"

"Insurance," said Lee grimly.

"Insurance?"

"Precisely. Life insurance. I am told that Mary has insured her life for fifty thousand dollars, naming you as the beneficiary."

"Who told you that?" asked the Major sharply.

"What does that matter? I am employing investigators. So are the police."

"Do you have to pry into *my* affairs?"

Lee drew a long breath to give him patience. "Look, Major, as one sensible man to another, you must know that when there is a mysterious disappearance and someone is discovered to benefit greatly, questions are bound to be asked. Is it true about the insurance?"

"Yes, so what? Do you dare to imply that I put my granddaughter out of the way for the sake of the insurance money?"

"Not at all! But all the circumstances must be gone into."

"Why shouldn't Mary take out life insurance and name me? I'm her only relative."

"Somewhat unusual for a young person to insure herself for the benefit of an old one."

"Oh, is that what is sticking in your crop? Well, as a matter of fact, Mary only named me because she had to name somebody. The policy was for her own benefit. It never occurred to either of us that I might outlive her. It's what they call an endowment policy; matures in twenty years. Mary took it out in order to force herself to save money. She was paying something like a hundred dollars a week on it. In twenty years she'd get it all back and more."

To one who knew Mary's extravagant habits, this was a plausible explanation. "You and she had talked it over?" asked Lee.

"Of course we had! Mary had even said that if there should be an accident, a theater fire or a railway smashup, I'd be provided for. Does that make me guilty of her murder?"

"Certainly not. . . . Of course," added Lee carelessly, "if Mary married she would naturally change the name of the beneficiary."

The old man shot a scowling glance at Lee from under his heavy brows. "Well, that question had never come up," he said.

Lee shot out an accusing forefinger. "You knew that Mary was going to marry Jack Fentress!"

The Major's glance shifted away from Lee's. "Well . . . well . . . yes, I did!" he said defiantly. "So what?"

Lee shrugged. "Nothing," he said. "It's a suspicious circumstance, that's all."

The Major mounted his dignity. "If you have concluded your cross-examination, perhaps I may be allowed to go out for my walk."

"By all means," said Lee. "I want to talk to Lottie."

The Major, twirling his stick, started downstairs. Odd that he had never asked Lee if there was any news of Mary.

Lee called up the stair well. "Lottie!"

She answered immediately. "Coming, Mr. Mappin!"

"Stay where you are," said Lee. "I'm coming up."

Mary's sitting room—or her "boudoir," as she called it with a grin—was flooded with late sunshine. The chintz coverings were as fresh as natural flowers; the brass fire irons gleamed. Lee looked around him, feeling a sickness at the heart; the pretty room was so empty now. The motherly Lottie guessed what was passing through his mind and her eyes filled with tears.

"Damn that old man!" growled Lee, to cover his feelings. "Always puts me in a rage."

Lottie wiped her eyes and nodded vigorously. "That's right, Mr. Mappin. It certainly is a trial to live in the house with him. . . . Is there any news?" she asked piteously.

Lee shook his head and Lottie turned away. There was a silence.

"I came to ask you a question, Lottie," Lee said at length. "Miss Dordress came to see me this morning. You know who she is?"

"Sure, the great heiress."

"She's no heiress, Lottie. She already has the money right in her fist."

"What about Miss Dordress, Mr. Mappin?"

"Were she and our Mary ever friends?"

Lottie shook her head. "Not in my time, Mr. Mappin. I suppose they met around different places, but not to say friends. . . . Wait a minute. I mind now that they did meet once and Miss Mary spoke about it afterwards. She said the rich girl was so rude—damned rude was what she said, if you'll excuse me, sir—that she, meaning Miss Mary, just walked out on her."

"Judging from my own experience, I can well believe that," said Lee. "Yet Miss Dordress evinced a sharp and ugly curiosity in regard to this matter that I cannot figure out."

"Maybe it is just the natural jealousy of an ugly woman for a beautiful one," suggested Lottie.

"Maybe so."

ON TUESDAY NIGHT Inspector Loasby came to Lee's apartment to discuss the day's developments. Meanwhile, the popular interest and excitement was rising with every new edition of the newspapers. Various scraps of information had leaked out to the press, and what they lacked in facts, they more than made up in comment and speculation. Lee's photograph was reproduced in the evening papers; so was Major Dunphy's in the rakish derby.

Lee described Miss Dordress' visit. Loasby said:

"The multimillionaire girl, too! Boy! what a case is shaping up for one of your books, Lee!"

"I doubt if I'll ever have the heart to write this one up," said Lee.

"Then let me have it for my memoirs!"

"We'd better wait until we solve it before we decide anything," said Lee dryly.

"In the meantime I'll have that rich dame shadowed."

"Let Stan Oberry do it."

"What!" cried Loasby with an affronted air. "So Oberry's detectives are better than mine, eh?"

"Not necessarily. They're amateurs and yours are professionals."

"And is it your idea that amateurs are better than professionals? That's something new."

"Only under certain circumstances," said Lee, smiling. "Your men and women look like detectives. How could they avoid it? It is therefore not difficult for a sharp-eyed person to spot them. Now if Miss Dordress discovers that she's being shadowed, she'll simply do a disappearing act and we'll learn no more. Lakewood for the cool spring weather, or Pinehurst, or any place where there's a de luxe hotel."

"Sure," said Loasby, "that's a chance you have to take. How could Oberry do any better?"

"Oberry has hundreds of operators on call. He may not use them in months. They come from every walk of life and cannot be distinguished from ordinary people. They may be inexperienced, but they are clever, and can follow instructions. Moreover, he could have the girl followed by a different operative every day. You can't waste the public money like that."

"All right, have it your own way," grumbled the inspector. "Where are *you* going to get all that money?"

Lee told him about George Restorick's offer.

Loasby struck the table. "By God! what a note!" he said, staring. "Never heard the like of it. . . . Well, that lets Restorick out. No man would offer a hundred grand to solve a crime he had committed himself."

"I'm not convinced of that," said Lee. "What's a hundred thousand to Restorick? No more than a dollar to you or me. He may have offered it in a spirit of bravado. It would be an astute move."

"He might offer it to the police," said Loasby ruefully, "because the police are supposed to be dumb. But not to Amos Lee Mappin. That would require a superhuman nerve!"

"Note well," said Lee, "that the offer is contingent upon secrecy. If any word of it gets in the newspapers, I don't get the money."

"It won't get out through me," said Loasby.

"Well, I have some more evidence," Lee continued. He told Loasby about the search of the wrecked coupé, and showed him what he had found in it. Loasby became freshly excited.

"What did I tell you?" he cried. "Restorick is out of this case. Blanding is our man. See how neatly it all fits together. We know that Blanding bought these, what's this?—Investia orchids, around eight o'clock on Sunday night. He then calls on Mary Stannard and presents them to her. She must have worn them because they are not found in her house after she's gone. So she goes with Blanding. . . ."

"Wait a minute," objected Lee. "There's no proof of that."

"She was never seen afterwards," said Loasby. "Perhaps Blanding hit her over the head or throttled her and *carried* her out to his car. He was not seen to leave the house. Shortly after nine o'clock, he smashes into a tree alongside Pelham Bay Parkway—you see, the time is just right. And certainly there was an unconscious woman in the wreck. It all hangs together. Blanding is our man. This faded flower is positive proof of it!"

Lee smiled. "You said that last night about the handkerchief I picked up at Black Maple."

"The picture is entirely changed now. Restorick is out of it. The handkerchief must have been dropped on some previous visit. Blanding is our man . . . There is only one other possible complication."

"What's that?"

"The old man may have made it up with Blanding to do the job for him. He could afford to give Blanding a nice cut out of the fifty grand insurance money."

"It's a possibility," said Lee, "but a slim one."

"We're handicapped in our search because we have no photograph of Blanding, but by God! I'll find that devil if it's my last act on earth! Just give me twenty-four hours, Lee!"

CHAPTER EIGHT

ON WEDNESDAY MORNING, Lee was making his way east on Forty-second Street, on the way to Stan Oberry's office. The sidewalk was thronged with people. At intervals during the past twenty-four hours Lee had had the uneasy feeling that he was being spied upon and followed, but he had not been able to spot his trailers. It was difficult to figure who had an interest in spying upon *him*. Could it be at George Restorick's order? Restorick had the means to hire spies. Or Amy Dordress?

In front of the Commodore Hotel he heard a voice at his ear, saying: "Can I speak with you for a moment, Mr. Mappin?" It was an agreeable male voice, but strained with anxiety.

Lee turned his head to see what kind of a touch this might be. He found a stalwart young man at his shoulder; Lee was aware of fine blue eyes, tortured with anxiety. The whole face was reassuring; it had nothing of the abject quality of a panhandler.

"Who are you?" asked Lee.

"Charles Foster," said the young man hurriedly. "You don't know me. . . . I'm not a beggar!" he added.

"You don't look like one," said Lee. "What can I do for you?"

"I can't talk to you in the open street, sir," faltered the young man, "among all these people. If you'd be kind enough to sit down with me for a moment or two in the Commodore bar . . ."

"All right," said Lee.

"Oh, thank you, sir!" The young man darted into the bar in advance.

74

They seated themselves at a little table against the wall. At this hour there were few customers. Lee ordered two beers and studied his young companion. He looked exhausted—from lack of sleep, perhaps. The blue eyes were rimmed with red.

"It's about Miss Mary Stannard, sir," he began imploringly. "What has happened to her? The newspapers are full of silly stuff. I can't make head or tail of it. The suspense has nearly driven me out of my mind. I can't bear it any longer. What is the truth, sir?"

"What's your interest in Mary Stannard?" asked Lee.

The young man turned his head aside. "I should think that is obvious."

"You mean you're in love with her."

He said nothing.

The truth like a great light suddenly broke on Lee's mind. "You're Ewart Blanding!" he exclaimed.

The young man looked at him with eyes full of terror. "Oh, no, sir," he stammered. "Nothing like that. Miss Stannard was scarcely aware of my existence; I was just one in the crowd that fell for her. You've got me wrong. My name is Ned Foster."

"You just said Charles Foster," murmured Lee, smiling.

With a gesture of surrender, the young man allowed his chin to fall on his breast. There was a silence. As he studied him, Lee's face warmed with feeling, then hardened again. He must not allow this young man's comely features, his fine physique and his voice charged with emotion to blind him to the fact that there was strong testimony that Ewart Blanding had been the last to see Mary Stannard alive, or dead.

Blanding lifted his eyes imploringly. "What has happened to Mary, sir?"

"I don't know," said Lee dryly. "We were beginning to believe that you were the one to answer that question."

Blanding was neither excited nor alarmed by this charge. He even smiled bleakly. "I know," he said, "I gathered as much from the newspapers. It's ridiculous. I couldn't have harmed Mary. I love her."

"If you're innocent," said Lee, "why didn't you give yourself up at once so you could help us discover the truth?"

Blanding looked at him in surprise. "It never occurred to me that I could help. I was nothing in Mary's life. I didn't give myself up because I couldn't take the charge against me seriously. I expected every hour to read that you had found the real criminal—if a crime has been committed. Moreover, if the police persisted in their suspicions of me, why, I had no money to hire a lawyer."

"Tell me everything that happened on Sunday," said Lee. "I already know about the fight you had with Jack Fentress on Saturday night."

"How much else do you know?" asked Ewart naïvely.

Lee laughed briefly. "Never mind that. Tell me what you know—and stick to the truth."

"I shan't lie to you," said Ewart with an indifferent air. "Why should I? Certainly not to save my own skin. I don't value my life any more than that!" He snapped his fingers. "And there's nobody in the world to grieve for me. . . . But there are others to be considered."

"The truth won't hurt anybody except the guilty," said Lee.

Ewart smiled at him almost pityingly. "It's not as simple as that, sir."

"Get on with your story," said Lee, slightly nettled.

Ewart considered for a moment, and began: "Last fall, when Mary made her big hit and had her salary doubled . . ." He raised his eyes to Lee's face. "Do you mind if I call her Mary, sir?"

"Of course not. Go on."

"She bought a car and engaged me to drive her around town. I fell for her at sight. It was not her beautiful face that attracted me; more than that; it was her goodness of heart, her fun, her honesty. There was never anybody else like Mary. From the first, no other woman existed for me, and none ever could. She made a friend of me, but I didn't misunderstand her. I knew I never had a Chinaman's chance. We had wonderful times together, always laughing, though my heart was aching for her like sin . . ."

"Never mind your heart," growled Lee. "Stick to the facts."

"As time passed," Ewart went on, "my feelings got so strong I couldn't hide them. I tried to make a joke of it, to get her to take me for granted, but that hurt her, too, she was so tenderhearted. It embarrassed her to have me around. So she made up a story that she couldn't afford to keep a car in the city. She sold the car and let me go. But she didn't cut me off altogether. She was too kind to do that. She would include me in a party once in awhile. I was never alone with her.

"It wasn't until last Saturday night that I learned she was going to marry Jack Fentress. Of course, I knew that she went around with him. I knew . . . well, I knew too much about them. It hurt me like a stab!" Ewart struck his breast. "It wouldn't have been so bad if it had been a man I could respect. But *Fentress*! I knew I was a better man than he. It seemed like more than I could bear! And when I learned she was going to *marry* him . . . Well, you're not interested in my feelings."

"Suppose she had accepted George Restorick?" suggested Lee, curious to see how he would react.

"That would have been easier to bear, sir. Because then I could have imagined her safe and happy, like a queen on her throne, like a lady bountiful dispensing gifts."

"Hm!" grumbled Lee. "You are eloquent."

"Sunday I walked the streets like a crazy man," Ewart resumed. "After I learned she was going to be married, I didn't want to see her again. Not alone. Because I was afraid I wouldn't be able to hold myself in. But I had told her I was going to bring the flowers Sunday night and so I had to go. I meant to stay a few minutes only. As a matter of fact, Miss Dordress had ordered the car for later."

"For what purpose?" asked Lee.

"She gave a big party on Sunday night; dinner followed by music and dancing. I was instructed to call for Miss Damaris Forsman, the opera singer, at nine-thirty and take her to Miss Dordress', and carry her home again after she had sung."

"Go on," said Lee. "What time did you call at Miss Stannard's house? That's extremely important."

"It was a few minutes past eight, sir. That's the closest I can come to it."

"All right. What happened?"

"I knew that Mary and Fentress were planning to get married, but I didn't know it had been arranged for that very night. As soon as I saw her costume and the shine in her eyes, I knew." Ewart paused, with hanging head.

"Was she all ready to go out when you came?"

"Yes. She even had her little overnight bag in her hand."

"Go on."

"I lost my grip then," Ewart said simply. "I knew I was a fool, but I couldn't hold back the words. I told her everything I had been saving for so long. I begged her not to marry Fentress. I told her what other men thought of him. Even then she was kind—kind but firm; told me I had better go . . ." He stopped.

"Well, what happened?" prompted Lee.

"Nothing happened. Mary pinned my flowers on the breast of her jacket and I ran out of the house like a crazy man, carrying the picture in my mind of Mary wearing my flowers and standing up to be married to another man. I jumped in the car and drove north . . ."

"What time would this be?"

"I couldn't say. I couldn't say. I was in the house about a quarter-hour."

"Where were you heading for when you drove away?"

"I don't know. Anywhere. My only idea was to get out of the city. I forgot all about my employer. Up on Pelham Bay Parkway I took a curve to the left at too great a speed; both my right-hand tires blew; I lost control and crashed. You read all that in the papers."

"How you escaped death I cannot understand," said Lee.

"I saw it coming. I slid from under the seat and wrapped my arms around my head."

"Can you tell me the exact time that you crashed?"

"Sure!" Ewart held out his left wrist. "Look! my watch stopped at ten minutes to nine. It's broken and it's still stopped."

"And what became of Mary?" asked Lee softly.

Ewart stared. "Mary? What are you talking about?"

"Mary was beside you in the car."

Ewart laughed scornfully. "That's silly! Would I have been driving like a madman if Mary was beside me?"

"Across the road from the spot where you crashed, there is a house," said Lee. "The householder heard the crash and ran to the window. He saw you lift the body of a woman from the wreck. Then another car came along and picked you both up."

"Nothing in it," said Ewart quietly. "Either he was deceived by the darkness, or he is plain lying. I was alone in the car."

"I wish I could believe you," said Lee.

"Did anybody else see a woman?" demanded Ewart. "My own movements after the crash were perfectly open. I went direct to a garage in Pelham and gave them an order to tow the car in. I wanted to get the wreck out of the way before the police heard about it. Then I thumbed a ride back to town."

"There is more evidence against you," said Lee regretfully, "more and deadlier."

Ewart looked his question.

Lee put his hand in his inside pocket. "Yesterday when I examined the wreck of the red coupé, I found this. It had slipped behind the seat." He opened the envelope. "Bear in mind that you have just told me Mary pinned your flowers to the breast of her jacket."

Lee laid the faded flower on the table between them. "Badly damaged," he said, "but you can still see that it is a blossom broken from a spray of the Investia orchid. There is no other flower like it."

Ewart stared at the flower with his eyes starting from his head. "The orchid!" he whispered. "How could that be?" Then he broke into a high-pitched laugh. "It was planted on me! It was planted!"

"That's what they always say," murmured Lee, putting the flower away.

Ewart seemed to collapse in his chair. "Then you don't believe me," he said, looking at Lee reproachfully. "I don't care about the police, but if you're against me, I'm a goner, certain!"

"I'm not against you!" said Lee sharply. "I only want to bring out the truth!"

"What's to be done now?" asked Ewart hopelessly.

"You must understand that I have to turn you over to the police."

The young man was electrified. Leaping to his feet, turning his chair over backwards, he cried, "No, by God!" and like a flash was out of the door—not the front door on Forty-second Street, but a rear entrance to the bar, giving on one of the great passages leading to the Grand Central Concourse.

Lee followed as fast as he could, but there was a throng of people moving each way in the passage, and when he got to the door, Ewart Blanding was already lost among them. Lee, with a shrug, returned to his little table. There was a curious mixture of feelings visible in his face. Perhaps he was not altogether displeased that his prisoner had escaped.

The waiter came to him. "What bit the young fellow so sudden?" he asked.

"He discovered he only had a minute to catch his train," said Lee calmly.

Paying the check, he resumed his walk in the direction of Stan Oberry's office.

WHEN HE ARRIVED, Stan said: "Inspector Loasby just called up to see if you were here. Ewart Blanding has been nabbed."

"The hell you say!" exclaimed Lee.

"Sure enough! Loasby is tickled pink about it. Blanding was picked up a few minutes ago at Grand Central, and he is being taken down to headquarters. Loasby wants you there while he's questioning him."

"Okay," said Lee.

He stopped only long enough to instruct Oberry to find the nurseryman in Madison, New Jersey, who grew the Investia orchids. Lee wanted to learn if there had been any other sales of this blossom on Sunday. He then took a taxi to headquarters.

In a private room he found Loasby, a clerk, a uniformed officer, and Ewart Blanding, looking stiff-lipped and stubborn.

"Won't talk," said the inspector disgustedly. "Says he has told his whole story to you."

"That's right," said Lee, ". . . or what he says is his whole story." Lee described his meeting with Ewart. "How was he taken?" he asked.

"Ask him," said Loasby, nodding toward the man in uniform.

"I was on fixed post outside the main door of Grand Central Station," said the officer. "I hears a little disturbance in the station and I looks in. Sees this prisoner making for the door, and everybody gaping at him. Nobody offered to interfere with him, but I hears a voice from the back somewheres shouting: 'Stop that man! It's Ewart Blanding!' So I collars him. He made no resistance."

"Did you see the man who denounced him?" asked Lee.

"No, sir. I holds the prisoner there for a few minutes, expecting the man to come up and identify himself, but he didn't. Then, as the prisoner admitted he was Blanding, and knowing he was wanted, I took him to the station house and telephoned headquarters."

"Ewart," asked Lee, "did you hear the voice that named you? Did you recognize the voice?"

The prisoner unbent a little toward Lee.

"No, sir. I was too excited, I guess. Wasn't paying any attention."

Lee ran over the main points of Ewart's story for Loasby's benefit.

"Well, we can check that on the spot," said Loasby. "Bring in the two men who are waiting in the anteroom," he said to his clerk.

The clerk presently brought in two blond, well-dressed young men, obviously brothers, whose name was McVeagh. They were evidently strangers to headquarters, and looked around them curiously.

At sight of the two, all the color drained out of Ewart Blanding's face. He stepped forward before anyone else spoke and said beseechingly: "Be careful what you say, men! For God's sake, be careful!"

"Silence!" roared Loasby, "or I'll have you put in a cell!"

The elder of the brothers said to Blanding: "I'm sorry, fellow, but I can't lie for you if it's a police matter. I wouldn't dare!"

Blanding lowered his head and said no more.

"Do you recognize this man?" asked Loasby of the McVeaghs.

"Yes, sir," said the elder. His brother corroborated him.

"Describe the circumstances under which you met before."

"It was last Sunday night, Inspector, around nine o'clock. My brother and I were driving up Pelham Bay Parkway on our way to New Rochelle where we live. I was at the wheel. Half a mile or so this side of Pelham Manor we heard a crash. Well, a red convertible had just passed us at a dangerous speed, and I said to my brother: 'It wasn't long before he got his.' A minute later we saw the wreck. This man was staggering around the car, sort of dazed. He lifted up the smashed top and drew out the limp body of a woman. We had stopped, of course, and he brought her over to our car and said: 'Can you give me a lift to the nearest hospital, fellows?' and I said, 'Sure!' and asked how badly she was hurt. He said: 'Not bad, I think; I can't find any broken bones; she's not bleeding anywhere. She's just been knocked cold.' So he climbed in the back of our car, holding the girl in his arms."

"Describe her," said Loasby.

"He was carrying her sort of crouched over, Inspector, and neither of us ever got a good look in her face. My brother wanted to take her from him, but he wouldn't let him. I can only say that she had a slender figure, was wearing a black, tailor-made suit, and had no hat. Her hair was a medium blonde."

"How was it dressed?" asked Lee.

"I couldn't describe it to you, sir. Just a mess of curls like all the girls have."

"Did she have a spray of small orchids, green and black, pinned to the breast of her jacket?"

"I couldn't say, sir. He was holding her too close to his own breast for me to see that."

Lee took a photograph of Mary Stannard from his pocket. "Was it this girl?" he asked, dreading the answer.

The two young men studied it with their heads close together. "It is possible," said the elder, "but I couldn't swear to it. I never got a look at her in the light." His brother made a similar answer.

"One more question," said Lee with a stony face. "Is it possible that this girl was dead when he brought her to your car?"

"Oh, my God!" exclaimed the startled youth. "Such a thing never occurred to me. You see, he said she had been knocked cold. But she neither moved nor spoke; maybe she was . . . I couldn't answer that question either way, sir." His brother replied to the same effect.

Lee glanced at Loasby to signify that he had no more questions. Loasby asked: "Where did you carry them?"

"To the Pelham Hospital, sir. Wasn't but about three minutes' drive. This man got out, still carrying the girl. Wouldn't let my brother take her. He started up the steps with her. We didn't wait, so I couldn't testify that he actually entered the hospital with her."

"Did you have any other conversation with him during that short drive?"

The brothers glanced at each other. "Just a little bit, sir."

"What was it?"

"Well, he said he was anxious to protect the girl's name, because she was married and her husband didn't know she was out. And my brother and I promised that we wouldn't say anything about a girl. We have not mentioned her up to now. But of course, if a crime has been committed, we couldn't keep such a promise."

"Certainly not. Do you understand that that was what he was referring to when he spoke to you awhile ago?"

"Why, yes, sir."

"Nothing else was said on the way to the hospital?"

"Not a word, sir."

"Then that will be all today, gentlemen. And thank you for coming forward to testify."

The brothers retired.

Loasby addressed Ewart. "Do you wish to make a statement at this time? It is my duty to warn you that anything you say may be used against you."

"Nothing to say," answered Ewart stonily.

Loasby sent for a warder and had him taken away.

"Well, I guess that cleans up the Stannard case," said the pleased inspector. "I was right, you see."

"We are far from the end of it," said Lee gravely.

"Hey?"

"We have still to find the body!"

CHAPTER NINE

As LEE CAME DOWN the steps of police headquarters, he ran into Jack Fentress among the perennial loungers on the sidewalk. They talked in undertones.

"Thank God, here you are!" exclaimed Jack. "I'm near out of my mind, not knowing what is happening."

"Blanding has been arrested," said Lee.

"Good! I'm glad that swine is safely locked up. . . . Look, Mr. Mappin, my car is parked around the corner. Can I take you any-where?"

"Surely!" said Lee. "I have to stop in East Thirty-sixth Street. And many thanks."

As they pushed their way through the gaping onlookers, Lee studied his companion's face. The dark young man looked pretty bad. He was even jerkier than usual in his movements.

Jack, guessing what was passing through Lee's mind, said: "I suppose I look as if I had been put through a wringer. Haven't had much sleep since this thing happened. Well, you don't look very bright yourself, sir."

"It's getting us all down," said Lee.

As they started uptown in Jack's car, the young man burst out: "I'm the person most concerned in this case but I have no stand-ing in it! I couldn't go up to Inspector Loasby's office to find out what was happening."

"You're mistaken about that," said Lee. "Loasby is quite hu-man. He would understand your position."

"What happened up there, Mr. Mappin?"

Lee told him.

"Then we've *got* him!" cried Jack in angry satisfaction. "He hasn't a loophole! Thank God for that much!"

As Lee did not echo these sentiments, Jack turned to him in surprise. "Aren't you satisfied that he's the man, Mr. Mappin?"

"Frankly, no!" said Lee. "The evidence *looks* conclusive, but I have a hunch that Blanding is not the man."

Jack cast an astonished glance at him. "Do you go by your hunches, Mr. Mappin?" he asked with a touch of sarcasm.

"Yes and no," said Lee. "Naturally, I do not offer my hunches as *evidence*, but I follow them in *looking* for evidence. And when the evidence is all in, I generally find that my original hunch was not deceiving me."

"What *is* a hunch, anyhow, sir?"

"A prompting, a whisper, from the little fellow who sits inside every man's breast."

"And what does your little fellow tell you about Blanding?"

"That he was speaking the truth."

Jack's eyebrows ran up. "But the two guys from New Rochelle *proved* him a liar!"

"That's right. Still . . . I never saw a man with such an open, honest glance. If Blanding was lying, he is a better actor than any I ever saw on the stage. To act a *simple* part must be the hardest."

"You're right," agreed Jack. "But it is done. It's not for me to set up an opinion against yours, sir, but I have always thought that this open look you speak of was simply an accident of nature. Some are born with it, some not."

"True."

"I've known men who could look you straight in the eye and lie like Ananias."

"Of course. I can do it myself when necessary. But it's not easy to deceive the little fellow inside. . . . And apart from the question of whether Blanding is lying, there is a lot about this case that is still unexplained. Nearly every day something happens that does not jibe with the accepted theory."

"For instance?"

"When Ewart Blanding cut across the Grand Central Concourse, somebody hollered, 'It's Ewart Blanding!' His photograph has not been published. Who could that have been?"

"Oh, there must be a certain number of people around town who know Blanding. One of them happened to be in Grand Central. It was pure accident."

"Perhaps."

"What other things have you in mind, Mr. Mappin?"

"There are certain things I must not speak of. Things that hang by a hair."

Jack looked startled, but said no more.

"The body must be found before we can know where we stand," said Lee.

"What are the police doing about that?" asked Jack.

"Loasby is concentrating all his resources on the search. Pelham is within the city limits, so he has a free hand. If everything else fails, he will make a house to house search."

"If Blanding had no car, he couldn't have carried the body far," said Jack.

As he put Lee down in front of the Restorick Estate office, Jack said anxiously: "Can I see you again, sir? You're my only source of information."

"Stop around at my place any time," said Lee. "Better telephone first."

"I'll do that, sir."

THIS WAS THE FIRST TIME that Lee had come face to face with Mr. Eversman, head agent for the Restorick Estate. He was a finished, soft-spoken gentleman, beautifully dressed in a somewhat old-fashioned style. He had been associated with the affairs of the rich for so many years that he had come to look more like a millionaire than any actual millionaire Lee had ever known.

"What are the latest developments, Mr. Mappin?" he asked when Lee had introduced himself.

By way of answer, Lee wrote out a telegram for George Restorick, giving a brief résumé of the events of the morning.

Mr. Eversman said: "I'll put this into code and dispatch it at once, Mr. Mappin."

Lee's next stop was at Stan Oberry's office. Here he learned that no shipments of the Investia orchid had been made to New York on Saturday or Sunday except the two sprays that were already known.

WITHIN AN HOUR OR TWO the news of Ewart Blanding's arrest was out on the streets. Lee's connection with the case could no longer be hidden, and the reporters camped on his trail, seeking further particulars. All the rest of the day they hung around the entrance to his apartment house, and on Thursday morning they gathered early.

Jermyn came to Lee in his study to say that a lady was calling on the phone. "Her name is Mrs. Carlyle, sir, but she says you don't know her. It's about the Stannard case, sir."

"Oh, another reporter," said Lee. "Tell her there is nothing to be given out this morning."

"Excuse me, sir, but this one doesn't sound like a reporter."

"What in thunder does a reporter sound like?" demanded Lee.

"Well, confident and self-assured, sir, if you know what I mean. Smooth. This young lady has a modest voice, sir. Sounds almost as if she had been crying."

"Well, switch her in here," said Lee. "If it's just another reporter, I'll flay you, Jermyn."

He presently heard a timid, breathless voice over the wire: "Mr. Mappin, I just came to your apartment. My husband is with me. We found a lot of reporters waiting outside in the street, and they started asking questions to find out if we had come to see you. My husband got angry and so we went away again. Mr. Mappin, I was wondering if you would be kind enough to let me speak to you for a few moments outside somewhere."

"Well!" said the surprised Lee. The gentle voice had half won him. "What's it about?"

"I can't tell you over the phone, sir. It's very important."

"But I must know before I can run out and see you. The reporters are laying for me, too. Are you using a dial phone?"

"Yes, sir. In a pay station."

"Then there is no danger of the wire being tapped. You may speak freely."

"Mr. Mappin . . . Mr. Mappin," faltered the gentle voice. "I am the woman who was in the car with Ewart Blanding on Sunday night when he crashed."

Lee's face became one great O of astonishment. "Well! . . . Where are you now?"

"Speaking from a pay station on First Avenue."

"We cannot talk in the street," said Lee. "Take a taxi and go to Thirty-nine West Forty-second Street. Meet me there in Room 918. There's no lettering on the door; you walk right in. It's the office of my friend, Stanley Oberry. Have you got the address?"

She repeated it.

"I'll be there in ten minutes," said Lee.

Jermyn, who had overheard this, stood waiting with his hat and topcoat. Lee went down in the elevator, taking care to wipe all signs of excitement from his face before the reporters tackled him. Putting them off with a bland platitude or two, he hopped into a waiting taxi.

"Metropolitan Museum of Art," he said, to put off the eager listeners clustering at the cab door.

Waiting in Stan's outer office he found a pale, pretty woman, who bit her lip and raised her eyes to his apprehensively. A sharp pain struck through Lee's breast because she reminded him vaguely of Mary. Beside her sat a young man, scowling and grim, but since he had his wife's hand in his, it was evident that he intended standing by her.

Lee led them into Stan's private office; Stan was away. The young woman was trembling piteously.

"Take it easy," said Lee in a friendly voice. "Now that you have made up your mind to tell the story, the worst is over. I'm not a terrifying person."

"You are kind," she murmured. They all sat down. Moistening her lips, she made an effort to begin, but could not get the words out.

"Let me tell him," said her young husband with gruff sympathy.

She shook her head. "I must do it." Finally she got started. "My husband and I spent Sunday at the house of some friends in the country. On the way home we quarreled. . . . Don't misunderstand me, Mr. Mappin. We are *very* fond of each other. That's what made it so bitter . . . Must I tell you what we quarreled about?"

"Not unless it concerns Blanding," said Lee.

"Oh no!" she said. "I had never heard of him then."

"I'll tell," the young man blurted out, "because it was my fault. There was a red-haired girl at this house in the country, sir. I made up to her just to tease my wife a little, but she took it seriously, and on the way home she reproached me so bitterly that I lost my temper."

"Oh! red hair!" said Lee.

"The quarrel got worse and worse," resumed the girl, "and finally, when we stopped for a red light on First Avenue, I opened the door and got out and he . . . he drove on without me. I didn't expect him to do that."

"I don't know what got into me!" groaned the young man. "God knows, it has taught me a lesson. I didn't mean to leave her really. I drove around a couple of blocks and went back to pick her up. But she was gone. When I got home she wasn't there. She didn't come. I was wild with anxiety."

Mrs. Carlyle picked up the story. "I started to walk home. At the next corner I was stopped again by the light. A car drove up beside me and stopped. The young man jumped out of it; he was looking at me very strangely. 'Mary!' he said. I told him he'd made a mistake. 'I know,' he said. 'You look like somebody I was crazy about, and I lost her!' There was nothing fresh about him and I couldn't get angry. He was so gentle. And he looked absolutely heartbroken.

"Well, I imagined I was heartbroken, too. Something more was said, and when he asked me to take a little drive with him so he could cheat himself that he had Mary beside him . . . well, I got in the car. It was an insane impulse. I suppose I had some notion of teaching my husband a lesson.

"You know the rest. We drove north and crossed a bridge. I regretted what I had done and asked him to take me home. 'Just a little farther!' he pleaded. Not much else was said. He never told me who he was and of course I didn't tell him my name. 'So like Mary!' he murmured once or twice. He drove very fast. Suddenly the car left the road and crashed. He flung himself in front of me to save me. Then I knew nothing more.

"When I came to my senses, he was carrying me up the steps of a hospital. I begged him to put me down. I begged hard not to be taken into the hospital because then everything would have to come out. When he put me down I could stand. I was shaky but I wasn't injured any place. So we left the hospital. We sat down on a bench until I was able to walk. Then we went to the railway station. He left me there while he went to the garage to order the smashed car towed in. Then he came back and we took the first train to town. He took me home in a taxi. It wasn't yet eleven o'clock.

"I was so glad, so glad to get safely home. I made up a story to tell my husband. I thought my foolish adventure was forever buried, until last night when I read in the paper that Ewart Blanding had been arrested, and that he was suspected of having killed the woman who was riding in his car. Then I knew I would have to come forward.

"I tossed all night trying to nerve myself up to it. This morning I told my husband the truth. I couldn't let him learn it for the first from the newspapers. He forgave me. Your name was mentioned in the newspaper stories and we thought it would be easier to tell you than to go to the police. So we came."

"Have you got the courage to repeat your story to the police?" asked Lee.

"Must I?" she asked piteously.

"If you want to get Blanding out of jail. You couldn't expect the police to release him just on my say-so."

"If I must!" she murmured.

"Does it have to appear in the newspapers?" the young man asked anxiously. "If all our friends read it, it will be so much harder to live it down!"

"I see no necessity for publishing your names," said Lee. "But of course I can guarantee nothing."

"Well, come on, Vera," the young man said gruffly. "We can't back down now."

Half an hour later, Vera Carlyle was telling her story to Inspector Loasby in his private office. Loasby did not take it too well. He was a man who hated to have his ideas upset. He listened, grumbling throughout, and when Vera had come to the end, he put her through a sharp cross-examination with a view to establishing a previous connection between her and Ewart Blanding. But the young woman was transparently honest. Her tale never varied by one iota.

Finally Loasby said he would confront her with Blanding. She pleaded so piteously to be saved from this ordeal that Lee intervened.

"What do you expect to gain by that, Inspector?" he asked mildly.

Since Loasby could not answer the question, he was obliged to give up the idea. He made Vera sign a deposition—to protect him, he said, if questions were asked later; he agreed grudgingly that it was not necessary to give her name to the press.

"All you need give out," said Lee soothingly, "is that the police have found the woman who was in Ewart Blanding's car when it was wrecked, and let it go at that."

When the Carlyles had left, Loasby paced his office in a very bad temper. "Damn it! we're back just where we started! What am I to do with Blanding now?"

"Release him!" said Lee promptly.

"I wouldn't be justified in doing that," said Loasby, swelling a little. "Perhaps he made away with Mary before he picked Vera up."

Lee smiled. "Impossible! We know that the accident took place at ten minutes to nine. It is twenty minutes' fast driving from the spot where he picked Vera up. Say she got in his car at eight-thirty. We also know that it was some time *after* eight before Blanding ever got to Mary's house. He must have driven directly from Mary's house up First Avenue."

"There's the unexplained orchid that was found in Blanding's car," objected Loasby.

"That's a mystery," said Lee, "that you and I have to clear up. In itself it doesn't make a case against the man."

"Well," grumbled Loasby, "let's have him upstairs."

Ewart Blanding looked much worse today, and Lee suspected that he hadn't been allowed to get much sleep during the night. The question of the third degree was a sore subject between Lee and Loasby. Naturally, under a modern administration, a prisoner was not assaulted, but he could still be questioned for hours on end by relays of policemen. Blanding had not weakened. Lee knew that by Loasby's ill-temper.

When Loasby told Ewart what had happened, the young man's harassed face cleared a little. "So you see I was not lying," he said. "That certainly was decent of her! I hope she won't suffer for it."

"She told her husband before she came down here," said Lee. "He forgave her."

Loasby took Ewart over the ground covered by Vera Carlyle. Now that he had nothing to conceal, Ewart's story tallied with the girl's at every point.

"Well, I'm going to release you," said Loasby. "On one condition."

"What's that, sir?"

"That you agree not to leave town, but to hold yourself ready to appear whenever wanted."

Ewart smiled. "That's easy, sir. I'm just as anxious to see this mystery solved as you are."

"What are you going to do now?"

"Look for a job."

"Don't be in too much of a hurry," put in Lee. "I expect to need your help. Drive uptown with me and let us talk things over."

"You are very kind, sir."

Lee and Ewart departed from headquarters in a taxi. Lee gave the driver the address of the Restorick Estate. He said to Ewart: "I telegraphed George Restorick yesterday morning that you were locked up. Now I'll have to let him know you're out again."

In the office in Thirty-sixth Street, the face of the elegant Mr. Eversman wore an excited smile. When Lee proposed sending another telegram to Mr. Restorick, he said: "That's hardly necessary, sir. Mr. Restorick is here!"

Lee's jaw dropped. *"What?"*

"It seems that when Mr. Restorick got your telegram yesterday morning, Mr. Mappin, he immediately chartered a plane and flew to New York."

CHAPTER TEN

GEORGE RESTORICK, hearing voices outside, entered from the rear office. He and Lee, while shaking hands, studied each other with strong curiosity. Lee beheld a formidable figure, tall and power-fully made, with a heavy, determined face. It amused Lee to note that while his agent resembled a millionaire, the millionaire him-self looked more like a cow-puncher or a stevedore in his Sunday suit.

"So this is what you're like!" they said simultaneously, and laughed.

Then Restorick caught sight of Blanding over Lee's shoulder and his jaw dropped. "Blanding!" he cried. "What the hell? I thought you were locked up!"

"How are you, Mr. Restorick?" said Ewart. "I have just been released, thanks to Mr. Mappin."

"The case against him has collapsed," explained Lee.

"Hm!" said Restorick sardonically. "That changes the whole face of things." He turned to his agent. "Mr. Eversman," he said, "call up La Guardia Field and get Captain de Mercado on the wire. He's my pilot. Keep on trying until you get him, and find out from him how soon he can take off for the return journey."

"Going right back?" said Eversman with a falling face.

Restorick did not deign to answer him.

While this was going on, Lee murmured to Ewart: "Take a taxi to my apartment and wait there until you hear from me. Restorick will talk more freely if you are out of the way."

Ewart made his exit.

Lee said to Restorick blandly: "You and I should have a talk before you leave."

"Charmed," said Restorick carelessly, "but is it necessary?"

Lee stared. "Aren't you interested in the case against Blanding?"

"I don't give a damn about Blanding—as long as they're not going to railroad him."

Lee shook his head. "I don't understand you, Mr. Restorick."

Restorick laughed briefly. "Why should you?"

"Are you no longer interested in solving this mystery?"

"Certainly I am. Go to it! My offer stands."

Lee was growing a little warm. "How can I accomplish anything without your co-operation?"

"Look, Mr. Mappin," said Restorick. "Blanding's not the man. So what? Go to work and dig up another suspect and I'll back you to the limit. In the meantime I'm returning to Mexico."

"Why did you come back?" persisted Lee.

"Come in here," said Restorick, jerking his head toward the back room. Over his shoulder, he said: "Hope you won't mind if we use your room for awhile, Mr. Eversman."

In the inner room behind a closed door, he said with a more courteous air: "You must excuse my brusqueness, Mr. Mappin. I hate to be questioned! Always did!"

Lee spread his hands. "There are a few questions I must have the answers to."

"Well, shoot! But I won't promise to answer them."

"Why did you come back to New York?"

"I've already answered that one. It was to get Blanding out of jail."

"You said you didn't give a damn about Blanding."

"I don't, but I couldn't let him be railroaded. I happen to know that he's not guilty of this charge."

"How do you know that?"

Restorick smiled obstinately. "That's one I won't answer."

Lee turned away in helpless exasperation. "With one hand you offer me a fortune to solve this mystery; with the other you with-hold essential information. There is no sense in such an attitude."

"You'll have to make what you can of it," said Restorick coolly.

"This is what I will make of it," said Lee angrily. "From this moment I wash my hands of the whole business!"

"Suits me," said Restorick, lighting a cigarette.

There was a silence while they stared at each other, each pair of eyes striving for mastery. Finally Restorick laughed. "I have called your bluff, Mr. Mappin!" he said. "I can see that your blood is up and that nothing under heaven could force you to abandon this case until you solve it."

Lee shrugged and laughed, too. "You have me there," he said. "I haven't touched your money yet, and I will continue to get along without it. But I shall not drop the case."

"Good!" cried Restorick. "Shake and call it a day, and let me fly back to Mexico."

"Wait a minute," said Lee. "I'm not quite through with you."

The millionaire's haughty eyebrows ran up. "Through with me?" he demanded.

Lee's face was quite bland again. "Exactly. I have to explain that since Blanding has been eliminated, I *have* another suspect."

"Who is that?"

"You," said Lee.

"Well, I'll be goddamned!" said Restorick.

It was Lee's turn to laugh, then. "I am quite serious," he said.

"Damn it, be sensible? Would I offer you a hundred thousand dollars to find the criminal if I was the man?"

"I wouldn't put it past you. It would be a clever move."

"This is ridiculous," said Restorick.

"Did you drive up to your country place on Sunday night?" asked Lee suddenly.

Restorick gave him a keen look. "So you know that?"

"Isn't that the sort of thing I'm paid to find out?"

"Sure, I drove up there. So what?"

"What was your purpose in making that late trip?"

"I decline to state."

"Did Mary Stannard accompany you?" asked Lee softly.

"Certainly not!" cried Restorick heatedly.

"There is evidence that she did."

"I talked to my farmer while I was up there," said Restorick excitedly. "Ask him! Ask him!"

"That wouldn't help. It would be easy to conceal Mary's presence from the farmer."

"What is the evidence you refer to?"

"I found one of Mary's handkerchiefs under a peony bush in the garden."

"It must have been dropped on a previous visit."

"This was one of her wedding handkerchiefs. Embroidered with a spray of Investia orchids. She would hardly have carried that on an earlier occasion."

"Are you serious?" said Restorick, scowling.

"I have it in my safe at home with some other exhibits," said Lee. "I'll show it to you if you care to drive up there."

Restorick paced the room, scowling, without answering.

"Did you ever threaten Mary?" asked Lee.

"Threaten her?" he said, staring. "How ridiculous! No!"

"Did you not on one occasion a couple of years ago say to her: 'If I can't have you, no other man shall!'"

"Yes, I did," said Restorick unexpectedly. "Who told you that?"

"I decline to answer," said Lee with a dry smile. "Mary told it, but not to me."

"It is one of those things anybody might say in the heat of passion," Restorick went on. "I was beside myself at the time. If such threats were taken seriously, half the population would go to the chair."

"I know that," said Lee. "At the same time, a jury is always powerfully swayed by that sort of thing."

"The hell with juries!" said Restorick scornfully. His face softened. "Mary could drive me wild," he went on, "but it would have been impossible for me to harm a hair of her head. I loved her! . . . It was more than five years ago, Mappin, when Mary went on the stage. I saw her in her first insignificant part and fell head over heels in love. For the first time in my life! I was thirty-five years old, and when a man is hit for the first time at that age, he is hit hard! I got somebody to introduce me. Any other woman would have fallen at sight for a man as rich as I. Not Mary! My money was a handicap there! Mary leaned over backwards to show me she didn't give a damn for it. Maybe if I had been a poor man she would have had me!"

The big man had forgotten his arrogance. He paced the room, his face haggard with feeling. Though he still addressed Lee, he appeared to have forgotten his existence. "I saw you smile to yourself when I said I was wild with passion. Hard to believe, isn't it, of a stony-face like me? That was the last time it happened. Maybe you think it was easy to get the best of it. What I have been through! But I *did* get the best of it. During these years my love for Mary strengthened and became tender. I gave up all thought of winning her. My only desire was to see her happy. If it is of any interest to you, I have made a will leaving her everything that I could leave outside the family."

"Certainly it interests me," said Lee. "I'm glad you told me this."

Restorick already regretted having betrayed his feelings. "Okay! Okay!" he said, trying to pass it off. "Now can I go and board my plane?"

"You haven't yet told me how you knew that Ewart Blanding wasn't guilty," Lee pointed out.

Restorick paced the room thoughtfully without answering. Lee gave him his own time. Finally he said: "Very well. I've made up my mind to tell you the whole story now. I hope it won't get in the newspapers! I hate to see them bandy Mary's name back and forth."

"I give nothing to the press unless it is to aid justice," said Lee.

"The police suspected Blanding because they thought he was the last to see Mary alive," said Restorick abruptly. "Well, he wasn't. On Sunday night after Blanding had left her, I saw Mary and talked with her."

"Good!" said Lee. "That is the first rift of light on this case. I was faced by an unbroken blank wall."

"It was about half-past eight on Sunday night," Restorick went on, "Mary came to my house in Sutton Place. As you may know, I

have never opened up that house. I don't care for formal entertaining. I occupy a suite on the second floor with one manservant.
Living in that fashion gives me a degree of privacy that I couldn't
have otherwise. There is also an old caretaker and his wife who
live somewhere down in the basement, but I rarely come in contact with them.

"On Sunday my man had the night off. I heard the bell and went
downstairs to open the front door. It was not a part of the caretak-
ers' duties to answer the doorbell. Anyhow, as I discovered later,
they were out also. I opened the door and there stood Mary, smiling. A great surprise. I knew she was going to marry Fentress some
time or another, and when I saw the perfection of her costume, I
guessed it was going to be that very night. It was a blow! Fentress
was never the man to make her happy. A second-rate guy! I took
Mary up to my living room . . ."

"You were alone in the house?" put in Lee.

Restorick smiled at him grimly. "Setting the stage for your
drama, eh? Yes, we were alone in that big house, but I didn't know
it then. . . . Upstairs, Mary confirmed my suspicions about a wedding. Well, I told her exactly what I thought of what she was doing.
We had always been extremely frank with each other. What I said
didn't have the slightest effect, of course. She only smiled, and I
felt as ineffective as a wave beating against the base of a cliff."

"Let me interrupt," said Lee. "Did Mary give you any reason
for this unexpected visit?"

"Yes, she had two reasons. In the first place, she was afraid I
was angry because I had refused to come to her party the night
before. Such a foolish woman's notion!—to give a party on the eve
of her wedding for the men who were in love with her! I had refused to go and I'm glad I did! . . . Well, I soon showed her I wasn't
sore about that.

"Her second reason was to ask for her letters to me. There was
a big bunch of them; perfectly innocent letters, but Mary and I had
fallen into the habit of chaffing each other in the most outrageous
fashion, and they would have sounded terrible to an evil-minded

person. The letters were in my little wall safe at Black Maple, and I promised her I would get them and destroy them. Mary was in a tearing hurry, because the unexpected call from Blanding had detained her. She didn't stay more than ten minutes in all."

"Can you tell me the exact time she left?" asked Lee. "It's important."

"Yes. She was continually looking at the living room clock. As she was going out of the door, she asked if the clock was right and I said it was. It was then twenty-two minutes before nine."

"Go on," said Lee.

"There isn't any more," said Restorick somberly. "Mary scampered down the stairs ahead of me and got the front door open before I could reach it. . . . Wait a minute! I forgot something. She said she had to go home for a moment, that she had forgotten something. I stood in the open doorway and watched her turn into Fifty-second Street. That was my last sight of her."

"You let her go alone?"

"Why not? It was still early in the evening and her house is not more than two hundred yards from mine."

"Can you describe her costume?" asked Lee. "That also is important."

"Sure!" Restorick closed his eyes. "If I had the skill I could paint her from memory! . . . She was wearing one of those marvelously fitting little tailored suits, black; something green at her throat; a pair of green lizard pumps, an absurd little green hat like a bunch of chicory, and a spray of the green-and-black orchids pinned to her jacket. She had walked from her house to mine and she was carrying a little alligator overnight bag."

"How many blossoms in the spray of orchids?"

"Six."

"Did she tell you where she was going upon leaving your house?"

"Not in so many words. I assumed she was taxiing to the church."

"She never got there!" said Lee heavily. "What did you do after she had gone?"

"I walked the floor," said Restorick grimly. "Without Mary— without even the little I had had of her—my life seemed to stretch ahead of me like a desert."

"But wouldn't your relations with Mary have remained the same after her marriage?" put in Lee.

"When she was married to Fentress?" cried Restorick violently. "No! I would have been forced to kill him! I knew I could never see her again."

"Go on," said Lee.

"The trip to Black Maple provided a distraction," Restorick resumed. "I telephoned to the garage for my car and drove up to Connecticut. But Lord! everything about the place reminded me of Mary's visits there and I hated it! I got her letters from the safe and destroyed them. I drove back to New York. In the morning I gave my man a bonus and let him go. I instructed the Estate office to arrange with local agents to sell Black Maple and its contents as it stood. I bought out a man who had a reservation on the plane to Mexico City, and I took his place. That's all."

Mr. Eversman entered to say that he had Captain de Mercado on the phone. The pilot reported that the plane had already been serviced for the return journey, and he was ready to take off at any time.

Restorick signed to Eversman to wait, and looked at Lee. "Do you want anything more of me?"

"Not I," said Lee. "But I am in honor bound to work with the police. Won't you talk to Inspector Loasby before you leave town?"

Restorick's face darkened with anger. "What! Submit myself to the questions of an ignorant policeman? No, by God! I've told you the whole story. You can tell him what you like." He turned to Eversman. "Tell Captain de Mercado that I will come to LaGuardia Field as fast as a taxicab can bring me!"

Eversman went out.

"Does my agreement with you still hold?" Restorick asked Lee.

"It holds," said Lee.

"Very well!" Restorick thrust out his hand. "Then good-by! Whenever you find the guilty man I will return to see him tried."

He left the room. Lee presently heard the outer door of the office close.

Without leaving the rear office, Lee immediately got Inspector Loasby on the telephone. "Loasby," he said, "I have just had a talk with George Restorick."

"What!" interrupted the inspector excitedly. "What brought him back so suddenly? What did he say?"

"Listen!" said Lee peremptorily. "There's no time to go into detail. Restorick is already on his way back to LaGuardia Field. He told me his story. It clears Ewart Blanding without the shadow of a doubt. . . ."

"In that case Restorick himself is the man!" cried Loasby. "I'll have him stopped at the airport!"

"Wait a minute!" said Lee. "Restorick's story neither convicts him nor does it clear him. It leaves the case against him just about where it was!"

"But the trip up to Connecticut on Sunday night, the finding of the handkerchief. I will arrest him!"

Lee said nothing.

"What's the matter?" demanded Loasby anxiously. "Don't you approve?"

"It's your responsibility, Inspector. I am only doing my duty in letting you know."

Loasby was seized by a doubt. "I know! I know! But, my God, man, tell me what you think. . . . To arrest a man like Restorick would raise a hell of a stink. I've already arrested one man and been forced to let him go. If I had to let Restorick go after detaining him, it would react against me terribly. Public opinion . . ."

"Why consider public opinion?" said Lee mildly. "You have your duty to perform."

"Sure! But tell me what you would do in my place."

"Very well, I would let him go. You can't proceed against him with the evidence you have. If you get additional evidence, you can always reach him, Mexico City or wherever."

Loasby let out a great sigh of relief. "Okay, I'll let him go. . . . Where can I see you, Lee?"

"Could you come up to my place to lunch? Blanding is there."

"I'll start in a quarter-hour."

CHAPTER ELEVEN

LEE, STOPPING ONLY TO WARN JERMYN by telephone that there would be three to lunch, walked home from the Restorick office, because the exercise of walking stimulated his mental processes. He had much new material to turn over in his mind.

He and Loasby arrived at the door of his apartment house simultaneously, Loasby having driven uptown in a red police limousine. The eyes of the solitary reporter on guard at Lee's door goggled at the juxtaposition of Mappin and Loasby; however, it did him no good. Both men were polite but firm.

"Nothing to say!"

Upstairs, Ewart Blanding was waiting for them. Loasby's greeting to the young man was a little distant. It hardly consorted with the inspector's dignity to sit down to eat with a prisoner he had just set free, and at that an ex-chauffeur. Jermyn, who prided himself like a Chinese cook on the ability to produce a meal for any number at a moment's notice, did not keep them waiting long. While they ate, Lee described his talk with Restorick.

When he had come to an end, Loasby asked: "What are your general impressions of the man?"

"I haven't made up my mind about him," said Lee. "He's a contradictory character. Seems like a good fellow at bottom, but one has to bear in mind that he was an only child, and from birth the heir to a great fortune. That's not good for a child's character. He's been accustomed to having his own way all his life. It has made him arrogant and contemptuous of others. A man naturally of strong will, he's accustomed to riding over all opposition

103

roughshod. One can also see that he is by nature passionate and violent. On ordinary occasions, he has himself under tight control, but in such a man there is always the danger of an appalling explosion of rage."

"What does the little fellow tell you about him?" asked Loasby slyly.

"The little fellow has not yet spoken," said Lee.

There was a silence at the table.

"Restorick *could* have done it," ventured Ewart.

"I'd go further and say that Restorick was the only one who could have done it," added Loasby.

"Wait a minute," said Lee. "We haven't explored the whole field yet. . . . Certainly Restorick *could* have done it. According to his own account he was alone in the house with Mary. She told him something that might have induced an explosion of rage. He could have killed her and telephoned for his car. In front of the Restorick mansion there is a sort of porte-cochère. That is to say, a car drives in from the street and stops close in front of the entrance door. The car was left standing there. Restorick could have carried a body downstairs and thrust it into the car without danger of being seen by anybody in the world. And then have taken it up to Connecticut and disposed of it."

Blanding's face was working with pain. "Then why did you let him go?" he burst out.

"Hold on!" said Lee. "This is only a theory. It is not yet sufficiently supported by evidence. Loasby had no choice but to let him go."

They continued discussing the case from every angle. Finally Loasby said: "Lee, can I speak to you alone for a moment?"

Blanding immediately arose and left the room.

"Shoot!" said Lee.

"I have another theory," said Loasby. "Suppose Blanding drove Mary around to the Restorick house in his car. Suppose he had offered to drive her down to the church afterwards, and waited for her. He wouldn't wait immediately in front of the house, naturally, but somewhere close by. And when Mary got in his car again, he killed her."

"There wasn't time," said Lee.

"It doesn't take long to kill a woman with a gun or a knife."

"There wasn't any blood in the car."

"With his bare hands, then. That's the most likely way."

"What about the story of Vera Carlyle and her husband?"

"Probably old friends of Blanding's and lying to save him."

Lee smiled and shook his head. "It won't hold water, Loasby. Mary left Restorick's house at eight-thirty-eight and the crash took place at eight-fifty, twelve minutes later. I don't know exactly how far it is to Pelham, eight or nine miles through traffic. It's a mathematical impossibility, you see. Why don't you send a cop over the route to see how short a time it can be covered in?"

Loasby said no more.

"Ewart, you can come back," called Lee.

The young man entered with a scowl. "Has the inspector fetched up something new against me?" he wanted to know.

"No," said Lee. "Sit down and forget it."

When they had finished eating, Loasby returned to his office. Lee looked up a number in the book and reached for a telephone. Blanding looked astonished when he heard the number.

"Is Miss Dordress at home?" asked Lee. "Just ask her if it will be convenient to see Mr. Mappin for a few moments. . . . Thank you very much. I'll be right over.

"What do you expect to get out of her?" asked Ewart.

"I don't know," said Lee. "I'm working in the dark. . . . That young woman has some unexplained connection with this case."

IN THE GRANDEST of the grand apartment houses on Park Avenue, Lee was shown into an immense salon or living room with a ceiling twenty feet high. He looked around him curiously. It was filled with *objets d'art* expressing the last word of the mode in decoration on Park Avenue. Everything was very new or very old, and scandalously expensive. Down at one end was a collection of

Cambodian figures sculptured in wood with a frank attention to anatomical detail that made Lee's eyebrows run up. At intervals around the floor stood immense wooden bowls filled with colored glass balls. Many abstract paintings hung from the walls, of which he could make nothing. On a table to one side stood a short-bodied Chinese horse of the Ming period; on the other side of the room, a Greek vase in terra cotta with a circle of amorous figures.

The mistress of all this did not keep him waiting long. She pattered into the room wearing a scarlet negligee costume as extraordinary as the other furnishings. It had tight breeches to her ankles and an abbreviated skirt above. With it she wore scarlet clogs and a little beanie with a long tassel. Today her face was smooth, and she seemed well content with herself.

"Mr. Mappin!" she gushed. "How sweet of you to come and see me! What's the news? Do sit down."

"I was hoping you might have some news for me," said Lee. "I am pretty well up a tree."

"Really!" she said. "I thought the case was sewed up. You have the guilty man safe in jail. All that remains is to find the body."

Lee had come to get information, not to give it, and he felt under no obligation to inform her of the latest developments. "That doesn't appear to be so easy," he said with a rueful air.

"Oh, the police are sure to find it," she said. "Murder will out! . . . Surely you didn't expect me to help you there!" she added archly.

"Of course not!" said Lee. They laughed together. ". . . Can you tell me how far Blanding had driven the car when he crashed?" he asked, because he had to ask her something. His object was to loosen her tongue.

"Yes, I can tell you," she said. "I kept a close watch on the speedometer. He hadn't driven it any distance. Only as far as from the garage to Pelham and maybe two miles more."

"Had he ever taken the car before without permission?"

"No. I had told him he could have it all day Monday if he wanted."

"Why Monday?"

"Well, that was his day off and I had no use for it."

"Tell me, Miss Dordress," said Lee, trying another tack, "have you ever seen anything that would lead you to suppose he was a dangerous character?"

She laughed again. It had an affected sound. "Oh, my dear Mr. Mappin, how would I know? One never looks at one's chauffeur. I'm sure I couldn't tell you what passions were concealed behind his pink cheeks and his baby blue eyes! Mary Stannard could have told you, I'm sure."

Lee let that pass.

He wasn't making very good progress with the lady when a manservant entered with an afternoon paper. He was putting it on a table when his mistress said sharply: "Bring it here. . . . I have to read them as fast as they come out," she added deprecatingly to Lee. "Though there's seldom anything new."

The servant handed her the paper and left the room. Amy Dordress, affecting a bored air, unfolded it. An involuntary cry escaped her; she stood up suddenly and the paper fluttered to the floor. Lee could read the staring headline:

EWART BLANDING SET FREE!

She dropped back in the chair. Her face was paper-white. "It can't be true!" she said faintly. ". . . Is it true?"

"Why, yes," said Lee. "I thought you knew it."

She snatched up the paper. Her teeth sunk deep into her lower lip as her eyes skimmed over the lines of the story. "Who dared set this man free?" she demanded of Lee when she had come to the end.

"The police," said Lee.

"It's a scandal! It's a disgrace!" Her face was red now.

"When the Carlyles testified . . ." Lee began.

"They were lying!" she interrupted shrilly. "Any fool could see that! Ewart Blanding is as guilty as hell! That inspector must have been bribed! He can't get away with anything like that! I'll have him broke!"

"My dear young lady!" protested Lee in seeming astonishment—his glasses were glittering wickedly. "What is it to you if Ewart Blanding was set free?"

She turned on Lee with baleful eyes. She tore off the little red cap and flung it on the floor. Her hair seemed to stand on end. "What is it to me?" she screamed. "Wouldn't you like to know, old man? You knew what had happened and you never told me! You came snooping in here to entrap me. I can see it all now! You've been bribed, too!"

"Upon my soul, I don't know what all the excitement's about!" murmured Lee.

Running across the room, she pressed a bell beside the door. "Get out!" she screamed. "You dirty spy! Posing as a nice old gentleman!" She added other epithets. "Get out before I have you thrown out!"

The manservant appeared.

"Show this old man the door!" she screamed. "And if he ever shows himself here again, shut it in his face!"

The servant looked at Lee appealingly. "This way, sir, if you please." Evidently it was a common scene in this house.

Lee made his way out with dignity. His scalp crawled on the back of his head, because he half expected to feel her claws there. However, he reached the door without being assaulted.

"I'm sorry, sir," murmured the servant.

Lee was suddenly struck by the funny side of the scene. "That's all right, Joe," he said, laughing. "It wasn't your fault."

At home Ewart Blanding evinced no surprise when he heard the story. "That's the way she carries on," he said.

"But why should the news of your release from jail excite her so?" asked Lee.

"You can search me, sir."

"Has she fallen for you?" demanded Lee.

Ewart grinned widely. "Don't sound much like it, sir."

"But if you had turned her down . . . Hell knoweth no fury like a woman scorned."

"Nothing to it, sir. Right from the beginning she treated me like the dirt under her feet. It's her way with servants. It didn't gripe me because the wages were good, and apart from that I despised her."

"How did you get the job?"

"Mary sent me to her. She had heard somehow that Miss Dordress was looking for a chauffeur. But Mary told me not to say that she had sent me, or that she had fired me. Miss Dordress hired me on the spot when I told her I was working for Mary. She thought she was getting back at Mary by taking her chauffeur, and of course I never let on. She hated Mary like poison."

"Why?" asked Lee.

"That I could never tell you, Mr. Mappin. I never got any hint of the reason for it."

The telephone rang and Jermyn presently reported that it was Inspector Loasby.

Loasby's voice sounded excited over the wire. "Lee . . . Lee, is Ewart Blanding still there?"

"Yes."

"Thank God! . . . Don't let him get away from you, Lee. Don't let him out of your sight!"

"What's new?" asked Lee.

"The body has been found!"

Lee's heart sank. Up to the end he had been hoping against hope. "Mary?"

"Yes. In a cellar opposite the hospital in Pelham. I'll stop for you on my way up."

Lee shuddered.

CHAPTER TWELVE

LEE TOLD EWART BLANDING the news.

The young man paled. "Mary!" he cried in a voice charged with pain.

There was a silence in the room. The two men avoided each other's eyes.

Finally Ewart said: "How could she have been brought to a house opposite the Pelham Hospital?"

Lee dumbly shook his head.

After another silence, Ewart said: "Mr. Mappin, you don't think that I? . . ."

"I do not," said Lee.

Inspector Loasby, accompanied by two plainclothesmen, entered the apartment full of a grim satisfaction. His glance at Lee said, as plainly as if he had spoken the words: I told you so! To Ewart he said: "You're under arrest." And to the two officers: "Take him in charge."

Loasby went on to Lee: "We must get going. I have only two men up at Pelham and they will have difficulty controlling the crowd. The body will not be disturbed until we have viewed it. The medical examiner and the photographer are already on the way. Blanding will go with us."

Ewart flinched. "Oh no!" he cried. "You don't need me to identify her. I couldn't stand it!"

"I'm afraid you'll have to," said Loasby with a hard smile.

Lee was forced to speak. "Why burden ourselves with him?" he said with seeming indifference. "He can see the body later."

Loasby acquiesced with a shrug. To the officers he said: "Take him down to headquarters and lock him up. Let him have no communication with the outside until I get back."

They went down in the elevator. Ewart and his two guardians were dispatched to headquarters in a taxi, while Lee and Loasby entered the police limousine. Accompanied by two outriders on motorcycles equipped with sirens, they headed north up First Avenue at great speed.

Lee said to Loasby in his mild way: "In my opinion you were too hasty in ordering the re-arrest of Blanding."

"What!" cried Loasby. "When Mary Stannard's body has been found not fifty yards from the spot where Blanding was seen carrying the unconscious woman in his arms!"

"But that woman was *not* Mary Stannard," Lee patiently pointed out.

"The Carlyles were lying!" cried Loasby violently. "I have said so from the first."

"I don't believe they were lying," said Lee. "And even if they were, I have shown you that it was mathematically impossible for Mary to have been in Blanding's car at the moment of the crash."

"There's an error somewhere in your calculations," said Loasby. He struck his breast. "I, too, have my hunches! . . . If it wasn't Blanding, who hid the body there, who was it?"

"I don't know," said Lee.

"And anyhow," Loasby went on, "when the news of the finding of the body gets out, public opinion will demand the arrest of Blanding. I have been seriously criticized for releasing him this morning."

"The hell with public opinion," murmured Lee.

"You saw how he flinched when I threatened to confront him with the body," said Loasby heatedly. "That tells the story!"

"Sure! The poor wretch was in love with Mary. . . . I suppose you don't suspect me of murdering her? Well, I tell you, Loasby, to have to look at her now is one of the hardest ordeals I have ever been faced with!"

"You're too softhearted!"

Lee shrugged. "Well, when you're forced to release Blanding, let it be on your own head!"

"I'll take my chance on that!"

They relapsed into silence.

In Pelham the house in question was a small, detached, frame building standing in a yard across the street from the hospital. Neither new nor old, it had a neglected look and wanted painting. It was vacant, and a sign nailed to a porch post advertised it for sale. The yard was overflowing with people who milled around, trying to peer through the windows. The agent had been brought there with the keys, and he stood at the front door, keeping out curiosity seekers. Another red police car was waiting in the street.

Lee and Loasby were taken through the empty house and down cellar by one of the headquarters men. Floodlights had been led in from the yard and the place was brilliantly illuminated. Lee, wrenched with pain, was forced to look at what he dreaded. The body lay where it had fallen against the side wall of the cellar below a window. The slender shape was horribly contorted, the bright head bent down against the breast and the legs forced upward. Her blonde hair was soiled and matted, her face streaked with dirt; the neat suit was stained with muddy water, the skirt half torn away at the waist. Around the upper part of the body there was a deep crease, as if made with a rope. This crease passed under the arms. Near by the smart green hat and the alligator overnight bag lay on the cellar floor. Lee noticed at once that the spray of orchids was missing; he could see a broken end of the stem still pinned to her jacket.

The police photographer was setting up his camera while the medical examiner spread out his paraphernalia on a folding table ready for use after the pictures were taken. There were several other men staring at the gruesome object.

Inspector Loasby said in his official voice: "First we must have a formal identification of the remains."

Raising his head, Lee said quietly: "It is the body of Mary Stannard."

There was no need for him to remain while the horrible preliminaries were conducted. The desecration of that dear body, so beautiful in life, was more than he could bear. He returned to the street floor of the house. One of the headquarters men described to him the finding of the body.

"We had instructions to make a house to house search of this part of the village, but naturally the vacant house so near the hospital seemed like the best place to begin, and we didn't have to look any further."

"Did those who brought the body here break into the house?" asked Lee.

"They didn't have to, Mr. Mappin. They never bothered the house, but simply shoved the body through the cellar window and made off. The original sash in that window had rotted away. A wooden frame had been nailed up on the outside. The murderer had only to prize that off. After he had got rid of the body, he didn't attempt to nail the frame back again; the sound of a hammer in the night would have betrayed him to the neighbors. He simply leaned the frame back against the window and that's the way we found it. When I stuck my head through the window, there lay what I was looking for on the cellar floor. It looks like a one-man job."

"Did you find any tracks?" asked Lee.

"No, sir. Presumably the murderer brought his car in from the street by the driveway leading to the garage at the back. The driveway is only a couple of yards from the cellar window. It is paved with cinders, and after years of use has become as hard as a stone. It shows no tracks. Some of the weeds outside the window were broken down; now they're broken down all over the yard. It was impossible to keep the people out."

"Did the weeds that you found broken in the first place look freshly broken?"

"No, sir, not to say fresh."

Lee shrugged. It was clear to him that this man had already heard the headquarters version of what had happened, and was bound to support it. Lee was familiar from of old with this foible of the police. Dismissing the man, he tried to make an examination of the yard for himself, but he found nothing of any significance. There were too many people in his way.

Later he met the medical examiner leaving the house upon the completion of his work. "The victim met her death as the result of strangulation," he said in business-like tones. "Apparently she was throttled by strong fingers. She has been dead about five days. Impossible now to say for certain. Having been kept in a cool place, the body is in a fair state of preservation. Apparently she was taken by surprise; there are no indications that she put up a struggle for her life. No wounds, lacerations or fractures. There are certain contusions on the body which may have been received after death."

He went his way.

Lee, with a stony face, conducted his own examination of the body while Loasby looked on. The other men had been sent upstairs.

"What about her jewels?" Lee asked Loasby.

"Robbery was not the motive for this crime," answered the inspector. "She was wearing a string of pearls and a beautiful little wrist watch studded with diamonds, also a gold ring with an empty setting. The stone has fallen out. Want to see the things?"

"Only the ring," said Lee.

It was a ring that Lee had often seen on Mary's finger. It had contained a small solitaire diamond. Inside the ring was some lettering: A.J. to M.B. Mary Stannard's right name was Mary Brown, which explained those initials. Lee had never heard of any man in her life whose initials were A.J. The private mark of Tiffany and Company was also engraved inside the ring. Lee handed it back to Loasby without calling attention to any of the marks.

Lee took note that, though the cellar was dry, Mary's clothes were damp, damp all the way through to the skin, as if her body had lain in water previously. Her clothes were beginning to mildew. There was another sourish smell about her clothes that he could not identify. Clinging to her clothes and to her hair were some shreds of a blackish, fibrous substance that rotted between the fingers. Lee collected some of these shreds in an envelope.

"What is that?" asked Loasby.

"Don't know. Rotten straw, perhaps. My glass will tell me."

When Lee finally rose to his feet, he muttered something about "clumsy work."

"What's clumsy?" asked Loasby.

"The attempt to pin this crime on Ewart Blanding."

Loasby was nettled. "Lee, you're like a bird that can only pipe one note," he said with a smile of attempted superiority.

Lee looked into the little alligator case. The contents were now tumbled together. It contained nothing but what a girl might carry for an overnight stay: a gown, a negligee, cosmetics and other aids to the toilet. Loasby said that the officer who first opened the case reported that it was very neatly packed, and had the appearance of not having been opened since Mary had carried it away from home.

Lee started out of the cellar with a backward glance of farewell at the poor body. "What will you do with her now?" he asked Loasby.

"To the morgue for an autopsy," said the inspector.

Lee gritted his teeth. "Is that necessary? There's no dispute as to the cause of death."

"It's essential," said Loasby. "There's no knowing what the defense might spring on us if it was omitted."

"Please see that I am notified when the police are through with her," murmured Lee.

Upstairs the reporters pressed forward with questions.

"Nothing to say," said Lee.

"You may say that immediately upon the discovery of the body in this neighborhood, Ewart Blanding was rearrested," said Loasby importantly.

"Have you got the goods on him, Inspector?" one asked eagerly.

"I leave that to your own deductions."

"Can't you give us a little statement, Mr. Mappin?" they begged. "The public expects it from you."

"Please let me off this afternoon," said Lee. "Mary Stannard was a dear friend of mine, and I am a bit overcome. . . . You may say, though, that I hope the public will not make up their minds about this case until all the evidence is in. For myself, I am not yet convinced that Blanding is guilty."

Loasby strode on with an expression of heavy injury.

Later in the car, he said with dignity: "I don't think you ought to expose our differences of opinion to the press. It's bad for the public morale."

Lee's feelings were raw and he had less than his usual patience with the handsome, conceited inspector. "Piffle!" he said rudely. "I take it your theory is that Mary Stannard was strangled downtown; that she was already dead when the McVeagh brothers picked up Blanding after the crash; that after the McVeaghs had driven on, Blanding carried her body across the road and thrust it into the cellar of the vacant house, all on Sunday night."

"Sure!" said Loasby.

"Then please explain to me," said Lee, "why Mary's body has stiffened in that cramped position? How did her clothes become wet in that dry cellar? Where did she pick up that foul substance that is clinging to her clothes and her hair?"

Loasby had nothing to say, but only looked more deeply injured. They drove the rest of the way to town in silence.

Lee had Loasby put him down at the office of the Restorick Estate. "I'll have to send Restorick a night letter to tell him what has happened," he said.

Lee's last words to Loasby were: "Inspector, if you're aiming to put that boy through another course of sprouts tonight, you'll be sorry for it."

"What's this?" demanded Loasby, swelling out his chest. "A threat?"

"No, a warning."

"It's my duty to obtain a confession from the prisoner by any legitimate means."

"You tried it before with no success. Any further *pressure* you bring to bear will react against you when the truth comes out."

"Leave that to me," said Loasby stiffly. However, a look of un-certainty appeared in his eye, from which Lee took hope that Ewart would be allowed to sleep in peace.

LATER THAT EVENING, Jack Fentress called Lee at his apartment. "Can I come around for a little while?" he asked pleadingly.

"Come ahead," said Lee.

By this time an extra, announcing the finding of Mary Stan-nard's body, was being cried through the streets. When Jack Fentress arrived, he had a copy of the paper. It contained only the bare fact without particulars.

The young man's gray and haggard face showed the ravages that the last few days had made in him. Unable to keep still, he paced Lee's living room jerkily. "Did you see her?" he asked with a pain-ful intensity.

"Yes," said Lee.

"Where is she now?"

"At the morgue."

"Will they want me to . . . to . . ."

"I don't think it will be necessary. I have identified her."

"But I would like to look at her for the last time."

"Oh, no!" cried Lee earnestly. "It is too horrible!"

Jack clutched his head between his hands. "If I could only get my hands on that fiend!" he groaned. "I am the one most concerned in this. They ought to let *me* . . ."

Lee poured him a stiff drink.

When he had swallowed it, Jack asked eagerly: "Have they got a complete case against Blanding? There is no chance of his going free?"

"The police think they have a perfect case," said Lee.

"Oh, the hell with the police! What do you think?"

"I am not satisfied."

This threw Jack into a fresh turmoil of excitement. "Why? Why?" he demanded. "What reasons have you for saying that?"

"I can't discuss them," said Lee.

"Surely you could tell me!"

"I'd tell you as soon as anybody. It is a cast-iron rule that I adopted years ago, never to discuss my speculations and theories until they were supported by evidence."

"Oh, God! If this thing could only be ended one way or another! The suspense is driving me out of my mind! . . . What will be your next move, sir?"

"First I must wait until I see how Restorick reacts to my latest wire."

"If I could only assist you in some way! If I could do some work in connection with the case I wouldn't suffer so much! It's awful to be kept in the dark!"

"If I can use you in any way I will call on you," said Lee.

CHAPTER THIRTEEN

ON FRIDAY ABOUT ELEVEN, Lee, unable to contain his impatience, drove down to the office of the Restorick Estate.

"Nothing for you as yet, Mr. Mappin," said Mr. Eversman. "Perhaps Mr. Restorick has not yet reached Mexico City. He would not be in so much of a hurry on the return journey. No need to fly at night. They have probably grounded the plane some place en route where they could get a bed."

"It is possible," said Lee, "but I doubt it. Mr. Restorick is like a man pursued by devils, unable to rest."

Eversman shook his head sadly. "Of late, sir, that has been only too true!"

Lee sat down to chat with Eversman while he waited. He liked the nineteenth century New York atmosphere of the Restorick office. Nothing had been changed there since the time of George Restorick's grandfather. In the front corner of the room on a round stool before a high desk, sat a bookkeeper as old as the furniture, writing in an immense ledger. Near by was the desk of a stenographer no younger, with a boned collar reaching to her ears and a pompadour. She was pecking at the keys of an archaic Hammond machine. This was all the employees there were, though Lee knew that hundreds of thousands of dollars passed through the old office monthly.

"I suppose you have been following the Stannard case?" Lee said to Eversman.

"Every word!" said the elegant old gentleman. "It is so sad, so dramatic, so mysterious! But I suppose they have the right man now."

"Maybe," said Lee. "Were you acquainted with Miss Stannard?"

"Yes, indeed! She came here on several occasions to call for Mr. Restorick."

"What were their relations?"

The old man gave Lee a sharp look. Through having to code and decode the telegrams, he was familiar with all the details of the situation. "Most friendly, always," he said. "They were forever chaffing each other. I confess that my old-fashioned ears were often scandalized by the freedom of their talk, but that, of course, is only the modern way. One could never mistake the depth and strength of their friendship."

"Only friends?" asked Lee.

"Only friends, Mr. Mappin. In the early days of their acquaintance, I used to hope that it would turn out differently. I am old enough to dislike seeing so rare and fine a young lady displaying herself on the stage. How beautifully she would have graced that big house up on Sutton Place as its mistress! Or the country place. But after awhile I gave up hope of it. They were too good friends."

"*Too* good?" queried Lee.

"Oh, you know what I mean, Mr. Mappin. About a courtship there must be a certain strangeness and mystery. The utter frankness of those two killed romance."

"What about Mr. Restorick's side of it?"

"He would have married her like a shot if she had been willing. Now, I expect he will never marry and this great estate that I administer will some day pass into the hands of strangers. It is a pity!"

Eventually the looked-for telegram arrived and Mr. Eversman applied himself to decoding it. While it was addressed to him, the contents clearly were for Lee. Lee read:

YOUR LATEST NEWS THROWS THE CASE INTO COMPLETE CONFUSION. I CAN MAKE NOTHING OF IT. YOU SEEM TO EXPECT THAT I SHOULD

RETURN TO NEW YORK, BUT I CAN SEE NO REA-
SON FOR DOING SO. I HAVE ALREADY DEMON-
STRATED TO YOU THAT EWART BLANDING IS
INNOCENT. FOR GOD'S SAKE DIG UP SOME-
THING NEW AND THEN I WILL COME BACK.
                    GEORGE RESTORICK

"Sounds like Mr. Restorick," murmured Eversman. "So down-
right!"

"Quite!" said Lee dryly. ". . . Mr. Eversman, may I sit quietly in
your private office while I go over things in my mind?"

"By all means, Mr. Mappin!"

In the rear office, no less old-fashioned than the other, Lee
lighted his pipe and, sitting at the broad-topped desk of old wal-
nut, applied himself to discovering the "something new" that
Restorick demanded. He considered Restorick's own relation to
the case from every angle. Half an hour later he came out.

"Mr. Eversman," he asked, "does Mr. Restorick happen to pos-
sess a copy of his deed to the property at Black Maple?"

"Yes, Mr. Mappin. We have such a copy in our safe here."

"I'm not interested in the deed itself," said Lee. "But if there
happens to be a plat or sketch attached to it, I'd like to see that. I
want to recall certain features of the place. It may save my making
a trip up there."

"There is a sketch, Mr. Mappin. I'll get it for you."

In due course he brought it to Lee in the rear room. Spreading
out the sketch plan on the desk, they studied it together. Almost
immediately, Lee called attention to a little circle marked in the
middle of the south lawn.

"I see that that is marked 'icehouse.' I found no ice-house on
that spot, but only a little rustic pavilion that Barmby, the farmer,
said Mr. Restorick called the gazebo."

"That is the icehouse, Mr. Mappin," said Eversman, "or rather,
it covers the spot. Originally it was the usual farm icehouse; that
is to say, a pit dug in the earth and covered with a conical roof.
The former proprietor considered it an eyesore. He tore it down

and substituted the summerhouse you saw there. The pit for ice is still beneath it. There's a trap door in the floor. Every winter it used to be filled with ice from a near-by pond until electric refrigerators came in. Then it was no longer used."

"Strange, I should have overlooked it," murmured Lee.

"My dear sir, the trap door has not been lifted in ten or twelve years. Mr. Restorick considers the floor dangerous, and will not allow the little house to be used. I suspect the opening has become quite obliterated under the leaves and dirt."

"Yes," said Lee, still thoughtful. He made some calculations on a page of his notebook. "Mr. Eversman, what do you think of Barmby?" he asked suddenly.

Eversman was surprised. "Why . . . a very good farmer, sir. He has been working for Mr. Restorick for five years. The place has bloomed under his care. And such an intelligent and agreeable young fellow! Mr. Restorick thinks the world of him."

"And what does he think of Mr. Restorick?"

Eversman's expression clearly signified: What the devil has this got to do with the Stannard case? However, he answered the question: "Devoted to Mr. Restorick, sir; absolutely devoted!"

"That's the impression I got," said Lee. Pursuing the same line, he presently asked: "Mr. Eversman, do you keep the receipts and the expenditures at Black Maple in a separate account?"

"We do, Mr. Mappin."

"Have you any objection to letting me see the latest figures?"

"No objection, sir. Of course, I do not understand what it has to do with the case. But I have received explicit instructions. You are acting for Mr. Restorick, and your wishes are law here."

Returning to the front room, they applied to the ancient bookkeeper, who dutifully turned up the desired account in his ledger. Lee saw what he wanted, and led Eversman back into the private office.

"There is only one item that interests me," said Lee. "The payment of $1,000 to Archie Barmby last Monday."

"Surely," said Eversman. "The day Mr. Restorick first departed for Mexico."

"Exactly," said Lee, "and the day after Miss Stannard disappeared."

The old gentleman shook his head in a bewildered fashion. "I just don't see what you're driving at, Mr. Mappin."

"Why was Barmby paid this large sum of money?"

"Mr. Restorick wished to recompense him because he had decided to sell the place."

"But as a farmer Barmby could not be put off his land without at least six months' notice. That is the law."

"I know. I know. But Mr. Restorick did not want Barmby to suffer in any way through the sale of the place. The thousand dollars, as I understood it, was to enable Barmby to make the down payment on a place of his own if he could find what he wanted. Mr. Restorick had promised to stake him further, should it be necessary."

"It seems like a very large reward."

"Mr. Restorick always deals generously with a faithful servant," said Eversman rebukingly.

Lee picked up his hat and stick.

"What will be your next move, Mr. Mappin?" asked Eversman anxiously.

"I'm going to drive up to Black Maple," said Lee.

The old gentleman's agitation increased. "Mr. Mappin, you are putting me in a dreadful position. I have been instructed to assist you in every possible way. But if your investigation is leading you . . . leading you . . ." He could not name his fear. "What am I to do?"

Lee clapped his shoulder in friendly fashion. "Do not distress yourself, my dear fellow. I have to follow every opening that presents itself right to the end, but most of them turn out to be blind alleys. Why don't you wire Mr. Restorick in code and tell him what you fear? It won't be any shock to him because I have already told him myself. And he told me to go ahead and be damned. You know his way."

Eversman looked partly relieved. "May I accompany you to Connecticut?" he asked. "We have several cars at our disposal here."

"I'm sorry," said Lee. "I should enjoy your company; but on an errand of this sort I must go alone or take an expert assistant."

"I understand," agreed the old gentleman with a sigh. "I shall await your return with the keenest anxiety. . . . Will you use one of our cars?"

"Thanks, I will," said Lee. "I have no car of my own, and it will save time."

Eversman picked up the telephone. "You had better take the limousine. In that car you can talk to your assistant without danger of being overheard. Servants have long ears. And of course they're all mad with curiosity about this case."

"Thank you very much," said Lee.

In a few minutes the car and the chauffeur were at the door. On the way uptown, Lee had the man stop at Stan Oberry's office.

After giving Stan a brief résumé of the latest developments, Lee said: "I may need help today. Have you got a smart man available?"

"There is me," said Stan, grinning, "if you consider me smart enough."

"Get your hat," said Lee.

UPON ARRIVING at Black Maple, Lee and Stan Oberry went in search of Archie Barmby. They found the young farmer, stalwart, ruddy, slow-spoken, planting onion sets in the kitchen garden with the assistance of a boy. During the last four days, naturally, Barmby had read the newspapers and he now knew who Amos Lee Mappin was. He greeted Lee somewhat warily.

"Can you take time out to answer a few questions?" asked Lee.

"Sure, Mr. Mappin." Barmby gave the boy some instructions and the three men strolled away out of hearing.

"Mr. Restorick got you out of bed late last Saturday night?" said Lee.

"That's right, sir. He blew his horn outside my window and I came down."

"What did he say?"

"He told me to put on a few clothes and come over to the big house."

"And you did?"

"Yes, sir. He didn't wait for me in the car. I followed him over to the big house, and when I got there he was sitting in the living room burning some letters in the fireplace."

"How did he look, Barmby?"

The young farmer hesitated before answering. "He looked upset."

"Did he tell you what had upset him?"

"No, sir. Of course, later when I read of the disappearance of Miss Stannard, I knew it was that."

"Did he mention Miss Stannard's name?"

"Oh no, sir. He wouldn't, to me."

"What was the first thing he said to you? I want his own words."

"Well, sir, as near as I can remember, Mr. Restorick said he was going to travel; that he didn't know how long he would be out of the country, and so he had decided to sell Black Maple."

"And then?"

"You could have knocked me over with a feather, sir. He always seemed so interested in everything up here, I couldn't understand it."

"Didn't he tell you why he had come to this sudden decision?"

"No, sir."

"Didn't you ask him?"

"No, sir. Mr. Restorick was friendly, but he was not a man you could be familiar with. I knew my place."

"What was said then?"

"I told him how sorry I was; that this was the best job I ever had, and so on."

"And then?"

"That's all, sir. There wasn't any more."

Lee looked at the young man sternly. "You have left out the most important thing."

Barmby's ruddy face paled slightly. "What's that, sir?

"Mr. Restorick offered you a gift of a thousand dollars."

Barmby looked down at the ground. "That's right, sir."

"Why did you try to conceal it, Barmby?"

The young man jerked his head up. "I wasn't trying to conceal anything, sir. I looked on it as a private matter between him and me. . . . Besides, Mr. Restorick told me not to tell anybody."

"Oh, he told you not to tell!"

"Mr. Restorick never wanted his gifts known."

"Why did Mr. Restorick give you this money, Barmby?"

The farmer looked at Lee uncomprehendingly. "No particular reason, sir. He said I had done a good job up here. He said he would like to see me on a little place of my own."

"Had you performed any other service for Mr. Restorick beyond that of farming?"

"I don't get you, sir. . . . No, sir! . . . I was nothing to him but his farmer."

"How long did he remain up here on Sunday night?"

"Not long, sir. Half an hour, maybe. When he finished burning the letters he was ready to go back."

"What did he leave with you, Barmby?"

"Nothing, sir." Suddenly a change came over the farmer's face. His mouth fell open; his eyes protruded. "Oh, my God! Now I see what you're getting at! Oh, you're wrong! You're wrong!"

Lee took another line. "What cars have you on the place?"

Barmby's lips were trembling. "There's . . . there's my little Chevvy that I take my family out in. And a pick-up truck that belongs to the place. The Chevvy's in the yard at my house, the truck in the big garage."

"I'll look at them before I go," said Lee. "Let us see the icehouse first. . . . Take over, Stan."

Stan Oberry, ordinarily so easygoing, could, when it suited him, assume a terrible air and a voice that bit like steel. He put Barmby through a searching cross-examination as to the events of Sunday night, firing questions without giving the young man time to catch his breath. Barmby, in complete distress, trembled and stuttered, but made no damaging admissions. Meanwhile, they were making their way slowly around the house.

When they reached the little rustic summerhouse, Lee walked all around it, searching the bed of hyacinths. There was a section of the bed where the gay flowers were drooping. Lee dropped to his knees to examine the latticework inside the bed, but rose again without speaking of what he had found.

"You knew there was an icehouse under this, Barmby?"

"Yes, sir. I've always known it. But it hasn't been opened in my time."

"Let's see. Unhook the chains at the entrance."

Barmby did so.

Lee said: "Can't you see that there are a lot more leaves, fresher leaves, scattered on the floor than there were when I was here before?"

"Yes, sir," said the trembling Barmby. "It's something I would never have noticed if it wasn't pointed out to me."

"Look closer, Barmby. Notice that these new leaves are not wistaria leaves that have fallen from the vine that covers the building; there are several shapes of leaves among them—oak leaves, elm leaves, dogwood leaves. How did those leaves get in there?"

"Maybe . . . maybe they blew in, sir."

"Impossible! There are no such leaves lying in the grass or the hyacinth bed outside."

Lee went down on his knees outside the entrance to the little building. He lightly brushed the leaves aside and immediately the lines of a double trap door began to appear in the floor. They were clearly visible now, because the trap had lately been opened. As he brushed the loose leaves further back, it could be seen that when the trap was raised after so many years, one side of the door had pulled the screws of one hinge clean out of the rotting wood.

"Now do you say this place has not been opened?" Lee asked Barmby.

"Not by me, sir! Not by me!" the farmer cried despairingly. "I swear it!"

When the trap doors were thrown back, a dank breath rose from the pit beneath that turned Lee a little sick. He recognized the same sourish smell that was clinging to Mary's clothes. "We are on the right track," he murmured.

The end of a descending ladder could now be seen. "I am going down," said Lee.

"It looks rotten," said Stan. "Better let me go first. I'm heavier."

"I know how to test out my weight on a doubtful ladder," insisted Lee. ". . . Besides, you can see from the rungs that this ladder has lately been used. As a matter of fact, it was used no longer ago than last night."

Lee, after making sure that his flashlight was in order, started cautiously down the ladder. The pit was about eighteen feet deep. In the bottom lay the straw which had been used to cover the ice years before, now a sodden, rotting mass, into which Lee sank halfway to the knees. The reek of it well-nigh suffocated him.

Switching on his light, he cast it all around. On top of the straw lay a rope in sprawling loops, just as it had dropped from above. It was a new rope and had not been there long. There was nothing else visible. Lee, aided by his light, started a minute search of the place, back and forth, covering every square foot, squelching deep into the saturated mass at every step. At intervals Stan Oberry, growing anxious, would call down.

"Are you all right?"

"All right. Just making a search."

"Shall I come down?"

"No. You'd only be in my way."

In the end, Lee found a bit of evidence that brought his heart slowly into his throat. A less keen eye might easily have missed it. It was like a part of the straw. He took an old letter from his pocket, and laying the limp object between the sheets, returned it to his pocket. He then tied the end of the rope around his waist, because he needed both hands for the ladder, and started slowly up, trailing the rope.

When Lee issued out into the light of day, Stan Oberry, seeing his face, said: "You found something!"

Lee, when he stepped out on the ground, opened the letter sheet and showed him a faded spray of small green and black flowers. There were five blossoms on the stem. In the cold, wet pit they had been preserved to a certain extent; they were still recognizable as the Investia orchids.

"That's conclusive," said Oberry solemnly.

"I wish I could think so," murmured Lee. "However, it makes many things clear. Mary's body was dropped in this pit at some time *after* my visit here on Monday morning. There it lay until last night. Wednesday night the man who had hidden it here hauled it up with this rope. You can see where the rope chafed the sill under the trap door. The marks are fresh. To drop the rope back in the pit was the quickest way of getting rid of it. He then carried the body to Pelham and thrust it in the cellar opposite the hospital. His idea was to pin the crime securely on Ewart Blanding. The real murderer did not know, of course, that Blanding had by that time cleared himself. It was his fatal error."

Archie Barmby listened to this with a face of horror and dismay. "How can you prove all this by a faded flower?" he demanded.

"Because only two sprays of that particular flower were sold in New York last Sunday," said Lee, "And we know where the other one is."

"I don't understand it at all!" cried Barmby. "I didn't do it! I swear before God I had nothing to do with it!"

"I don't know whether you had or not," said Lee. "The truth is bound to come out now."

"All last night I lay quiet in my bed!" protested Barmby. "I swear it! I swear it! Ask my wife!"

"A wife is not a competent witness."

"What do you want of me now?" wailed the farmer.

"Nothing, now," said Lee. "Go ahead and plant your onions."

Barmby followed them miserably to the garage, where Lee gave the little truck a careful going-over. It revealed nothing.

"Of course, if he used this the body would have been well wrapped," said Lee. "I see you leave the key in the switch," he remarked to Barmby.

"Well, it's always been done," said poor Barmby. "Don't seem likely a thief could come in from the road and steal it right out of its garage."

"Why not?" said Lee. "Your house is a good three hundred yards away. A stranger could run the truck out of the grounds without you hearing anything if the big house was empty."

"That's right! That's right, mister," said Barmby, seeing a ray of hope ahead.

"Does the speedometer tell you anything?"

The farmer's hopes fell again. "The speedometer's off," he said. "Didn't seem worth while fixing it, as it's only used around the place."

"What about the gasoline?"

Barmby turned the switch and watched the indicator. "Just the same as when I left it, as far as I can tell," he said gloomily.

"Well, the tank could have been filled again, of course."

Before leaving the place, Lee and Stan examined Archie's own car. It revealed no evidence.

They carried away the rope with them. Returning to New York by way of Danbury, in the principal farmer's supply store of that city the rope was identified as a length that had been sold to Archie Barmby a week or so before, and charged to the Restorick account. Lee was shown the item in the ledger.

Bowling along Route 22 on the way to town, Stan said to Lee: "It *must* have been either Restorick, or Barmby acting under Restorick's orders. Nobody else knew of the existence of that pit."

"Not so fast," said Lee. "I made a new discovery today. I didn't speak of it because Barmby was there. . . . You noticed, I suppose, that the flowers in a certain part of the hyacinth bed were drooping. When I examined the lattice at the bottom of the summer-house in that spot, I found that a section of it had lately been removed and put back again."

"By God!" murmured Stan. "That changes everything."

"The drooping flowers gave it away," Lee went on. "It is clear that to avoid breaking the hyacinths, the murderer carefully dug them up and laid them to one side. He then pulled off a section of the lattice and shoved the body under the floor. After putting back the lattice, he replanted the bulbs in line with the others and neatly raked the bed over. On my first visit to the spot, I saw nothing amiss. That may have been because it was then too soon after they had been disturbed for the flowers to wilt."

"I get you," said Stan.

"This suggests two new possibilities. First, the body may already have been in the pit when I visited Black Maple last Monday afternoon. Second, it may have been put there by one who was a stranger to the place. Perhaps he thought only of thrusting it under the floor, and got the surprise of his life when he heard it fall to the bed of straw in the bottom. He raised the trap doors only when he came back to get the body out in order to plant the crime on Ewart Blanding."

"What fiendish cleverness!" said Stan.

"I don't agree," said Lee. "I have never yet come upon one of those fiendishly clever murderers, Stan. Certainly, this one went to a hell of a lot of trouble to save his skin, but it wasn't very clever of him not to realize that the wet clothes on the body would give the whole thing away." After a little silence, Lee added: "I feel somewhat encouraged by this, Stan."

"How, sir?"

"Even when the body was safely hidden—after another day or so the replanted hyacinths would have taken hold and there would have been nothing to show that they had ever been moved—even so, the murderer was afraid. This indicates that there is evidence against him somewhere. Well, if it exists, we can find it."

"Yes, sir. . . . The preponderance of evidence still points to George Restorick as the man."

"Surely."

"Do you suppose he will return of his own free will or will he have to be fetched back?"

"Who can tell?" said Lee. "At any rate, I am not ready to fetch him—yet!"

Stan looked his surprise.

"There is a fatal flaw in the evidence against him, Stan."

"What's that?"

"In a dead body, *rigor mortis* does not set in until an hour or more after death. Figure that one out."

Stan scratched his head.

CHAPTER FOURTEEN

Upon returning to town, Lee did not send a telegram to George Restorick, neither did he consult with Inspector Loasby. Both of these moves could wait until he felt surer of his ground. It seemed to Lee that the case against Restorick rested on a pretty rickety foundation. The violent and headstrong millionaire might have killed Mary Stannard in a burst of rage, but it was hardly consistent with his character to go to such pains to hang the crime on another man. Neither did it seem likely that the simple Archie Barmby would have the gumption to act on his own initiative. Could Restorick have *another* agent working under cover, a cleverer man who had given Barmby his orders?

There were two vital questions to which Lee required answers: (a) Supposing that Restorick had killed Mary and had brought the body to Black Maple on Sunday night, where had it been hidden until after it had become rigid in death? (b) What communications, if any, had passed between Barmby and Restorick after the latter had flown to Mexico on Monday?

The key to the situation still lay in Barmby, and after Lee and Stan had threshed out the matter during the drive home, Stan agreed to return to Connecticut next day for the purpose of grilling the farmer further. In order to save time, he was to take an express to Bridgeport and hire a car there.

"If that guy is hiding anything I'll get it out of him," promised Stan. "I'll tackle his wife, too. While she couldn't be put on the stand, she may let something drop that will give us further leads."

The morning newspapers on Saturday provided an additional sensation, albeit a mild one, to share the front pages with the latest commentary on the Stannard case. Miss Amy Dordress, "the richest girl in America," announced her engagement to Mr. Wilbur Foulkes. The wedding would take place in six weeks, she said.

Lee did not know Foulkes, though the name was vaguely familiar to him. Photographs of him were printed, representing a little fellow with a flat face devoid of character, and the interviews he gave made him sound like a very silly fellow indeed. Since Amy could have had the pick of the basket, Lee felt a good deal of curiosity as to why she had chosen this poor specimen.

He drove over to the Oberry office after breakfast to study the reports of the various operatives who had been placed on Amy's trail. Already, by noon on the previous Monday, Amy had engaged a chauffeur in Ewart Blanding's place, so Stan had missed out there. Stan's attempts to get in touch with the new chauffeur had been without success. The young fellow evidently figured that loyalty to so rich an employer would profit him more in the end.

Various operatives had been assigned to tail the Dordress car. Miss Dordress was using an imported town car for visits and shopping. As everybody knows, it is an uncertain business trying to follow a car through the traffic of New York streets with the ever-changing light signals. The gist of these reports was that Miss Dordress never walked. She was a highly suspicious person who always looked sharply from side to side when she crossed from her front door to the step of her car, and she continually glanced through the car's rear window to discover if another car was following. This, of course, might be due to the natural caution of a rich and conspicuous character, who feared attack or robbery in the streets. When an operative did succeed in following her car for awhile, it only led him to a fashionable shop or restaurant or some such place. It was curious to note that Miss Dordress always drove alone. Sometimes the newspapers called her "the poor little rich girl."

Naturally, there was a heavy servant turnover in the Dordress triplex apartment, and on Wednesday morning Stan had been lucky enough to introduce a female operative as an upper housemaid. Unfortunately, this did not bring her in close touch with the mistress. In her first report, the operative said that in addition to the listed telephone with extensions to different rooms, which was always answered by the butler, Miss Dordress had a silent wire to her own sitting room where she carried on long conversations in a low voice.

Stan's operative was a clever woman and would no doubt have secured valuable information—but unluckily, in forty-eight hours she was fired. She wrote in her report: "This morning, for some imaginary fault, she burst out at me like a crazy woman. I have never seen such a display. I would hate to have to repeat the language she used. I didn't mind being cursed; it's all in the day's work with me; but it put me on a spot because I couldn't judge just how I ought to appear to take it. I suppose I was too meek, because that made her suspicious and she fired me out of hand. She's obsessed with the idea that she's surrounded by spies."

The story of the engagement in the *Herald-Tribune* was signed by a reporter called Tom Cottar, a friend of Lee's. At this time of day Tom was just getting up. Lee got him on the phone, and a few minutes later he dropped in, redheaded, lively, and sniffing for a story.

"What do you know about the engagement of Amy Dordress?" asked Lee.

Tom's eye brightened.

Lee took note of the brightness. "There's no story in this," he hastened to add. "At least not today. This is off the record."

Tom shrugged away his disappointment. "Well," he said, "I interviewed the two of them yesterday afternoon in the immodest triplex. La Dordress was her usual gracious self. She thinks it's smart to be insulting."

"Who is this Foulkes fellow?"

"Oh, a harmless little panty-waist, a writher, a sucker-up; his nickname is Imby, short for Imbecile, and he loves it. Nobody knows anything about his beginnings. He's asked out a lot; almost everybody tolerates him because he's always got a choice new morsel of dirt on his tongue."

"Why does Amy Dordress want to marry such a one?" asked Lee.

"Bless your heart, she has no intention of marrying him. When she announced it yesterday she scarcely troubled to hide her contempt for Imby. You could see, too, that he knows this is only a stall of some kind. But of course he's tickled pink to enjoy even a day in the sun."

"It's a strange world!" said Lee.

"Rotten!" Tom agreed cheerfully. "I don't know what La Dordress' game is, but I'm offering five to three that they won't be married in June. Do you want to take some of it?"

Lee, busy with his own thoughts, shook his head inattentively.

Tom leaned toward him eagerly. "Mr. Mappin, is there any connection between this and the Big Case?"

Lee raised a pair of eyes as innocent as a babe's. "Why, how could there be?"

"Well . . . Ewart Blanding was La Dordress' chauffeur!"

"Speculate as far as you like," said Lee, "but don't print your speculations."

Lee felt a good deal of sympathy for Ewart Blanding, who was still unjustly locked up at police headquarters. He drove down there to cheer him up. It was necessary to see Loasby first, and Lee immediately guessed from the inspector's glum face that he had begun to doubt the wisdom of his course of action toward Blanding. To cheer him, Lee now told the story of the previous day's journey. Loasby's face cleared.

"Then Restorick is the guilty man!" he said, striking his desk. "At bottom I have always thought so!"

Lee looked at him *very* dryly and murmured the words of the ancient wheeze: "Off again, on again, Finnegan."

Loasby made believe not to hear him. "Are you sure he went back to Mexico City, Lee?"

"Had a wire from him yesterday. Stan Oberry's keeping him shadowed there."

"Shouldn't he be arrested?"

"Give me a day or two longer, Inspector. We don't want to make a second slip. . . . Can I see Blanding?"

"What for—if he's innocent?" demanded Loasby suspiciously.

"Just for friendliness today. I want to make up to him for his durance vile."

"I dare not let him go until I have the real criminal to show the public," said Loasby.

The pass was written.

EWART'S FACE LIGHTED UP at the sight of Lee. He felt instinctively that the older man was his friend. Lee, for his part, saw no reason why he should not tell Ewart that the last vestiges of the case against him had collapsed.

"Then why don't they let me out?" said Ewart.

"Have a little patience," said Lee. "It can't be much longer delayed."

Ewart had read the morning papers.

"What do you think about this odd move of Amy Dordress'?" asked Lee.

"Don't ask me," said Ewart. "Just one of her senseless impulses. The woman is wacky."

Lee said thoughtfully: "When a woman flies a kite in this manner it is usually for the purpose of diverting attention from another man. Can you suggest who the real man in the case might be, Ewart?"

"No, sir. There was a whole crowd of them. None seemed to have anything on the others. There wasn't a one who was like her *friend*, if you know what I mean. It was her securities they were courting."

"Quite! . . . She mentioned to me one day that she had been going to let you have the coupé on your day off last Monday."

"That's right, sir."

"Was she in the habit of doing that?"

"No, sir. It was a complete surprise."

"Had you *asked* for the car?"

"No, indeed, sir! Catch me asking her for a favor!"

"Had you made any plans for Monday?"

"No, sir. There wasn't anything seemed worth doing without Mary."

"Did Miss Dordress have a key to the garage?"

"Yes, sir."

"How many cars did she keep there?"

"Just the coupé and the town car. . . . What are you trying to prove, Mr. Mappin?"

"I don't know, Ewart. I'm like a man standing before a locked door with a big bunch of keys. I'm trying one key after another, but so far I haven't found a key that will open the door. . . . I'll try another. When did you order the orchids for Mary?"

"On Saturday, sir. As soon as Mary asked me to the party at La Perouse for that night. I was hoping the orchids would come in time for her to wear them, but they didn't."

"Did anybody know you had ordered those flowers?"

"Mary did. I told her at the party and she scolded me because she knew how dear they were. She wanted me to cancel the order, but I told her I had already paid for them."

"Where did this conversation take place?"

"In her dressing room after the show. That's where the party met."

"Did anybody overhear it?"

"They were all there. They could have heard."

"Was anything further said about the flowers?"

"Yes. I told Mary I would bring them around Sunday evening and she said to come early because she'd be going out about half-past eight."

"Did she say anything about her intention of calling on George Restorick that night?"

"No, sir."

"Think, Ewart! This is important."

"So far as I can recall, sir, Mr. Restorick's name was not mentioned all evening."

Stan Oberry returned to town in the late afternoon. Lee went to his office. "Wasted day, Mr. Mappin," he said with a glum face.

"A certain number of days have to be charged off," said Lee. "What did Barmby have to say about the rope?"

"He readily admitted purchasing it. Said he wanted it as part of a homemade contraption for sweeping the chimneys. He hadn't

used it yet. It was hanging in the garage and the garage door wasn't
locked. Anybody could have lifted it. He had had no occasion to
enter the garage yesterday, so he hadn't missed it.

"I questioned Barmby for several hours," Stan went on. "He
stumbled and stuttered and sometimes contradicted himself, but
that was due to the fact that he was scared. I never succeeded in
shaking his first story. Afterwards I questioned his wife apart from
him. She corroborated his story in every particular. She's quicker
witted than her husband. They have a young baby. She says she
was up with the baby three times on Thursday night and it would
have been impossible for Barmby to have left the house without
her knowledge during the night."

"What about telegrams and telephone calls?" asked Lee.

"The Barmbys are on the Danbury exchange. They have sent
no telegrams recently and have made only one toll call. It was to
New York yesterday, after we had left. I got the number."

"That's the Restorick Estate," said Lee, when he heard the number.

"The Danbury long-distance operator said she heard nothing
of the conversation that took place," said Stan.

"Well," said Lee, "until something else turns up, we must assume that Barmby is telling the truth."

WHEN LEE REACHED HOME Jermyn said dryly: "Major Dunphy is waiting in the living room, sir."

Lee murmured a heartfelt imprecation under his breath.

There sat the old man in all his elaborate panoply for the street.
His granddaughter, the only relative he had in the world, had been
found the day before brutally murdered, yet he still had a carnation in his buttonhole. He hastened through some perfunctory expressions of grief. When he came to the real object of his visit, his
old eyes glittered. "The newspapers said that you identified poor
Mary's body, Mr. Mappin. So you are the right one to sign these
affidavits for the insurance companies giving proof of death."

Lee looked at him without speaking. His expression suggested
that he wished with all his heart he could bring the old man to

book for Mary's death. But he had made no progress in that direction. All you could say in excuse of the old creature was that he had lived too long; he had become senile. His manhood was already dead; only vanity and appetite remained.

While Lee was signing the papers, the Major said fretfully: "I hope they'll pay promptly now. I can see no further excuse for delay, can you? I am entirely without money. I have been put to the humiliation of borrowing from the servants!"

"You should let the servants go and move out of that big house," said Lee dryly.

"I can't. The lease runs to October."

"The lease was in Mary's name, and Mary has left us," said Lee. "The owner has no hold on you. In any case, a house so charming could be sublet within twenty-four hours."

"Where would I go?"

"To a hotel."

"I don't like hotels," said the Major peevishly. "The service is terrible!"

Lee shrugged. "There's a question I want to ask you, Major. Restorick has said that when Mary left his house, she told him she was going home for a moment. He watched her cut across the street and turn into Fifty-second Street. This would be about eight-thirty-nine."

"I don't know anything about that," said the old man with a curious indifference. "I didn't know she had ever left the house until Nina Gannon called up at nine-fifteen to ask for her. I don't believe she came back after she first went out."

The old man asked many questions about the case. The combination of mean curiosity with an entire absence of grief was too much for Lee. "I can't discuss it," he said, ringing for Jermyn.

"In any case, I'm glad the police have got that Blanding fellow by the heels," said Major Dunphy. "I never liked him!"

Jermyn came in.

"Major Dunphy is leaving, Jermyn," said Lee.

Jermyn handed the old man his hat and stick.

WHEN LEE DINED ALONE he was fond of chatting with Jermyn. Very improper, he would have admitted, had he been caught at it, but Jermyn had been so admirably trained by his former master, the Duke of Senlis, Lee would have said, that it was impossible to spoil him now. Jermyn's dearest ambition was to engage in detective work, and his cup of happiness was full whenever Lee condescended to discuss one of his investigations.

"Jermyn," said Lee, "how is the Butlers' Club getting along?"

"Quite as usual, sir, I believe. The financial situation is excellent. I do not frequent the club much myself because I find the conversation of the members somewhat tiresome. They talk about nothing but the personal habits of their employers."

"Miss Dordress has a butler. I don't know his name. Is he a member of the club?"

"Yes, sir. His name is Rathbun. He is quite prominent in the club because his employer is so rich. Her money gilds the butler, so to speak. Personally, I have found Rathbun rather an insignificant fellow."

"Could you cultivate him for awhile?"

"Why of course, sir, if you have an object in it. He would be flattered, I believe, if I paid him a little notice."

"Good!" said Lee. "Miss Dordress has a silent phone in her private sitting room. I am told she holds long conversations over it. See if you can find out who calls her up on this wire, or whom she calls, and what they talk about. If you can't find out anything else, get me the number of this unlisted phone."

"Very good, sir. I might drop down to the club tonight after I finish my work."

"Let the dishes wait until you get home," said Lee.

While Lee was finishing his little pastry, the doorbell rang. Jermyn, when he went to answer it, shut the dining room door so that Lee could not be seen from the gallery. In three minutes Jermyn returned. His usually inexpressive face was all agog.

"Mr. Mappin," he stammered, "it's . . . it's Mr. George Restorick!"

"Ah!" said Lee, flinging down his napkin. "Serve coffee and liqueurs in the living room, Jermyn."

CHAPTER FIFTEEN

RESTORICK, TALL, BROAD-SHOULDERED and scowling, stood waiting in the middle of the big room, a terrifying figure.

Lee said mildly: "Well! What led you to change your mind in such a hurry about returning?"

"This!" said Restorick, thrusting out a telegram.

It was from Eversman. Since it was in code, Lee could make nothing of it. He handed it back.

"This was sent from New York at five yesterday afternoon," shouted Restorick, rapping the paper. "Eversman says that he had just been talking to Barmby, my farmer, up at Black Maple. Barmby told him that you and another detective had been snooping around the place all afternoon, and that you claimed to have found positive evidence that Mary Stannard's body had been thrown into the old icehouse. Barmby said that he suspected he had had a hand in it and he didn't know what he ought to do under the circumstances."

"That's right," said Lee.

Restorick's voice rose to a roar of rage. "What damned nonsense is this, Mappin?"

"Don't shout at me!" said Lee calmly.

"I'll shout as loud as I damn please!"

Jermyn was bringing in the coffee tray at that moment and the cups rattled as he placed it on a table. But Jermyn was game. He lingered, ready to go to his master's aid against this wild man.

Lee appeared quite unruffled. "Thank you, Jermyn," he said. "You needn't wait."

Jermyn went out with a dubious, backward glance. It was a safe guess that he was lingering in the gallery.

Restorick was still roaring. "What infernal mischief have you been up to, Mappin? God! I thought you were a man of sense! Barmby is as honest as the day! I refuse to hear a word against him!"

Lee was busy with the cups. "Coffee?" he asked.

"The hell with your coffee!" shouted Restorick. "You listen to me! Do I hire you to go spying around my place in my absence and interfering with my employees?"

Lee put down his cup and stood up rather quickly. His glasses sparkled. "Look here, Restorick! I haven't touched a penny of your money and I don't mean to! It's true I borrowed one of your cars, but I'll pay for that! You can't hire me!"

"Oh, I can't, can't I?"

"No, you can't! What's more, you can go plumb to hell!"

Restorick stared at him in amazement. Suddenly he roared with laughter. "By God, you're a spunky little half-pint!" His anger was gone. "Mappin, that's the first time in my life that a man ever told me to go to hell!"

"It would have been better for you if they had," grumbled Lee.

Restorick laughed again. "I believe you, old man! Forget it! Forget it! Give me a cup of coffee."

Lee handed it over. "Sugar and cream on the tray if you want it."

Restorick sat down. "Now explain all this damned foolishness," he said. "Pardon my language."

"It's all right when you smile," said Lee. ". . . In the first place, after prolonged questioning, I am satisfied that Archie Barmby is not implicated in any way."

"Well now, that's nice of you," said Restorick with heavy sarcasm.

"It is, however, certain," Lee went on, "that Mary's body was dropped into the icehouse and lay there for three days."

"I can't believe that," said Restorick stubbornly.

"Jermyn," said Lee, raising his voice slightly. "Bring me that little package I placed in the refrigerator last night."

Jermyn's retreating footsteps could be heard.

"He was listening!" growled Restorick with a scowl.

"Only because he thought you were going to attack me," said Lee. "I would trust Jermyn with my last dollar."

"I wish I had a man like that," muttered Restorick. "Go on with your story."

"Wait until I show you what I found in the bottom of the ice pit."

Jermyn came back. Lee had placed the faded spray of flowers between two thin sheets of cotton wool saturated with water.

"I'm preserving it as long as I can," said Lee. "You can still see what it is."

"Mary's orchids!" gasped Restorick.

Lee replaced the spray and handed it back to Jermyn to be returned to the refrigerator.

To Restorick he said. "Mary was wearing that spray when she came to your house on Sunday night."

"I know! I know! But it had six blossoms then and now there are only five!"

"The sixth one was found in Ewart Blanding's wrecked car."

"God!" groaned Restorick, turning away. "This is maddening! What earthly connection can there be between Blanding's car and my icehouse!"

"Somewhere there is a simple explanation," said Lee. "But we have still to find it."

"Do you think *I* had something to do with it?" demanded Restorick, flinging back.

Lee met his angry eyes squarely. "Possibly!"

Restorick's fist doubled. "Damn you, Mappin! . . ."

Lee waved his hands soothingly. "Now don't lose your temper again. That won't get us anywhere."

"Then don't bait me!" growled Restorick.

"The trouble with you is, you are not accustomed to meeting men on an equal footing."

"Damn it! I didn't fly three thousand miles just to bandy words with a little cock sparrow like you!"

"Oh, for heaven's sake, what's my size got to do with it?" said Lee disgustedly. "Did I ask you to come back this time?"

"No," admitted Restorick. "But now I'm here, I'm going to stay until this matter is cleared up."

"Good!" said Lee coolly. "Then try to be of some help instead of doubling your fist at me every two minutes."

Restorick looked at him queerly. The millionaire was having a new experience. Lee perceived that at least he was winning his respect. "Well . . . what do you want of me?" Restorick asked quietly. "Give me an honest-to-God drink. I can't stomach those syrupy liqueurs."

Jermyn was summoned again, and the makings of a man's drink were quickly forthcoming. The big man sat down as quiet as a lamb now, and Jermyn glanced at his master with a new admiration.

Lee said to Jermyn: "I won't need you any more tonight. You can go to your club."

"Yes, sir, thank you, sir."

To Restorick Lee went on: "You asked me just now if I suspected you, and I said yes, meaning in a general way. I haven't found the guilty man; consequently I must suspect everybody who *could* have committed the crime. Instead of taking it out in cursing me, why not go to work and eliminate yourself from any possible suspicion?"

Restorick grinned hardily. "You're a card, Mappin! But damned if I don't like you! . . . Okay, I'll take you up. . . . You tell me you came up to Black Maple late Monday afternoon. At that time, the body had not yet been dropped in the icehouse, you say."

"Wait a minute," said Lee. "That's all changed now." He described the new evidence furnished by the hyacinth bed and the wooden lattice. "So you see the body *may* have been in the pit at the time of my first visit."

"Very well. Let that go for the moment. You say further that the body was hauled out of the pit with a rope some time during Thursday night."

"I have positive proof of that."

"All right. On Thursday night I was in Mexico City. I can prove that a hundred times over."

"I don't doubt it. But you are a very rich man, Restorick. You could have hired a man or a dozen men to carry out your orders while you were away."

"Sure," said Restorick, "but I suppose you will concede that it takes real money to hire an assassin—or even an accessory after the fact. Not to speak of putting yourself in his power forever. You can easily satisfy yourself that I have paid out no money for that purpose."

"How?" asked Lee.

"I never carry any amount of money on my person," said Restorick. "I don't have to. My name is so well-known around this town that credit is thrust on me wherever I may be. At the end of the month the bills come in to Eversman and he pays them. His accounts are in admirable order. You can find out from him every penny I have spent and what I have drawn in cash."

"But Eversman is the soul of loyalty," objected Lee. "Could I trust him not to hide a payment or two?"

"Hire a public accountant. We'll turn you loose in the office of the Estate. If the books balance, there could not be any missing sums."

"How much have you had from the Estate this week?" asked Lee.

"A thousand on Monday morning and two remittances of five hundred each by wire since. Not too much, considering that I paid my way to Mexico City on an air-liner with a big premium, and have since chartered two private planes. . . . I don't know exactly how much I have left. I dare you to do the sum with me right now."

"I accept the dare," said Lee.

It worked out to Lee's satisfaction. Except for a few dollars, Restorick was able to account for all the money he had spent.

"Tomorrow," said Lee, "I'll take up your offer to put a public accountant to work on the Estate books. He needn't know, of course, what I'm looking for."

Restorick shrugged. "It's nothing to me whether he knows or not."

"Don't you want to keep it out of the papers?"

"Let the papers rage. They can't touch me where I live!" Restorick sprang up and began pacing again. "The man who did this thing must have visited Black Maple beforehand," he muttered.

"Not necessarily," Lee pointed out.

"Anyhow, he must have had the place in mind. He went there. When Blanding worked for Mary he brought her up on several occasions."

"Blanding is out," said Lee. "Blanding would never have carried the body down to Pelham to convict himself."

"Sure! Sure!" Restorick struck his forehead violently. "Damn it, I'm no detective! Who would want to hurt Mary? I haven't an idea in my head, Mappin!"

"I have several theories," said Lee.

The big man whirled around. "What are they?"

"I can't discuss them until I have supporting evidence."

"Oh, sure! Sure!" said Restorick angrily. "Mystery is your stock in trade, isn't it? You are the celebrated sphinx, the great question mark!"

Lee took no offense. He could see that the man was suffering.

Their talk was interrupted by the ringing of the doorbell. Lee was surprised, because when Jermyn went out the boys in the hall were instructed never to bring any visitor to Lee's apartment without first telephoning his name. Still, it might be a telegram or a special-delivery letter. Lee went to the house phone in the gallery.

"Who is ringing at my door?" he asked quietly.

The scared voice of the boy at the switchboard in the lobby answered: "It's Inspector Loasby and a couple of cops, sir. I couldn't refuse him, sir. He ordered me not to telephone you he was coming."

"That's all right," said Lee calmly. "I just wanted to know who it was."

The bell sounded again. Lee, letting it ring, hastened back to the living room. "It's Loasby," he said.

"So what?" demanded Restorick, running up his eyebrows.

"He's apt to go off at half cock," warned Lee. "He knows I'm here, and I've got to admit him. But you can wait in my study until he goes."

"What!" roared Restorick. "Hide from the damned cop! The hell with him! Go and let him in!"

The bell was ringing continuously now. The moment Lee opened the door Loasby cried out: "I want Restorick!" Thrusting Lee aside, he marched in, followed by two plainclothesmen. Lee, with a shrug, closed the door. The matter was out of his hands.

In the living room, Restorick and Loasby faced each other. Loasby was a big man, but he had run to fat somewhat; Restorick was even bigger and as lean as a boxer. Loasby said pompously: "Mr. Restorick, I have to ask you to accompany me to police head-quarters."

"Says you!" sneered Restorick with contempt. He lit a cigarette with insolent deliberation and dropped the match in an ash tray.

Loasby turned a brickish red. "Do I have to warn you of the penalty of resisting arrest?"

"What am I wanted for?" asked Restorick coolly.

"In connection with the murder of Mary Stannard."

Restorick turned angrily on Lee. "Is this your doing?"

"No," said Lee.

"How did you know you'd find me here?" Restorick demanded of Loasby.

"I had the airport watched," retorted the inspector. "Two of my men saw you arrive and followed you here. One of them telephoned me to ask for orders, and I said I'd come myself." It was Loasby's turn to sneer. "I couldn't do less for a man of your prominence."

"Never mind my prominence! You can go back to headquarters now and take your men with you. When I've finished my conversation with Mr. Mappin, I'll come to headquarters under my own power. I won't be taken there."

"That's not for you to say," said Loasby with an ugly smile. "You're going to be treated like anybody else. It's nothing to me how much money you have."

"Gentlemen, for God's sake!" remonstrated Lee. "You're acting like a pair of schoolboys!"

Both angry men turned on him simultaneously. "You keep out of this!"

Lee retired.

Loasby said to Restorick: "I don't have to take this from any citizen, rich or poor. Will you come with me or do I have to take you?"

"Try taking me," said Restorick with a hard smile. He backed away a little, looking around him to make sure he had room to swing in.

"Restorick, you can't buck the police!" cried Lee earnestly.

"If any man lays a hand on me, let him take the consequences," said Restorick grimly.

The two plainclothesmen started forward, but Loasby restrained them with a hand. "Better listen to your friend," he warned. "You can't defy the whole police force. If these men are not enough, I have more downstairs. If they are not enough, there are hundreds within call of the telephone."

"Try taking me," repeated Restorick.

Loasby addressed one of his men. "Go fetch the others," he said, jerking his head toward the gallery.

The officer turned to go. Restorick sprang into action. Moving with a swiftness astonishing in so big a man, he overtook the officer before he reached the door of the room, and with a blow on the side of the head stretched him on the floor. The other man ran in, drawing a short rubber club and raising it high. Restorick, turning, caught the raised wrist in one hand and with his other fist struck a blow that sent the man reeling to join his mate on the floor. The rubber club flew across the room. Lee quietly pocketed it.

Loasby ran to help. Restorick, hauling off, aimed a terrible blow in his face, but Loasby ducked under it. Restorick whirled helplessly under his own momentum; Loasby seized him around the waist and they crashed to the floor together, Restorick beneath. But Loasby could not hold him. "Help me here!" he cried hoarsely. The other two men scrambled across the floor and flung themselves on Restorick's body.

A mad scene succeeded. The men on the floor thrashed down the whole length of the big room with flying arms and legs. Restorick, under them all, leaped and twisted like a maddened cat. The others, in the effort to pin him down, only interfered with each

other. There was an appalling series of crashes as chairs went over
and tables, bearing whatever stood upon them. A body went
through the glass case of shelves where Lee exhibited his smaller
bibelots. They ended up against a commode between the windows.
It bore a priceless porcelain vase that swayed dangerously. Lee
clutched his head in despair. The vase toppled over and was shat-
tered on the floor.

In spite of the odds, Restorick succeeded in wrenching and kick-
ing himself free of those who tried to hold him. He scrambled to
his feet and backed away against the south wall of the room, looking around for a weapon. He snatched up an elegant light chair,
and held it in front of him. Blood was running down the side of his
face, but Lee noted with astonishment a kind of gaiety in his glance.

The other three got to their feet among the porcelain shards
and leaned against the commode, panting hoarsely. All three were
variously damaged and bloody. There was no gaiety in their faces,
but a look of outrage and surprise. A short truce was necessary to
enable all to recover a measure of breath.

The officers finally stood upright and moved away from the
commode, keeping close together and watching Restorick warily.
Restorick suddenly charged them with the chair, scattering them
right and left. Restorick himself crashed against the opposite wall
of the room and flung the broken chair aside. One of the officers
lay on the floor. The other made for Restorick.

Loasby followed his man, gasping out to Lee: "Telephone downstairs for help."

As Lee went out the door, he heard the crack of fist on jaw, and
a body fell to the floor. Then the smack, smack, smack of close
fighting. Lee himself was acting instinctively. Snatching up a knife
in the pantry, he sawed through the wires of the house phone. One
of the plainclothesmen came tearing through the gallery with
Restorick at his heels. The officer flung Lee to the floor and
Restorick fell headlong over him. The officer got through the front
door and slammed it shut behind him. When Restorick picked himself up and got the door open, they could hear the man pattering
like mad down the stone stairs a flight below.

Restorick turned his bloody face toward Lee and grinned. "Reckon he's had all he wants," he said.

Lee pulled him inside the door and closed it. "Listen!" he said urgently, "they'll be right back in a body."

"Well, why not?" said Restorick.

"Man, they'll beat you to a pulp if they take you now! Keep out of the way for awhile! Let everybody cool down! . . . This way! Go down the service stairs clear to the basement. The front of the house will be watched. Keep away from it! Listen! There's a row of windows in the basement looking east. Drop out of one of those windows to the rocks along the river shore. You can make your way along those rocks to the end of the next street. Get me?"

"I get you, cock sparrow! It was a good scrap, wasn't it? Best workout I've had in years. So long!"

Lee thrust a couple of tea towels in his hands to wipe away the blood, and Restorick started down the stairs.

Lee scampered back through the gallery to the living room and peeped in fearfully. Loasby and the second man were lying on the floor, out cold. Both were breathing stertorously, so Lee supposed they were not seriously hurt. He ran back to the front door to listen.

After a few minutes, he heard the elevator door slam back and the murmur of many voices on the other side of his door. Simultaneously the bell rang and fists pounded on the door. Lee was in no haste to open it. They waited a minute and then redoubled their pounding.

"Open! Open! Or we'll smash it down."

Lee opened at last, but by now Restorick had a long start on the service stairway. Lee sank back on the floor with a woebegone expression. The policemen poured through the door. Nobody had any regard for *his* supposed injuries. One cried out: "Why didn't you phone down when it started?"

"He . . . he cut the wires," said Lee faintly.

"Where is he? Where is he?" they cried, spreading through the rooms.

"I don't know," murmured Lee. "I must have passed out."

In a minute or two, one discovered the service stairway. "This way! This way!" he shouted.

But Restorick had gained more precious time.

Two men went down the service stairs and two more ran out the front door to commandeer the elevator. A wonderful quiet descended on the apartment.

Lee staggered back through the gallery, biting his lip to control a grin. When he entered the living room, the grin changed to a grimace of pain. The big room presented a ghastly scene of ruin. Loasby had come to and was sitting in a chair holding his head. A fifth officer was bending over his still unconscious mate on the floor. Lee quietly dropped the rubber club behind an upholstered chair and sank into another chair with a sepulchral groan. The man on the floor sat up, saying: "Where is he? Where is he?"

Lee's ears were stretched for sounds from below. All was silence.

Restorick had made good his escape.

CHAPTER SIXTEEN

POOR JERMYN WAS FLABBERGASTED when he got home. The police were out of the apartment, but an officer had been left on post in the lobby below on the improbable assumption that the fugitive might return. Jermyn's leathery old face worked with emotion when he came to his master.

"Oh, sir, are you hurt? Are you hurt?" he cried.

"Not a scratch!" said Lee cheerfully. "I was only a spectator—in a ringside seat! It was a lovely scrap!"

"I shall never leave you alone in the apartment again!" vowed Jermyn.

"Nonsense, man!"

Jermyn surveyed the debris in the living room with a tragic face. "All your beautiful things, sir! It will cost thousands to replace them!"

"Quite," said Lee. "Luckily Restorick is good for it. It was his show."

LEE AWOKE VERY EARLY NEXT MORNING, consumed with curiosity as to what the newspapers would say. Early as it was, Jermyn had already been out to buy the papers. Lee read them propped up in bed.

The story—practically the same in every paper—described how George Restorick had unexpectedly come to Mr. Amos Lee Mappin's apartment the previous night to demand that the famous criminologist lay off the Stannard case. Mr. Mappin was alone in his apartment. Like a good citizen, he had telephoned for the police. When the police arrived, they found the apartment partly wrecked and the wanted man gone in spite of Mr. Mappin's courageous efforts to detain him. Mr. Restorick was a tall and powerful man, a former athlete. He had escaped through the service entrance of the apartment house, and his present whereabouts were unknown. However, the entire police force was aroused to action by the outrage and the quick arrest of Restorick was assured.

Lee laughed when he read this, and laughed again as the implications of the story became clear. It relieved his most pressing anxiety. To resist the police in the performance of their duty is a grave offense. Supposing Restorick to be innocent of the murder, after the publication of this story the police could hardly press the other charge.

Restorick's flight, naturally, stamped him in the public mind as guilty of the Stannard murder. Ewart Blanding could now be released.

"Well, it's an ill wind that blows nobody good," Lee remarked to Jermyn.

Lee's private phone was unlisted in the book, but of course a certain number of people knew it; others knew the address of the apartment house. From eight o'clock on, Jermyn was kept busy answering inquiries from anxious friends and persistent reporters on both phones. The friends were assured that Lee was all right; the reporters were told that Mr. Mappin was in no state to be interviewed today, and that he had nothing to add, in any case, to the story already published.

After breakfast, Lee sent out for a discreet barber that he knew and ordered him to paint *on* a black eye. It was the first time the artist had ever received such an order, but he had dark pigments as well as flesh-colored in his box, and the task intrigued him. Over his realistic black eye Lee put a shield of pink celluloid which fitted under his glasses. Thus accoutered, he set off for police headquarters.

At first he was denied access to Inspector Loasby's private office. "The inspector is engaged on the Stannard case," he was told, "and left orders that he could not be disturbed."

"It is in relation to the Stannard case that I must see him," Lee remonstrated.

He was admitted.

The inspector's handsome face was liberally decorated with adhesive. His self-love had received a worse hurt than his face. He glowered at Lee with a hangdog expression.

As soon as the door closed, he blurted out: "I wasn't responsible for that story you read in the newspapers. My policy is to tell the whole truth or say nothing. But I was overruled. They said it would damage the prestige of the police to tell the whole story."

"Naturally," said Lee.

Loasby glanced at him sharply, suspecting irony. Lee's face was as a babe's. Loasby went on, fingering his bandages tenderly: "He ought to have been shot! He was wearing brass knuckles. Didn't you see them?"

"No," said Lee. "But I was terribly excited."

"How did you get your eye?" asked Loasby suspiciously.

"I don't remember exactly."

"It looked all right when I left last night."

Lee raised the shield briefly to give him a glimpse of the lurid green and blue pigments beneath. "Swelled up after you left."

"You weren't much help to us," said Loasby sourly.

"I did my little best."

"When did he get a chance to cut the telephone wires?"

"That must have been before you came. When I went to call for help I found them cut."

"Were you expecting him last night?"

"No. He had wired the day before that he wouldn't return to New York."

"What did he want of you?"

"Just what the newspaper said, to warn me to keep out of his private affairs."

"That hundred thousand he offered you in the beginning was just a kind of bribe!"

"Well, I haven't taken any of it," said Lee. "I'm still a free agent."

"Any news?" asked Loasby eagerly.

"No. I was hoping to hear some from you."

"Every newspaper in the country will run his photograph to-day!" said Loasby fiercely. "He's not a man who could easily be overlooked. In town here, his house and the Estate office are watched, also the place in Connecticut, and the telephone wires tapped." Loasby banged the desk. "He can't escape me long! . . . There is one thing that last night proved," he added. "There's no longer any mystery about the Stannard case. Restorick's as guilty as hell!"

Lee said nothing.

"Don't you agree?" demanded the inspector.

"No," said Lee.

Loasby stared. "Then why in hell should he put up such a fight to escape?"

"Restorick is a special case," said Lee. "He has a passion for personal liberty. Bear in mind that he has never submitted to restraint or confinement in his whole life. I might have persuaded him to come down to headquarters of his own free will if you had given me time."

"Humph!" snorted Loasby. "I think I can feel the influence of that hundred thousand dollars here."

"Not at all," said Lee. "Believe it or not, I am giving you the straight dope . . . There is a certain amount of evidence against Restorick, but you will not have a real case against him until you can find the man who acted for him while he was in Mexico."

"That was Barmby, his farmer."

"Barmby has an alibi."

"Why didn't you tell me this?" demanded the scowling inspector.

"I did tell you. But last night you went off at half cock." Lee suppressed the temptation to add, "as usual!"

Loasby jabbed his pencil into his desk blotter. "And now I've let Blanding go, I haven't got anything to show for my work on the case," he said gloomily. ". . . Just the same, Restorick is guilty," he growled. "I could swear to it! No man could put up a fight like that unless he had the fear of the chair before him!"

"Have it your own way," said Lee.

The telephone on the desk rang. Loasby answered it, and pushed the instrument carelessly toward Lee. "For you."

Lee heard a laugh over the wire. A well-remembered bass voice said: "Was that Loasby who answered?"

"Restorick!" gasped Lee. "Where are you?"

It was a marvel to see how the inspector pricked up his ears.

"Why, Mr. Mappin, how indiscreet!" Restorick's voice drawled mockingly. "I'm surprised at you! . . . As a matter of fact, I have a safe and delightful hideout, and the police will never find me unless I get tired of staying indoors."

Loasby, signaling urgently to Lee to keep the man in talk, slipped out of the room.

Lee said to Restorick: "There's only one thing for you to do."

"What's that?"

"Come down to police headquarters and give yourself up."

"You tell me that after helping me to escape last night!"

"There was a reason for that," Lee said earnestly. "Do not think for a moment that I condone your defiance of the police. I was forced to depart from my own lifelong rule of conduct, and I deeply regret the necessity. The reason I spoke of no longer exists. By giving yourself up promptly you can regain some of the ground you lost by your actions last night."

Restorick laughed lightly. "The hell with that stuff! I don't give a single damn for what the police or the newspapers or anybody else thinks of my actions. I'm not going to give myself up. Liberty's too sweet. Let them come and get me! A millionaire leads a pretty dull life, Mappin. I almost wish I had turned crook long ago, I'm having so much fun out of this!"

"You're talking like a schoolboy," said Lee severely. "You mustn't expect any further help from me."

"Is the Grand Panjandrum listening?" asked the laughing voice.

"No," said Lee. "He has left the room."

"Ha!" said Restorick. "Gone to trace this call, eh? He can't do it! It's a dial phone. So long, Lee! I'll be seeing you."

The connection was broken.

In a minute or two a discomfited police inspector returned to the room and flung himself into his chair. There was no need for Lee to ask if he had been successful in tracing the call.

"So he's still in New York!" he growled.

"That ought to make things easier for you," said Lee pleasantly. "You can keep the search for him all in the family, so to speak."

Loasby, jabbing the pencil viciously into his blotter, was silent for awhile. Lee gave him his own time. Finally, he said:

"Lee, what sort of a hideout would a man like Restorick be likely to choose?"

"Ask me something easy," said Lee. "Suppose he offers a thousand dollars a night for a lodging—or ten thousand—who could refuse it? And who would betray so generous a guest?"

Loasby thumped his chest. "That's the hell of it! It's wicked! It's wicked that a crook should have so much money at his command!"

There was another silence. Then Loasby, with a lowering glance, said: "I cut in on your conversation with Restorick."

"I know you did," said Lee coolly. "I heard the circuit open."

"So you *did* help Restorick make a getaway last night. I suspected it all along."

"I did," said Lee. "You provoked a situation that I couldn't handle. After the fight began, I wasn't going to let your men take Restorick if I could prevent it, because in that case I should have had to stand by and see them beat him into insensibility. You couldn't have subdued him otherwise."

Loasby had nothing to say to this.

Lee went on: "I hope you heard the rest of the phone conversation, in which I put myself on record with Restorick. As you know, I have always played ball with the police, and I always will, unless the police themselves make it impossible for me to do so."

"What about the Stannard case—from now on?"

"From now on, I reserve full liberty of action. I have refused to touch Restorick's money, and I do not promise to take you into my confidence either. Twice now you have hindered my plans by acting too precipitately. . . . Of course, as soon as I have a case, as soon as an arrest should properly be made, I will come to you. When the case is finally solved, it's nothing to me who gets the credit for it. You're welcome to it."

Loasby's face was a study in mixed emotions. "You could be prosecuted for last night," he growled.

"Certainly I could," said Lee. "But I'm sure you don't want the whole story of last night spread on the record."

Loasby was silent.

As the conversation had now become unprofitable, Lee arose and briskly took his leave. "No hard feelings," he said, offering his hand with a smile.

"None on this side," growled Loasby, taking it.

WHEN LEE'S TAXI TURNED into his own street, he saw a battered cab standing against the curb, just short of the door of his apartment house. As Lee's cab passed this other, an anxious face pressed forward and took a good look at him. By the time Lee had paid off his driver and stepped out, the passenger in the cab behind was also on the sidewalk.

"Mr. Mappin, can I . . . can I have a word with you?" he asked nervously.

It was not at all a dangerous-looking customer. "Surely," said Lee.

The man waited until Lee's cab had drawn away. He was elderly and stooped and scrawny; very neatly dressed; his prominent Adam's apple worked convulsively up and down. The mild face was familiar, but Lee could not instantly place it. Then it came; this was the old-fashioned bookkeeper in the office of the Restorick Estate. His name was Slocum.

"You remember me, sir?"

Lee nodded.

"I . . . I have been delegated to escort you to a certain party . . ."

Lee smiled. "Wait a minute! It is only fair to warn you that I have told this party I no longer feel bound to protect him from the police."

Slocum swallowed hard. "The party is aware of that, sir. He thought perhaps you would be good enough to allow yourself to be blindfolded while I conduct you to him . . ."

"Blindfolded!" exclaimed Lee

Then he saw that Slocum was holding out a pair of heavily frosted glasses. "These would let you out with the police," he faltered.

Lee laughed outright. This was so characteristic of Restorick's saturnine humor. He considered. The adventure was tempting. After all, he was his own man; neither Restorick nor the police had any strings on him. "Very well," he said, "I'll come."

Slocum's face cleared wonderfully. "Oh, thank you, sir! I scarcely dared hope I would be successful."

Lee entered the old cab and dutifully assumed the glasses. They had sidepieces pressing against the temples, and when they were in place, he could see nothing at all. Before he adjusted them, he had taken a good look at this odd outfit. The cab was a genuine taxi with the usual legend painted on the body: "20c 1/4 mile," etc., but the young man under the wheel was much too sleek and superior to be a regular taxi driver. One of Restorick's chauffeurs, Lee suspected.

Since he could see nothing, he was dependent on his other senses. The cab turned south into First Avenue; no mistaking the roar of heavy trucking here. After proceeding for several blocks and pausing for a light (which confused Lee's sense of distance) they turned west. What street was this? Not Forty-second, because there was no sound of traffic bound in the opposite direction, no trolley cars, no tunnel under Tudor City. Since they were heading west, it must be one of the odd-numbered streets. Not Forty-third, because that street is blocked by Grand Central Station and they kept straight ahead without further turns. Not Forty-fifth either, because that is rather a quiet street, and this one was noisy. Probably Forty-seventh.

Pausing at the corner of Fifth Avenue for a light, Lee could easily recognize the peculiar rubbery hum of the heavy traffic on the city's principal thoroughfare. Then a very long block to Sixth Avenue.

After crossing Sixth, Lee was more than ever sure it was Forty-seventh Street because of the heavy shuffle of feet on the sidewalks, the sound of a juke box through an open store front. It was mid-day, and he could hear the orders being given at sidewalk lunch stands, and soft drink counters. This part of Forty-seventh is one of the most diverting and disreputable streets in mid-town. It is like a perpetual carnival.

Another long block. When they must have been close to Seventh Avenue (Lee could hear the clang of the trolley cars on Broadway), the taxi drew up at the curb on the south side, and Slocum tenderly helped the seeming blind man across the sidewalk. "Three steps up, sir," he murmured. They passed through a swinging door and through a corridor with a mosaic pavement. There was neither sound nor smell inside to indicate what sort of building this was. They entered an elevator, obviously an old-fashioned elevator because the door closed with a clang and the car started with a strong draught of air. "Sixth floor, please," Slocum murmured to the operator.

They got out and paused before a door. It was presently opened to them and they stepped inside. They were evidently expected, because nothing was said. The door closed behind them, and Slocum murmured: "You may take off the glasses now, sir."

The first thing Lee saw was a smart, high-yellow maid wearing a coquettish lace cap and apron. She took his hat and stick with a smile. He found himself in a long and rather narrow hallway, typical of the better class apartment of forty years ago. It was carpeted with expensive oriental runners and there were good etchings hanging on the walls. The faint suggestion of an expensive perfume lingered on the air.

"This way, sir," said the maid, leading the way toward the front of the building.

Slocum disappeared and Lee did not see him again.

The handsomely furnished living room had windows looking down on the street. The blinds were lowered; lamps lighted in the room. George Restorick met Lee at the door.

"Hi, Lee! The sight of you is good for sore eyes!" he cried. His voice changed. "Why who hit you? I didn't know that you mixed it up last night."

"I didn't," said Lee. "That's camouflage."

There was a woman in the room behind Restorick. He brought Lee forward. "This is Amos Lee Mappin," he said to her, "whom I am proud to call my friend! . . . Lee, this is Miss Clara Moore, a very old friend of mine."

She was on the sunny side of forty, a pleasant, good-humored woman rather than strictly beautiful; marvelously groomed in the tailor-made fashion that New York has brought to perfection. The light of a wide knowledge of the world lay in her smiling brown eyes.

She said: "It is wonderful to have you here, Mr. Mappin. For years I have been following your cases in the newspapers."

"And now I am in the papers again!" said Lee. "And this is the hardest nut I have ever had to crack."

"But you'll do it!" she said. "I'm sure of it! If I were guilty I should be out of my mind with terror."

"Clara refuses to believe that I did it," put in Restorick.

"Don't be silly, George! . . . I know you men want to talk together, so I'm going to see about lunch. It's our breakfast, really. I hope you'll join us, Mr. Mappin."

Restorick answered for him. "Of course he will! Let him try to get away, that's all!"

She left them. Lee and Restorick lit cigarettes and sat down. Lee could easily have snapped up one of the blinds. He knew New York so well that a glance into the street would have told him where he was. But he had no desire to look. He wanted to see this situation through to the end.

"I suppose you're wondering why I had you brought here," said Restorick.

"I just took it for an example of your peculiar humor," said Lee.

"It was partly that. I can't help it if my humor is peculiar. But there is more to it than humor. These girls are good to me, but I can't stop thinking about the case. Not for a minute. I would go wild if I didn't have some source of information as to what is happening from hour to hour."

"So I am to be led blindfold through the streets every day to put you wise," said Lee dryly.

"No! No! of course not! Once is enough. Besides, as smart a guy as you are, would soon get onto the location of my hideout. No, I just wanted to establish contact with you. If I had called you up today you would only have laughed at me, or told me to go to hell, and hung up. But if we can reach an understanding, I can call you up after this at hours that may be convenient to you. Last night I still had a hundred questions to ask when the police broke us up."

"Ask them now," said Lee.

Restorick immediately started putting him through a searching questionnaire covering every step Lee had taken in the case. Lee answered him candidly; he saw no reason why he should not.

"Well," said Restorick at last, "if you are satisfied that neither Blanding nor me is guilty, are you stopped?"

"Almost," said Lee, "but not quite. I have a suspect, but no case."

"You are referring to Amy Dordress, I take it."

"Yes."

"If you are right, the motive was jealousy. She wanted to break up the marriage between Mary and Jack Fentress. Fentress has an ungodly attraction for women."

"That's right."

"She couldn't have done it herself."

"Of course not. On the night of the murder she gave a big party in her apartment. Dinner followed by dancing. She was on view every minute until the party broke up."

"Then if you are right, she hired somebody to do it."

"Somebody was hired," said Lee. "And a thumping big price paid. Mary was wearing a couple of thousand dollars' worth of jewelry, and it was not touched."

"That doesn't sound like a hired job," said Restorick, scowling.

"You're right, it does not," said Lee. "But it's all we have to go on at present."

"Supposing you're right, why in hell should the Dordress woman have chosen to hide the body on my place at Black Maple?"

"Well, she knew that you were an unsuccessful suitor. She may have gone on the general principle that she'd be safe in trying to hang it on you. The same applies to Ewart Blanding. It looks as if she had hesitated between you and Blanding. Or as if something had caused her to change her whole plan midway. That may prove to be a fatal mistake. Through that we may convict her."

"But all this is mere speculation," objected Restorick.

"Sure," said Lee, "that's how you must begin to solve a case; by speculating on what *could* have happened."

"Mary has been dead eight days now. Haven't you the least bit of solid evidence to implicate the Dordress woman?"

"Yes," said Lee. "One little acorn of evidence from which I hope to raise an oak tree."

"What's that?" demanded Restorick.

"What was in the beginning the most baffling feature of the case? The single blossom broken from Mary's spray of orchids that I found in Blanding's wrecked car."

"Go on, man! Go on!"

"When Blanding was told of my find, he cried out spontaneously: 'It was planted on me!' Well, in the light of later developments, that must be the truth. *Because the spray of six blossoms was still intact on Mary's jacket when she left you twelve minutes before the car crashed!*"

"That's right, by God!"

"Then who planted it? . . . The car stayed in a garage at Pelham until Tuesday morning. The flower could not have been planted there, because La Dordress did not know where it was until Tuesday. The car was then towed down to the Packard garage and that was where I found it. Well, just before I got there, Amy Dordress had been to the garage to inspect the damage."

Restorick sprang up. "That's wonderful!" he cried. "That's the first ray of daylight that has broken on this case!"

"Dawn in the east," said Lee, "but it seems as if the sun would never come up!"

"How could Dordress have got hold of the broken flower?"

"Why, I assume the murderer brought it to her as proof he had done his job."

"Has she been seeing Fentress during the past week?"

"Not so far as we have been able to discover. She's as secretive and suspicious as hell. There is no evidence that she is even acquainted with him. But it would be natural for her to lay off him for awhile. Only her incontrollable temper has betrayed her passionate interest in the case. If she had kept her mouth shut, who would ever have thought of suspecting her?"

"Well, anyhow you have lifted a weight from my breast!" cried Restorick. "We have something to go on!" A doubt occurred to him. "But Dordress has just announced her engagement to another man!"

"Considering all the circumstances," said Lee, "that is highly suspicious in itself."

"Sure! Sure!"

A bell tinkled in the back of the apartment.

"Come on, old cock, let's eat!" cried Restorick. As Lee rose, he hit him a clap on the back that almost forced him to his knees. "I have recovered my appetite!"

"Careful!" grumbled Lee. "You don't know your own strength!"

They passed through the long corridor. Various closed doors opened off it. In the dining room at the rear, a pleasant surprise waited for Lee. It appeared that the household included two beautiful young girls, a blonde and a brunette, perfect foils for each other. They were beautifully dressed, and in a gayer fashion than Clara, as befitted their years. The blonde was introduced simply as Dorothy, the brunette as Julia. The smiling high-yellow waited at table.

"Oh, Mr. Mappin!" said Dorothy. "I'm scared to death of you!"

"Why?" asked Lee.

"They say you write books!"

"Dorothy never read a book," remarked Julia dryly.

"I have so! I read, what was it now—the *Prodigal Nurse*."

They sat down amidst great laughter. The silver gleamed, the crystal sparkled, the table blossomed with pink roses and delphiniums.

Lee thought: There was nothing like this when I was young—but I wasn't a millionaire.

"What'll you drink, Lee?" cried Restorick. "We have something special in champagne."

Lee wagged his hands protestingly. "Too early, too early for champagne!"

"Oh, can we have champagne, George?" cried Dorothy, like a child at a birthday party.

"Sure!"

She addressed Lee. "And *such* champagne, Mr. Mappin. Champagne from France. I didn't know that such nectar existed until George came."

When the champagne was served, Lee was persuaded without much difficulty to try it. It was such a wine as he had not tasted since the fall of France. The grim subject of murder was banished for the moment and he proceeded to enjoy himself to the full. There was nothing languorous nor provocative about Dorothy and Julia; they were as natural as the lovely flowers on the table. In two minutes they were addressing him as Lee. Since they treated him as if he was their own age, he was never reminded of the fact that he was elderly and bald and fat.

Two hours later, he very reluctantly tore himself away from this charming scene. Slocum was produced out of one of the mysteriously closed doors in the corridor, and after affectionate farewells, Lee assumed the frosted glasses and was conducted home the way he had come.

His first act on reaching his own quarters was to thumb the telephone book. There it was:

Moore, Miss Clara, 88 West 47th

Lee chuckled. Such a human and natural oversight, after going to all those elaborate pains to mystify him! The telephone book! However, the mystification *had* saved his face. He felt under no obligation to inform the police where the much-wanted George Restorick was to be found.

CHAPTER SEVENTEEN

THE ESCAPE OF GEORGE RESTORICK and the subsequent search for him stimulated public interest in the Stannard case to a fever heat. Restorick, who had always kept out of the public eye as much as possible, was a romantic and mysterious character to begin with, and the tale of his riches approached the fabulous. Never before had the hunting instinct of the public been aroused by millionaire game. The case instantly became nationally famous—indeed, internationally, for every newspaper in the world that enjoyed telegraph service featured it.

Everybody said that a man so well known couldn't keep out of the hands of the police for more than a few hours, but one day succeeded another and Restorick was still free. It was reported to Lee that Inspector Loasby's chagrin had almost brought on a cerebral hemorrhage, a danger to which such full-blooded men are especially liable. Lee kept out of Loasby's way during this period.

Jermyn's attempt to obtain information from Rathbun, the Dordress butler, was attended with unexpected results. He spent an evening at the Butler's Club in friendly talk with Rathbun. Jermyn devoted this time to establishing a basis for future talks, and took care not to ask the butler any leading questions. And then Rathbun disappeared.

The second man in the Dordress household had lately been elected to the club. He saw Jermyn and Rathbun in close talk all evening, and the assumption was that he had reported it to his mistress, for Rathbun was summarily fired next morning—that is to say, he was no longer to be seen around the Dordress apartment and the second man got his job.

"That seems like a foolish move on the part of Miss Dordress," said Lee. "If the man really has got anything of interest to tell us, he ought to be eager to talk now."

Every night Jermyn waited for Rathbun at the club, but he did not show up.

Several days later, it was discovered through Stan Oberry that Rathbun had not been fired, but merely transferred to Miss Dordress' yacht as chief steward of that palatial vessel. The yacht was lying in the Erie Basin, where she was being reconditioned for the coming season.

Lee said to Oberry: "Rathbun is no doubt a virtual prisoner on board. But anyhow, see what you can do toward bringing us in touch with him. Meanwhile we'll try other lines."

Oberry established relations with an electrician who serviced the Dordress apartment on a monthly basis. After his next inspection of the apartment, this man reported that the little ticket on the base of the unlisted phone in Miss Dordress' private sitting room had been removed, the number scratched out and the ticket replaced.

"She thinks of everything," said Lee. "I've got one more thing to try."

Through a friend who was in touch with the telephone company, Lee secured the desired information. The number of Miss Dordress' unlisted phone was such and such. "But," added his informant, "an order has just been received from Miss Dordress to disconnect this line."

"Damn!" said Lee to Stan Oberry. "Either I am playing in hard luck, or I am up against the cleverest mind that ever set itself against mine!"

Subsequently Lee said to Jermyn: "There's no use trying to get anything out of the new butler at Dordress' for the present. He's too new a broom. Miss Dordress pays her servants very handsome wages. She has to, or she couldn't keep one more than twenty-four hours."

LEE LOOKED FORWARD with no little interest to his next encounter with Jack Fentress. He had not long to wait.

One evening Jack called up to ask, as usual: "Can I come around for a little while?"

"By all means," said Lee.

When he came, Lee saw that his appearance had not improved any. He looked like a fit candidate for a psychiatric sanatorium. Before Lee had said a word, he blurted out:

"Sure, I've been drinking. What else can I do? I can't rest; I can't sleep!"

"Why don't you go away for awhile?" suggested Lee.

"That wouldn't do me any good. I couldn't get away from the memory of Mary!"

He had a hundred questions to ask about the latest developments in the case. Lee answered them frankly enough, but of course said nothing about the whereabouts of George Restorick. Jack raged against Restorick.

"I wish I could get my hands on that fiend! I wouldn't care what happened to me afterwards. I dream of him at night and wake up sweating . . . Do you think they'll catch him?" he demanded. "They've got to catch him!"

"Sure," said Lee soothingly. "He can't live without money. As soon as he tries to draw any, they'll have him."

When Jack was quieted down somewhat, Lee asked offhandedly, "Do you know Miss Dordress?"

Jack gave him a sharp look. "Sure! Everybody knows Amy Dordress."

"How well do you know her?"

"No better than a hundred other men around town know her. You meet her everywhere. She asks me to her parties. She gives wonderful parties. They say she's tight enough in other respects, but when she gives a party, the sky's the limit."

"Have you seen her lately?"

"No. I expect I'm in the doghouse. She gave a hell of a big blow-out the night . . ." He swallowed hard. ". . . the night I thought I was going to be married. I didn't go, of course. I reckon I even forgot to send regrets. She expects everybody to treat her like the Queen of America and it would take her a long time to get over that. . . . The hell with her! . . . Why did you bring her up?"

Lee didn't answer the question. "It has come to me from various sources," he said, "that Amy Dordress hated Mary."

"Very likely," said Jack. "I wouldn't know."

"Why did she hate Mary?"

"That question answers itself," said Jack indifferently. "You take a woman like Mary and bring her together with a woman like Amy; the Amy type is bound to hate the Mary type."

"I suppose so," said Lee. "But I thought you might know of some particular reason for it."

"None whatever," said Jack.

"Before all this happened," Lee went on, "had Amy Dordress ever given you any reason to suppose that she had an inclination toward yourself?"

Another sharp look from Jack. "Well, I suppose you want an honest answer, though I can't see what the hell you're driving at. . . . Yes, there have been times when Amy gave me to understand by a look that I could be more to her if I wanted. I never pay any attention to that sort of thing. I picked my woman long ago, and the others simply do not interest me."

"But now," said Lee softly, "now that Mary is lost to you, has it not occurred to you that you might improve that look in Amy's eye?"

Jack sprang up. "What are you saying?" he cried. "You know Amy Dordress. Can you suggest that she might be Mary's successor?"

"Sure, I know her," said Lee coolly. "They say she's worth fifty million dollars."

"I don't care if it's fifty billion!" shouted Jack. He took a turn toward the windows and came back. "Besides," he said, sneering, "everybody knows that Amy Dordress is a damn good business woman, and tight as wax. All her husband will get of the fifty million will be a handout from the missus when he's a good boy and does everything he's told. What a life!"

"Still," Lee persisted, "if she wanted some particular man badly enough, maybe she could be induced to make a marriage settlement on him."

"Well, that's an academic question now," said Jack with a shrug. "She's going to marry Imby Foulkes."

Lee allowed the subject to drop.

ON THE FOLLOWING DAY Amy Dordress called Lee up. When Jermyn told him who it was, Lee smiled. Yet he was not altogether surprised.

Over the wire he heard a meek little voice: "Oh, Mr. Mappin, I scarcely have the face to call you up after the horrible way I acted when you came to see me!"

Here was a change in the weather! "Forget it!" said Lee comfortingly. "I assure you it has completely passed from my mind."

"How kind of you to say so!" Lee had to listen to a lot more apologies before she came to the point. "I know how interested you are in the outcome of the Stannard case, Mr. Mappin. That's my only excuse for troubling you today. Some new evidence has come to my attention that you ought to know about. I can't tell how much it may be worth, but you ought to hear it. Can I come to see you?"

This was a rare piece of condescension in the little queen. "Not at all!" said Lee politely. "I will come to you."

"How good of you to put it that way! I will be at your service at any hour that may be convenient to you."

"Could you tell me over the phone?"

"I couldn't do that, Mr. Mappin. There may be somebody listening in on the wire at this end right now. . . . I can't trust anybody," she concluded sadly.

"Very well," said Lee. "I'll be right over."

At the Dordress apartment, he was admitted by a younger and handsomer butler, who showed him directly into the fantastic living room with its too, too candid oriental sculpture, its colored glass balls, and its ga-ga paintings. The mistress was waiting for

him there, biting her thin lips, twisting the rag of a lace handkerchief between her hands. Today she essayed to look like a simple
schoolgirl in a cotton jumper dress, with her hair combed back and
tied with a ribbon. But all the dressing up in the world could not
hide the ugly expression in her narrow eyes. This was a highly
sophisticated schoolgirl.

"Oh, Mr. Mappin!" she cried. "What must you be thinking of
me for the way I acted the last time you were here!" And so on.

Her voice would have melted a heart of stone, but the expression of her eyes did not change. They bored into Lee like two gim-
lets, as she tried to figure out the effect she was creating on him.
Lee smiled and smiled and heard her out.

When he saw a chance, he said: "Do tell me the new evidence
you have heard. I am on fire with curiosity."

"Sit down, Mr. Mappin. And smoke up. This is going to take
some time."

Lee obeyed, amused by the show and curious to see what was
coming.

"Yesterday a man came to see me," she began. "He was a rough-
looking and rather boozy character who would ordinarily have been
turned away at once. I ought to tell you that I have been so an-
noyed lately by all sorts of idlers, curiosity-seekers and crackpots
that I have been forced to engage a detective who is posted in the
lobby of the building and interviews everybody who asks to see
me. His name is Rulon. Rulon phoned up to me about this man
who was calling. Said that it was a person I would not ordinarily
want to see, but the man insisted he had important evidence to
give about the Stannard case, so Rulon thought he ought to let me
know. The man refused to tell Rulon what it was. Why didn't he
take it direct to the police, I asked. No! he wouldn't tell anybody
but me. Well, my curiosity was excited and I told Rulon to bring
him upstairs.

"He was a disreputable-looking fellow, in his forties I should
say. He appeared to be sober at the moment, but his breath, even
at several yards distance, almost knocked me down. Saturated with

cheap whisky, I expect. He had a kind of grinning impudence that was very offensive to me. He refused to tell his story while my detective was within hearing, so I sent Rulon out in the foyer to wait. I wanted him to be within call if the creature should become abusive.

"He gave the name of Pat Murphy, but that we subsequently found to be false. He gave an address in New Rochelle. That was false, too. He lives in Mount Vernon, near Pelham. His story was to the effect that on Wednesday night of last week about two o'clock—that would really be Thursday morning, wouldn't it?—he was walking through a certain street in Pelham when a small farm truck passed him. It seemed odd for a truck to be in that side street at such an hour, and he took a good look at it. It bore a sign reading Black Maple Farm. After it had passed, he looked back and saw it turn in at the vacant house where the body was subsequently found."

"Well!" exclaimed Lee. "This is important indeed! Why didn't the man come forward at once with his evidence?"

"I asked him that, of course," said Miss Dordress, "and he said he didn't want to be mixed up in the case. He said he hadn't any business to be on that street at such an hour and he didn't want to get into trouble at home. It was only after he thought it over that it came to him it was his duty to tell."

"Why did he bring his story to you instead of the police?"

"That's easy to answer," she said with a sour smile. "He had read in the papers that I was interested in the case. As you know, the newspapers are always talking about how much money I have. He wanted to sell his story to me. That's why he held back the most important part. Mr. Mappin, you have no idea how I am hounded by people of all sorts who are trying to get money out of me, for one reason or another. It is enough to destroy one's faith in humanity!"

"I can well understand that," said Lee. "What was he keeping back?"

"The description of the man who was driving the truck."

"Ha! So he was prepared to give that, too!"

"He said there was a street light overhead as the truck passed him, and through the window of the cab he got a good look at the driver's profile. The driver was alone in the cab. Slavin—that's the man's real name—said he could identify him among a thousand!"

"How much did he ask for this information?"

"Five hundred dollars."

"You paid it?"

"I did not!" she said. "It was no business of mine! I don't know much about the law, but I had a feeling that if this information was *paid for*, it would have little value in court."

"Quite right," said Lee.

"When I refused to give him money," Miss Dordress resumed, "he began to get abusive. So I called Rulon in, and the man was shown out of the building. Unseen by him, I gave Rulon a sign to follow him. He was a stupid fellow. Apparently it never occurred to him that he might be followed. He took the Lexington Avenue subway to the end of the line, and a trolley car to Mount Vernon. Rulon learned that his right name is Clem Slavin, and this is his address." She handed Lee a slip of paper.

"You have handled this matter exactly right," said Lee with a bow. "I congratulate you. I'll turn it over to the police and let them deal with it."

"That's what I expected you to do," she said, "but I wanted you to hear it first."

"Very thoughtful of you," said Lee. After a few more pleasantries, he bowed himself out.

Lee took a cab to Grand Central Station. There is a train every few minutes to Mount Vernon. The address that Lee had was in a shabby little street ending at the railway tracks. There was a saloon at the corner of the through street. Lee went in and ordered a beer. At the moment there was only one other man in the place, nursing a beer glass at the end of the bar.

"Do you know a fellow called Clem Slavin?" Lee asked the bartender.

"Sure! He's a customer here."

The other man spoke up: "Clem's just been reinstated, mister. He paid up yesterday."

The bartender scowled at the too-talkative customer.

"What's Clem's job?" asked Lee offhandedly.

"Oh, he ain't no common workingman, mister. Clem's a professional man, he is. His profession is living without working."

"Shut up, blabber-mouth!" growled the bartender. "What might you be wanting of Clem Slavin, mister, if it's a fair question?" he asked, giving the mahogany a swipe with his towel.

"Oh, just a little business," said Lee, with a wave of his hand. Seeing that he was not likely to obtain any further information here, he swallowed his beer and left.

Slavin's house was the last one in the squalid little street alongside the railroad tracks. A frame cottage with a broken porch, it was still grimy with soot from the steam locomotives that were retired so many years ago. Squire Slavin himself came to the door, wearing pajamas and a dressing gown long overdue at the washtub. He led the way into a small, littered sitting room. Judging from the look of it, Lee had interrupted him while daydreaming over a pitcher of beer. A dark, heavy specimen, hairy as a bear, Lee saw at a glance that he was not the stupid man Amy Dordress had described. His little eyes sparkled with cunning; glib rascal was his type; Lee had had experience of it.

"Mr. Mappin, sir," he said, dusting a chair. "Sure, I know you well, sir, from reading the newspapers. 'Tis an honor to have you call, sir. Sit ye down, Mr. Mappin. Will you join me in a glass of beer?"

"Thanks, no," said Lee. "I just had a glass at the corner."

"What can I do for you, Mr. Mappin, sir?"

When he told his story at Lee's invitation, it departed in no particular from Amy Dordress' version.

As he came to the end, Lee said bluntly: "Describe the man who was driving the truck."

A sly expression came over Slavin's face. "What's it worth to you, Mr. Mappin?"

"Not a penny," said Lee cheerfully.

Slavin was not at all put about by this answer. Apparently he expected it. "You wasn't born yesterday, I can see, sir," he said with undisturbed good humor. "But there's no harm in trying. . . . I could only see the head and shoulders of the guy driving the truck. A big man, he looked to be, sir, about forty years old, maybe, dark-complected with heavy features."

"So," said Lee. "What were you doing over in Pelham at that hour?"

Slavin grinned impudently. "Well, sir, as between man and man, I was calling on a lady, but I was hoping that wouldn't get around."

Lee gave this unappetizing Romeo the once-over without saying anything.

Slavin shrugged with a resigned air. "I suppose I'll have to tell my story to the police now."

"Certainly," said Lee.

"I always want to do my duty as a citizen."

"Very creditable," said Lee dryly. "I'm going back to town now. I'd be glad to have you accompany me if you care to."

"Sure!" said Slavin.

"Perhaps we can hire a car here in Mount Vernon. It would be more agreeable."

"I know where we can hire a car," said Slavin. "It's a real nice day. Maybe we can drive with the top down. . . . If you don't mind waiting until I can put me clothes on, Mr. Mappin."

"Of course I don't mind."

Slavin drank the last of the beer and disappeared. Lee sat within view of the stairs, in case the man might take the notion of slipping out at the rear. In due course, he returned downstairs wearing his Sunday suit.

At police headquarters, Lee left him sitting in the outer office while he entered Inspector Loasby's sanctum. Loasby was looking very glum.

"Any news?" he asked eagerly.

"No news of Restorick's whereabouts," said Lee. "I was hoping you might have some."

Loasby struck his desk violently. "Damn! It's enough to drive a man mad! Every hour there's a new report, by telephone, by wire, by mail. Restorick's been seen in a hundred places and nothing in it! All a waste of my time!"

"I've brought you a new witness," said Lee.

"Hey? Sit down! What's his story?"

Lee told it, and told how it had come to him.

Loasby's face cleared a little. "Well, that's something! Let's have him in. This supplies the missing link in the evidence!"

"Wait a minute," said Lee. "It's only fair to say that I think his evidence may be phony."

Loasby's jaw dropped. "Why?"

"He is evidently prepared to swear that he saw Restorick driving that truck in the small hours on Thursday."

"Well, why not?"

"Restorick didn't get here by plane from Mexico City until about eleven on Thursday morning."

"There's no *proof* of that," said Loasby. "I have made my inquiries. A chartered plane from Mexico City piloted by a Captain de Mercado landed a passenger at La Guardia Field at eleven on Thursday, but we do not know that that passenger was Restorick. Perhaps Restorick never left New York. Perhaps he sent a dummy to Mexico City."

"I had a telegram from him in Mexico City on Tuesday."

"Easy enough to have it sent by somebody else in his name."

"Have it your own way," said Lee good-humoredly. "I have other reasons for thinking this man's story may be phony."

"What are they?"

"Firstly, the man's a natural-born liar. He enjoys lying."

"I would never question your judgment in reading character," said Loasby. "But even a confirmed liar must tell the truth sometimes."

"Secondly," Lee continued, "though Miss Dordress said she had given him no money, he has had money from some source. He's been paying his bills in Mount Vernon. Thirdly, that part of the story that the detective, Rulon, was able to follow him from Park

Avenue up to Mount Vernon without being spotted, is simply in-credible."

"I will take care of all that," said Loasby, mounting his dignity.

Clem Slavin was brought in to Loasby's office. "This is the man," said Lee. "As I have already heard his story twice, there is no need for me to wait. I leave him to your tender mercies, Inspector."

CHAPTER EIGHTEEN

LATE THAT AFTERNOON, George Restorick called Lee up at the apartment. "Anything new?" he asked eagerly. "I'm sick of staying indoors. I must be gaining a pound a day!"

"I've got an amusing story to tell you," said Lee. "I don't know how much there may be in it."

"Don't spoil it by telling me over the phone," said Restorick. "Clara and the girls want to know if you'll come to dinner."

Lee thought of the champagne, the delicious food, the charming company. "I'd love to come!" he said at once.

"Okay, I'll send over for you at seven-forty-five. It won't be Slocum today; he's too closely watched by the police. The man I will send answers to the name of Warren."

"Very good," said Lee.

He left the telephone with a smile. He had no intention of waiting for the conductor. After dressing himself with care, he set out about ten minutes before Warren was to be expected, and started walking across town to work up an appetite for the good meal he expected. He stopped at a florist's on the way, and bought half a dozen orchids made up into three corsages.

Number 88 West 47th Street proved to be, as he expected, a medium-sized apartment house of the better class style that prevailed forty or fifty years ago. Lee had himself carried to the sixth floor. There were but two apartments to a floor, and he rang the bell beside the door on the left of the landing. It was opened by the same smiling colored girl. Seeing Lee standing there alone and

178

without the opaque glasses, she checked her smile.

"It's all right," said Lee. "I didn't wait for Warren."

She admitted him, still confused and biting her lip. Taking his hat and stick, she led him to the door of the front room.

"Hi, Lee!" cried George Restorick gladly.

"So nice to see you again," murmured Clara.

Lee presented his orchids. "For you and the girls."

Behind Lee, the maid was making signals to Restorick. Lee could see her in a wall mirror. Restorick went out in the hall with her and she whispered to him agitatedly. He came quickly back.

"Where's Warren?" he demanded toweringly.

"Oh, I didn't wait for him," said Lee airily. "I wanted a walk."

The faces of Clara and Restorick presented a study. Restorick glared at the maid and she retreated out of sight down the hall.

"How did you find your way here?" demanded Restorick.

Lee answered innocently: "I got Clara's address out of the telephone book."

The two faces looked so exquisitely foolish, Lee sat down and treated himself to the heartiest laugh he had had in many days. Finally, Restorick had to laugh, too. Clara's face was still terrified.

"Will he . . . will he tell?" she whispered, looking at Restorick.

"No fear," said Restorick. "Not when he brings you flowers. He's as clever as a little Satan but he's no Judas!" He laughed again. "What a pair of boobs we were not to think of the telephone book!"

The atmosphere cleared.

The dinner which followed was a lively affair. In addition to the statuesque Julia and the flowerlike Dorothy, two keen young men came in for the meal. One of them was Warren, who was quite willing to join in laughing at the trick Lee had played on him. The food was ambrosial.

"How do you do it?" Lee asked Clara, "In these degenerate days?"

"Oh, I have a good cook," laughed Clara.

"The cook is Clara herself!" said Restorick. "But she won't bestir her stumps for an ordinary guest. We wish you'd come to dinner every night, don't we, kids?"

"That's right!"

Immediately after dinner, the two young men departed. Lee understood that they had to "return to their post," wherever that was.

Later, in the front room, Julia and Dorothy sang torch songs in two parts, soprano and contralto, Clara at the piano. Suddenly, a loud bell sounded in the corridor. It was not the doorbell. The music broke off in the middle of a bar and Clara turned a white face.

"He *did* tell!" she murmured reproachfully.

Restorick was already in action. "I don't believe it!" he cried. "Go on playing, girls! Come, Lee!"

Lee not unnaturally said: "Where?"

"Never mind where! A line of retreat has been prepared."

"Why should I retreat?"

"You couldn't lie to the police. The girls can. Come!"

Lee yielded to the imperious voice. They snatched their hats in the corridor and went out of the door. Restorick led the way softly *up* the stairs with Lee at his heels. There were two more flights, and then a door leading out on the roof of the building. Holding the door open, Restorick listened for a moment. They heard the elevator stop at the sixth floor below. Restorick softly closed the door and locked it behind him with a key.

"That will hold them up for a moment or two," he said, grinning.

It was not dark on the roof of the apartment house. The sky signs over on Times Square filled the air with a soft radiance. A continuous rumble of traffic rose from the streets. Alongside the apartment building to the east, a hotel building rose several stories higher. Restorick led the way across the roof toward a certain lighted open window in the hotel that was just above his head. He whistled softly, and instantly a ladder came down, lowered by unseen hands above. Lee followed Restorick up the ladder and, climbing over a window sill, found himself in a typical hotel bedroom. Warren and the other young man were there; they made haste to pull up the ladder.

"Douse the light," ordered Restorick. "They'll break out on the roof below at any moment."

When the ladder was drawn in and the window closed, he said: "Are you sure you've left nothing in this room to betray you? The hotel will be searched."

"Not so much as a card of matches, Boss," said Warren.

They passed out of the bedroom and started up a stairway enclosed in a fireproof shaft, the two young men carrying the ladder between them. There were three flights in this building, and Lee was puffing a little when they came out on the roof. On this broad esplanade, a wide, low shed had been erected that had the look of a prefabricated building. The young men busied themselves with the lock.

"On the level, Lee, did you tip off the police?" asked Restorick while they waited.

"I did not," said Lee.

"I didn't think you had. If you had, I would have lost face with the girls forever!"

The big doors of the shed were swung back and the two young men, with Restorick's assistance, rolled out the strangest looking machine Lee had ever beheld. It had an immense horizontal propeller overhead. It resembled a gigantic Mayfly or one of those attenuated insects called mosquito hawks multiplied to the nth degree.

"My heliocopter!" said Restorick, grinning.

"How on earth did you contrive to install it up here?" asked Lee.

Restorick chuckled. "The apartment next door and this hotel are both a part of the Restorick Estate. The police overlooked that."

The engine was started with a roar. They waited to let it warm up. There were two seats in the contraption, one in front for the pilot, one for a passenger behind.

"You'll have to sit in my lap, Lee," said Restorick. "Will she lift the added weight, Warren?"

"Sure, Boss. Won't be anywhere near her capacity."

"Okay, don't fly over Forty-seventh Street. Some cop might look up. Head south, then east toward the river."

They took their seats. Warren was the pilot. Restorick held Lee on his knees.

"Make yourself scarce!" he called down to the man left on the roof. "They'll be searching the hotel directly."

Warren gave his engine the gun; the wide propeller overhead whirled softly; the machine rose from the roof as gently as an insect taking to the air. Lee caught his breath; it was a weird sensation; so much more magical than the swift run of a plane before leaving the ground. The roof dropped away beneath them; all the roofs, leaving only a tower sticking up here and there; the R.C.A. Building to the north, with a group of lofty hotels beyond; to the south the Empire State Building, tallest of all. It became chilly as they rose; Restorick reached into the fuselage behind him and drew out trench coats.

The machine started moving in a forward direction, heading east, but at a more leisurely pace than the darting planes Lee had been accustomed to. He could study the strange pattern of the city as seen from above at night with its indirect lighting. Acres and acres of dark roofs divided by the canyons of the streets, strongly illuminated at the bottom by lighted show windows and street signs. Presently they were passing the fantastic needle of the Chrysler Building; a minute later, the broad, shining ribbon of the East River lay beneath them. On the Long Island shore the lights of the great parkways stretched in graceful festoons far inland.

There was a telephone between Restorick and the pilot. Restorick spoke: "Follow the north shore of the Sound until you pass Bridgeport, fifty-six miles. Six miles beyond you'll find the mouth of the Housatonic. Follow the course of the river for thirty miles or so, and come into Black Maple over the hills from the east. I'll tell you when to leave the river."

"Black Maple is watched by the police," ventured Lee.

"I know it. We'll have to chance that. It's our only refuge. We'll land in one of the lower fields of the farm. Our friends will telephone Barmby from New York that we're on our way, and he'll show a light."

"Barmby's phone is tapped."

"I was prepared for that. We have a way of fooling them."

"The empty hangar will be found," Lee persisted. "The police will send word to their men at Black Maple."

Restorick patted his shoulder, as one might try to soothe a child. "Sure! Sure! Even so, I still have a card or two to play. My principal anxiety is on your account. I didn't want to drag you into this."

"Oh, well," said Lee philosophically. "I'm enjoying the ride."

They passed over the far-flung bridges, Queensboro', Triboro', Hell Gate and Whitestone. Beyond, the wide waters of Long Island Sound spread to the horizon before them. The moon had risen over Long Island, casting a faint, steely radiance on the water against which the islands stood out blackly. "We could do without the moon," said Restorick a little anxiously. The mainland shore line was picturesquely serrated with inlets and broken with islands; the city's favorite aquatic playground. Towns succeeded each other so rapidly that the lights of one ran into the next: New Rochelle, Larchmont, Mamaroneck, Rye.

After passing Stamford, the suburban lights died out and stretches of dark countryside separated the towns. A deep inlet and a triple galaxy of lights revealed the Norwalks; after another stretch of dark, they looked down on the myriad lights of Bridgeport. These lights were still visible when they saw the steely ribbon of the Housatonic coming down from the north and changed their course. After following the river for a dozen miles, another town lay below them.

"Derby," said Restorick; "and Ansonia lying over the hill. Stick to the river for about fifteen miles further. Come down lower so I won't miss the two bridges at Sandy Hook."

When he had picked up the bridges, he said: "In two miles you leave the river at the outside edge of a wide bend to the east. Lay a course due sou'east. You'll pass over two railway lines about a mile apart and a country road close to the second line. A pond lies on the northerly boundary of Black Maple Farm. We'll land in the field beyond the pond. There are no houses in this vicinity, no trees or wires. You can come down lower."

They dropped to within a couple of hundred feet of the ground. The little pond appeared, shining like silver under the moon. "Circle a couple of times to give Barmby a chance to signal us," said Restorick. "If he isn't there, come down anyhow. You can see well enough. It's pasture land."

A sharp spot of light appeared in the middle of the field below them; blinked on and off a few times, then held steadily. In a moment or two, the machine dropped in the grass alongside it; bounced gently and lay still. The engine was shut off, and peace descended on their ears. As Lee and Restorick climbed out, a flash was thrown on them; they could see Barmby holding the light.

"Put it out!" said Restorick sharply. "There's no need of it. . . . Is the coast clear?"

"So far as I know, sir," answered the farmer. "There are four detectives posted at the big house. They take turns patrolling the place and sleeping. They have a telephone connection."

"Where do they sleep?"

"In the guest rooms over the game room, sir."

"Damned impudence!" growled Restorick. "If they've got a telephone they must be on the alert. Weren't they watching you tonight, Barmby?"

"I don't know, sir. I got out of my house through the shed at the back and made a wide detour through the fields. I took plenty of time to it, and I made darn sure I wasn't followed."

"Good!" said Restorick. "But if they were outside the house, there is a possibility they heard the engine. We must break this up. . . . Is my car safely hidden in the north barn?"

"Yes, sir. They have never found that."

Restorick clapped a hand on Lee's shoulder. "Lee, I have a car hidden a couple of fields away with a full tank and an extra thirty gallons of gas. I'm heading north. By cutting a wire fence, I can reach my neighbor's farm road without going near my own place, and so gain a back road that by-passes Danbury. Will you come with me? I can drop you off some place where you can get back to town."

"Better not," said Lee. "If the girls keep the secret, nobody need ever know that I accompanied you on the first lap. I can serve you better by working on the case in town."

"Okay. Barmby will put you over to Danbury in his car."

"No," said Lee. "I would certainly be found out if we tried that."

"Then what will you do?"

"Walk to Danbury."

"Six miles!"

"So what? I'm not a cripple."

There was a moment's silence. It was a moment Lee never forgot; the misty, moonlit field sloping to the pond, the gleam of water, the smell of spring in the air and the great peace of night enfolding them. He laid a hand on Restorick's arm.

"George," he said earnestly, "if they cut you off, if they get you cornered, promise me you won't put up a fight. It's not worth it, because I'm going to clear you anyhow."

Restorick laughed. "Okay, I promise to submit to arrest—if they find me. . . . How can you be so sure you're going to clear me?"

Lee hesitated before answering—and Restorick never was answered.

"What's that?" he asked sharply.

They listened. Barmby spoke up: "A car bumping down the lane without lights."

"They *did* hear our engine!" muttered Restorick. "Get that crate out of here, quick!"

Warren sprang for his seat, saying over his shoulder: "Good luck, Boss!" He switched on his engine with a roar; the rotor whirled overhead, and presently the machine rose from the grass. Meanwhile Barmby on the other side was pulling at their arms. "This way! This way!" he urged. "There's a dry ditch at the edge of the field." They set off, running, stumbling over the uneven ground. Lee, looking over his shoulder, saw a pair of automobile lights go on at the far side of the field. A man was throwing down the bars that blocked the car's entrance. It presently charged into the field. At the same moment, the three running men fell headlong into a depression and hugged the bottom. The car came on, zigzagging to throw its lights in a wide arc back and forth across the field. The rays passed harmlessly over the backs of the crouching men. The car stopped in the middle of the field and two men piled out.

"Only two," said Restorick. "We could handle them easy."

"Remember your promise!" said Lee.

The detectives were not more than forty or fifty yards from the hidden men. The roar of the heliocopter's engine was loud in the

air. The great insect, heading south, passed between the watchers
and the moon, and those in the ditch bit their lips to keep from
laughing at the frantic way the detectives shook their fists and
cursed. They were excited and took no care to lower their voices.

One said: "He dropped a passenger here!"

The other replied: "How the hell can we find him in the dark?"

"There's only one road out of this place. We'll watch that. Make
a circuit of the field to let your light shine in every corner of it.
Sound the horn continuously to let the fellows at the house know
he's at large."

"That's a city man!" chuckled Restorick. "It hasn't occurred to
him that fences can be climbed."

After circling the field, the car returned to the lane. Its lights
were turned off. Presumably it stopped there. The three men
climbed out of the ditch and headed north across the field. By passing around the far side of the pond and climbing a couple of fences,
they put a wide berth between them and the lane. After crossing
several more fields, they came to a hay barn.

Barmby and Restorick rolled back the big doors as softly as
possible. In the fragrant interior, Barmby seized a pitchfork and
started throwing aside the hay at the bottom of the pile. When the
edge of a canvas cover appeared, he and Restorick each picked up
a corner of it and lifted it back over a little coupé snugly hidden on
the barn floor. Restorick, with a flashlight, walked all around the
car to make sure the tires were standing up.

They parted then. Restorick climbed into the car and, starting
the engine, leaned out through the window to shake his friends'
hands.

To Lee he said with a grin: "I'll be calling you up from time to
time."

"Be careful!" said Lee. "They can listen in on my wire, too."

"They won't get any change out of me," said Restorick. "Besides, I'll be keeping on the move."

He rolled out into the moonlight and, turning north, went
bumping slowly over the field, lights out. Lee and Barmby watched
until the car was swallowed in the luminous mist.

The farmer said: "He'll be all right now. On that side he's only got to cut one fence to reach the back road. I'll mend the fence before our neighbor ever finds out it has been cut."

After closing the barn doors, Barmby and Lee continued their wide detour through the fields, climbing one fence after another. Finally they ascended a hill and, topping a last fence, found themselves on a main road.

"Danbury to the right," said Barmby. "My house about a quarter-mile to the left. I believe I could sneak you in the back door without discovery. It's only a little after midnight and the first train in the morning don't leave until seven. You could get a few hours' sleep."

"Many thanks," said Lee, "but they will certainly search your house. It's safer for me to put as much distance as I can between me and Black Maple."

"Just as you say, sir. Shall I walk with you to Danbury?"

"Bless your heart, no!" said Lee. "You'll have a day's work to do tomorrow."

They parted, Barmby turning one way, Lee the other. Lee, aware of the comic little figure he must be making, walking along the road in the middle of the night, all dressed in his best and thumping his stick, was careful not to let himself be seen. The detectives would certainly patrol this road. Luckily, he was always warned in plenty of time of the coming of a car by the shine of its lights in the air. When a car approached from either direction, he climbed the fence at the side of the road and lay down inside. There were few cars; even so, he became dreadfully tired of climbing fences.

It was all very well to dismiss a six-mile walk so airily. He was already tired from plodding over fields and climbing fences before he reached the highway. He tried to keep up his courage by telling himself how beautiful the night was; how a man should make a practice of walking alone at night; how this walk would be something to remember; but the muscles and tendons of his legs hurt him worse and worse, and the six miles stretched out like twelve.

It was a weary little body that limped slowly into Danbury about three o'clock. And now that he was there, he didn't know what to do with himself. He wouldn't try the door of the railway station to see if it was open, because that would be the first place they'd look for him. Uptown there was an all-night lunchroom with steam on the glass that tempted him sorely, but that was too public, too. Nothing for it but to tramp until morning, he told himself dismally, unless he could find a public bench on which to park his weary bones.

Lee ascended further into the town, always looking for a bench. There were no benches, but he came to a church, and a light in front illumined a sign on the door reading:

THIS CHURCH IS ALWAYS OPEN
FOR MEDITATION AND PRAYER.

That's my dish! thought Lee; meditation and prayer. He went in. The chancel was dimly lighted; the body of the church almost dark. These are true Christians! Lee said to himself upon discovering that the pews were cushioned. By piling several of the flat cushions upon each other, he contrived a very comfortable bed, and, stretching himself out, was almost instantly asleep.

WHEN HE AWOKE it was approaching traintime. With what dignity he could muster, he walked downtown, unhappily aware of his frowsy state and his unshaven chin. No one appeared to take any notice of him. The train, which was made up in Danbury, was standing in the station. Lee boldly bought a ticket. Let them stop me now if they want, he said to himself. I have as much right to visit Danbury as any other citizen. Nobody stopped him. He bought a New York newspaper and, boarding the train, settled down to read the leading story, the facts of which he knew so much better than the man who had written it.

Somebody had tipped off the police that George Restorick was dining with a Miss Clara Moore on West Forty-seventh Street. When they got there the bird had flown. For awhile they were baffled, but upon the finding of the empty hangar on the roof of the hotel adjoining, the method of his escape became clear. The manager of the hotel said of course he knew that Mr. Restorick kept a heliocopter on the roof, but he did not know that it had been flown away that night. Why hadn't he informed the police about the heliocopter? Why should he? Mr. Restorick owned the building, and if he wanted to keep a heliocopter or a hippopotamus on the roof, that was certainly his privilege.

About one o'clock the pilot, Captain Warren, had the effrontery to bring the heliocopter back and to stow it in its hangar. At first he had refused to tell the police where he had been. He was charged with having aided in the escape of a fugitive from justice, and locked up. Later, it became known that George Restorick had landed from the machine at his own place, Black Maple, in Connecticut. Police were watching there. They had heard the engine of the heliocopter as it came down and had even had a glimpse of it as it took off. But George Restorick had disappeared as if the earth had opened and swallowed him. The whole state of Connecticut was being combed for him.

The train started. Lee, satisfied that his part in the night's adventure was wholly unknown to the police, settled himself for a further sleep.

CHAPTER NINETEEN

ARRIVING AT HOME, Lee ate a generous breakfast in order to restore his forces. He had not by any means had a night's sleep, but he did not mean to go to bed again. After bathing and changing his clothes, he set out for the Pennsylvania Terminal. He had one clue that he had never taken any pains to follow up, since it had not seemed to have any importance; now that matters were approaching a crisis, he determined to find out if there was anything in it. It consisted of the two scraps of partly burned paper that he had retrieved from the fireplace in Mary Stannard's room. One scrap bore a person's name, McCallum, written in a flowing, masculine hand; the other the name of a place, Elkton, Maryland. The handwriting was the same, also the quality of both scraps of paper, and it was a fair inference that they had been parts of the same sheet.

Elkton is about a hundred and fifty miles south of New York, and Lee assumed that he would make better time by train than by hired car. By exerting a little influence, he got the station master at the terminal to order one of the fast Washington trains to pause and let him off at the Maryland town.

He found it a brisk and busy little city exhibiting every style of architecture from early colonial to General Grant. His first act was to consult the telephone directory. There were several McCallums listed; one was a minister, and he suggested himself as the most promising lead. The address given was on the main street, a little north of the center of town, and Lee proceeded in that direction on foot, since his was the sort of business one could hardly open to a stranger on the telephone.

He was astonished by the number of ministers in the town and by the way they advertised their profession. Every fifty yards or so along the main street, there was an immense sign in the yard of one of the little wooden houses, with provision for lighting at night and bearing the legend: MINISTER: MARRIAGES PERFORMED. There were more ministers than churches. Lee was reminded that Elkton had long served as a Gretna Green for runaway couples from the neighboring states. Even though the laws of Maryland had lately been amended to make hasty marriages more difficult, the ministers were still doing business, it seemed.

Mr. McCallum was a typical minister, tall and thin, with a self-acting Adam's apple, and dressed in black. He appeared to be disappointed upon seeing that Lee had no lady with him. However, he received his visitor with professional graciousness and led him into a prim little parlor. Lee looked around him uneasily; how many hundreds of couples had been linked together "for life" in that room, and what proportion of them had flown apart?

It immediately appeared that he had come to the right place. The Reverend McCallum readily acknowledged that the writing on the scraps of paper was his own. He said that the scraps had undoubtedly formed a part of one of the marriage certificates he was accustomed to issue. This confirmed Lee's fears, and his heart sank. The Reverend McCallum looked up his records and, to make a long story short, Lee obtained *half* a clue to the mystery that tormented him—but only half.

He was back in New York soon after three o'clock. On the first newsstand he happened to pass, he saw in black headlines four inches tall:

RESTORICK IN CUSTODY

This hardly surprised him. He knew that it was impossible for a man whose photograph had been published in every newspaper in the country to remain for long out of the clutches of the police.

The story under the headlines described how Restorick had been stopped by customs men at the Canadian border near Rouse's Point, New York and, being recognized, had been taken into custody. Upon being notified by telephone, Inspector Loasby had immediately dispatched men by plane to Plattsburg, the nearest commercial airport, and Restorick was already on his way back to New York in the care of these men. He was expected to arrive at police headquarters about four. He had made no attempt to resist arrest, and had willingly accompanied the New York detectives. So he had kept his promise!

Lee visited one of the most prominent of the theatrical agencies in New York, where he had little difficulty in matching up the other half of the clue he had obtained in Elkton. He now had the beginning of a real case, but his heart was sore. Naturally he did not care to take the theatrical agent into his confidence, and he left a burning curiosity behind him.

It was now after four o'clock, and Lee proceeded by taxi to police headquarters. Inspector Loasby was in high feather.

Lee, wasting no time in beating around the bush, said at once: "I want to see Restorick."

Loasby ran up his eyebrows, affecting to be greatly surprised. "Impossible, my dear fellow!" he said. "Nobody can see him until after the police have finished their examination. Not even you!"

Lee was not impressed by the exhibition of surprise. Fixing Loasby with a steady eye, he said: "In that case, I shall be obliged to tell the newspapers the true story of what occurred in my apartment a few nights ago."

Loasby undertook to bluster a little. "You dare not! You would only be convicting yourself of assisting in the escape of a fugitive."

"I'll take that chance," said Lee. "The man will soon be exonerated, anyhow."

"Have you got something new?" Loasby demanded eagerly.

"Plenty," said Lee.

"What is it?"

"I have no intention of telling you," said Lee. "I warned you some days ago that I no longer felt bound to work with you."

"Well, it wouldn't make very pretty reading that Restorick had offered you a hundred grand to get him off," said Loasby.

"Go ahead and publish," said Lee calmly. "When I get him off it will establish my rate of pay."

"You can't see him until the police are through with him," growled Loasby.

Lee maintained an unruffled front. "I am not a lawyer," he said, "and I have no legal standing. Nevertheless I am, as you have just pointed out, Restorick's duly constituted representative, and if I am not permitted to see him and now . . ."

"He didn't resist arrest this time," said Loasby. "Not a finger has been laid on him!"

"He promised me he wouldn't resist," said Lee.

"Have you seen him . . . since that night?" Loasby demanded in a voice sharp with curiosity.

"That is neither here nor there. If I am not allowed to see him now, I shall sue out a writ and the whole story will have to come out. Rather damaging to the morale of the police, as you said yourself. Particularly since an untrue version of the affair has been given to the press."

Loasby began to weaken. "If he's innocent, what do you want to see him about?"

"Just a friendly visit," said Lee, "to tell him to keep his heart up."

"Oh, all right," grumbled Loasby. "You'll have to submit to the usual conditions."

"If you want to have me searched first, it's all right with me," said Lee. "And I'm perfectly willing to have a policeman posted at the door to watch that I don't pass anything to the accused man. But I must insist on counsel's privilege of speaking to the accused without being overheard by a policeman."

"All right," said Loasby.

NOTWITHSTANDING Loasby's earlier boast that the multimillionaire should be treated just like any ordinary malefactor, Restorick was not put into a cell at headquarters, but was given one of the fairly

comfortable rooms that are used for the detention of essential wit-
nesses and such other persons. It had a barred window looking
out on the quaint little street that runs behind police headquarters. Besides the prisoner, there were two detectives in the room,
but upon Lee's entrance they went out. In fact, it might almost be
said that they beat a retreat. Restorick was walking up and down
the fifteen-foot space like a caged animal. A uniformed officer remained standing in the open doorway throughout Lee's visit.

"Well," Restorick said truculently to Lee, "You see I didn't get
away with it!"

"No need to reproach yourself for that," said Lee mildly. "I knew
it was impossible."

"What do you want of me?" demanded Restorick.

Lee, who was beginning to know the man, was not at all put
about by this graceless welcome. "Just a friendly visit," he said.

"Hunh!" said Restorick. "If you're a friend of mine I'm surprised
they let you see me."

"Well, I had to exert a little pressure!" said Lee airily. "I assume they have been questioning you pretty closely."

"Every minute since I was taken," said Restorick. "In relays. I
tell you, Mappin, I almost broke a blood vessel in the effort to keep
my promise not to slug them. But now I'm getting accustomed to
it. After all, I have nothing on my conscience."

They sat down in two chairs near the barred window, entirely
out of hearing of the policeman at the door.

"I wanted to reassure you," said Lee, "that they have only a *talking* case against you. It won't stand up for long."

"What have they that's new?"

"They have dug up a witness in Mount Vernon who is prepared
to swear that he saw you driving the Black Maple truck through a
street at Pelham, and turning into the yard of the house where the
body was found next morning."

"I was in Mexico City that night."

"I know it. The man is so obviously lying no jury will believe
him."

"I didn't make any friends in Mexico City," said Restorick, "but I am sure there are people there who will remember me and can testify that I was there that night."

"Don't worry," said Lee calmly. "You were under surveillance by operatives hired by me from the moment you landed in Mexico and every hour you were there. They can testify in your defense."

"Well, I'll be damned!" said Restorick, staring.

"Part of my job," said Lee.

"You're a caution!" said Restorick.

"I wanted to warn you," said Lee, lowering his voice, "that the police may keep up the questioning all night—in relays."

"That doesn't bother me," said Restorick indifferently. "I'm a healthy man. I'm not going to break down through lack of a little sleep. . . . Besides," he went on with a hard grin, "I have a way of getting back at them. Haven't you noticed how thin-skinned some cops are?"

"How do you mean?"

"They can't stand ridicule. I have already routed a couple of them."

"Good!" said Lee.

"The hell with my case, anyhow," said Restorick. "I didn't commit this murder and I defy them to hang it on me. What I want to know is, *who did?* You're supposed to be at the head of your profession, and God knows I've offered you a proper fee. Why the hell can't you find out?"

"I made some progress today," said Lee cautiously. "Enough, anyhow, to formulate a theory that holds water at every joint so far. I won't tell you what it is, because I don't want to raise any false hopes. You must give me a little more time to collect evidence to support my theory. I can promise you that I will find it."

Oddly enough, Restorick did not press him to say more. "Is it bad?" he asked, scowling blackly.

"Yes, it's bad," said Lee frankly. "It hurt me like hell, and it's going to hurt you. But it's the truth, and anything is better than this maddening uncertainty."

"You're right about that," said Restorick gloomily. "I'll give you your own time." His face changed. "You're a funny little son-of-a-gun," he said almost wistfully. "I'm beginning to feel that after this nightmare is over, you and I can be friends."

"Why not?" said Lee.

"I never had a friend," said Restorick harshly, "except perhaps Mary, and she was a woman; that's not what I mean. I couldn't let myself go with Mary; I was too crazy about her. The trouble is, I'm too damn rich. I've been surrounded since birth by lickspittles and toadies, and that seemed to make the good eggs, the decent fellows, sheer off."

"Well, you can have me for a friend, such as I am," said Lee. "And friendship is catching, you know. One friend always leads to others."

Restorick hit Lee a slap on the back that made him cough. "Get the hell out of here!" he said. "Get down to business and clean up this dirty mess."

"Okay," said Lee. "So long!"

LEE WENT HOME to get his dinner. Before he ate, he called up Stan Oberry at his home. Stan had nothing significant to report.

"I'm still keeping Amy Dordress under surveillance more or less," he said. "I use different operatives every day. All amateurs, and the cleverest I can get. It's a difficult job because that Jane suspects everybody who approaches her. She's as slippery as an eel."

"I know it," said Lee, "but you'll hook her in the end. Everything depends on it now. She must have some damn good reason for not leaving town, where she'd be out of our reach."

"I'll keep in touch with you," said Stan.

When Lee had eaten his dinner and smoked his cigar, he prepared to go to bed in order to make up his lost sleep.

He said to Jermyn, his leathery and angular manservant: "Jermyn, have you noticed at what hour of the morning it becomes fully light at this season?"

"About five, sir."

"Very well, I'll have to get up at four-thirty tomorrow. Would you mind having some coffee ready for me? I'll pick up breakfast later, wherever I may be."

Jermyn's face worked oddly. "Would I mind, sir? Certainly not. It shouldn't be necessary for you to ask such a question, sir."

"Just a matter of polite form, Jermyn. Good night."

CHAPTER TWENTY

AT FIVE O'CLOCK NEXT MORNING, Lee was standing on the corner of
First Avenue and Fifty-first, looking thoughtfully down the side
street. Mary Stannard's little house was about halfway through this
block on the north side. Fifty-first, like all the odd-numbered
streets, was westbound and if, as Lee suspected, Mary had been
picked up by a car in this block on the night she was murdered, the
car must have continued westward at least as far as Second Avenue.
But Lee had reason to believe that the car had made its way downtown by First Avenue, so he did not trouble himself to make the
long detour around by Second Avenue.

Continuing down First Avenue, he paused on each corner to
look into the cross streets. Lee's knowledge of New York streets
was both prodigious and precise. It was due to the fact that his
principal diversion was walking through the streets, particularly
out-of-the-way streets. Whenever he came to a street that he had
not walked through before, he could never resist the impulse to
explore it, and he never forget any salient feature.

Just at present, he was looking for a street that would make a
perfect setting for the kind of crime he had doped out. He remem-
bered the exact look of the street, and the fact that it ran east from
First Avenue to the river, but he had forgotten its number. Of
course, there might be more than one street that would serve
equally well, so he took care to examine every cross street to see if
it fitted the facts so far as known to him.

198

Some of these streets running east ended on a high terrace above the East River; others ran downhill to join the new East River Drive. It was one of the low streets Lee was looking for. The last time he had walked this way, this section of the drive had not been completed, and that altered the look of the terrain a good deal.

Lee had walked half a mile before he found the street he was looking for. It was East Fortieth Street, a block not more than two hundred yards long, stretching from First Avenue to the East River Drive. The left-hand side of the block was entirely filled by a meat-packing establishment, the right-hand side by a station of the Electric Light and Power Company. It had never been considered worthwhile to repave this block, and the original stones were still in place, now very rough and uneven. No motorist would have chosen to drive through it, unless he had a special reason for doing so.

Lee could see by the look of the pavements that many trucks were accustomed to come and go to the loading platforms of the meat-packing concern. Beyond that point, there was so little traffic that spears of grass were actually struggling up between some of the stones. The electric light station received its coal from barges in the river. After nightfall, the short street must be absolutely deserted; moreover, the loud hum of the huge generators in the electric light plant would drown any inconvenient noises. There were no openings in this building at the street level. In all New York, a man could hardly have found a more suitable place to commit a quiet murder after dark.

It was possible, of course, that the loading platforms of the meat concern might be open on certain nights, so Lee started his search lower down. Even in a one-way street, a motorist who draws up for a moment naturally pulls over to the right, and Lee started looking in the gutter on that side. With a magnifying glass in one hand and a tiny folding rake in the other (another tool of his trade), he scratched in the film of mud that covered the stones. There was at this hour nobody in sight who might have taken an interest in these odd proceedings.

When Lee undertook a search, he searched. It was beautiful to watch his skill and patience. First marking off the ground roughly in squares with chalk, he went over it inch by inch, alternately squatting on his hunkers or going down on hands and knees. His figure was ill-suited to this kind of exercise, and he often had to stop and sit down on the edge of the curb to rest and stretch his legs. I'll feel this in my knees for a week, he thought ruefully. It was in his mind, too, that it might not be on this side of the street, after all, and that he must search the whole pavement from curb to curb before he could give up. Also, somebody might already have found what he was looking for, but this seemed unlikely because the object was so small.

After two hours of grueling work, he actually found it. He cleaned the tiny object and looked at it lying on his hand with a kind of surprise. This was what he was looking for, yet it was wonderful that he had found it! It was an unset diamond, not very large nor greatly valuable, but a veritable diamond washed by the rains under a film of mud.

Lee hobbled back to First Avenue and, picking up a taxicab, had himself carried to a hotel where he could obtain the breakfast he was so badly in need of. By the time he had finished eating and smoking, the stores were open and he proceeded to the magnificent establishment of Tiffany and Company on Fifth Avenue. His card gained him admission to the office of one of the executives, to whom he showed the little diamond.

"This," he said, "came out of a ring sold by you, if my calculations are right. Can you help me trace the sale?" Lee told him the markings he had found on the inside of the ring and the approximate date of the sale, as suggested by the entry in the Reverend McCallum's register of weddings.

After a wait of some minutes in the office of the executive, his man returned. "A ring such as you have described was sold to Mr. Amasa Johnson shortly before the date you mentioned. It contained a diamond like this. Of course, nobody here could swear that it was this particular diamond, but if the ring is produced, one of our experts could almost certainly tell if this diamond had been knocked out of that setting. In the meantime, we can testify that the diamond in that ring was of precisely the same weight as this diamond, and was cut in the same style."

"That is all I could expect," said Lee. "The ring itself will be produced in due course. And thank you very much."

LEE IMMEDIATELY CALLED UP Stan Oberry. Stan had nothing to report. Shortly before one o'clock, however, Stan called Lee at his apartment.

"I've got something for you at last, Mr. Mappin. The operative I put on the trail of Miss Amy Dordress this morning succeeded in following her to the — Hotel without being discovered."

(The hotel mentioned by Stan is one of the most fashionable and expensive in New York. Its name will not be mentioned, because the management was in no wise responsible for what happened, and a hotel, like Caesar's wife, naturally must guard its reputation.)

Stan continued: "Amy Dordress often goes to such places to lunch with friends, or by herself, but today, instead of entering one of the restaurants, she went up in an elevator, without any suspicion that she was followed. My operative went up in the same elevator. Miss Dordress got out at the seventeenth floor. My operative could not follow her, because that would have meant instant recognition. She went on to an upper floor.

"The — Hotel, as you may know, keeps a telephone operator on every floor. My operative, by the use of a judicious bribe, learned from the switchboard girl on the seventeenth floor that Miss Dordress had entered Room 1709 without knocking. She is still there and evidently intends to remain for some time, for an order had just been received by room service to send up lunch for two to 1709. My operative learned at the office that 1709 is occupied by a Mr. Amasa Johnson, but I don't suppose that means anything to you. Undoubtedly an assumed name."

Lee was smiling broadly. "On the contrary, it happens to be the fellow's right name. We have them, Stan! I shall go around to the hotel at once, and I will telephone Inspector Loasby to follow me. This is a police matter now."

"Can't I get in on it?" said Stan wistfully.

"You can wait down in the lobby if you like, but you had better not come upstairs unless I send for you. We don't want to make too much trouble for such a high-toned hotel."

"Okay, Mr. Mappin."

Lee then called headquarters. Getting Loasby on the wire, he said: "Mappin speaking."

"Oh, how are you," said Loasby, in a pretty cool voice.

"You will remember," said Lee, "that I promised to call on you as soon as I considered that the time was ripe to make an arrest in the Stannard case. Well, the time has come. The murderer and his accomplice are in Room 1709 at the — Hotel. They have just ordered lunch served in that room . . ."

"My God!" shouted Loasby. "Who the hell? . . ."

"The murderer's name is Amasa Johnson," said Lee with a wicked smile. "He's registered at the —. Come right up and bring three men with you. Better wear plain clothes in order to avoid creating excitement in the hotel. But use your authority to gain entrance to Room 1709. Break down the door, if necessary."

"For God's sake, explain yourself!" cried Loasby.

Lee hung up, grinning still. He knew Loasby would come.

Five minutes later, Lee was getting out of the elevator on the seventeenth floor of the —. To the telephone switchboard operator who looked at him inquiringly, he said: "I'm expecting a friend. He'll be up directly."

"What room?" she asked automatically.

"He didn't say. Just said to wait for him."

She yawned delicately behind her hand.

"Not much doing on the floor switchboard, I suppose," said Lee sympathetically.

"You're right, mister. It's as dull as dishwater. There's some activity in the evenings sometimes, but I'm off then. If I don't get transferred I'm going to chuck my job."

Lee thought: There'll be plenty of excitement in a few minutes, my girl.

Two waiters got out of an elevator pushing a wheeled tray with luncheon under covers. Lee followed them idly down the hall, suspecting that the lunch was for 1709. It was. Knocking on the door, the waiters were admitted and went in, leaving the door slightly ajar. The temptation was too much for Lee. He pushed the door open and followed them into the room.

Amy Dordress, very stylishly attired, was lounging in an easy chair near the window. On the other side of the room stood Jack Fentress, watching the waiters arranging the luncheon on a table.

"Hello, you two!" said Lee. "I saw you when they opened the door and I took the liberty of barging in."

Neither answered. Lee loved to watch the changing expressions of the human countenance, and this provided him with an exceptional opportunity. The woman and the man stared at him, exchanged a lightning glance, then stared at him again. But whereas the woman's face turned red with anger, the man was both angry and frightened.

Not a word was said until the waiters had finished arranging the lunch table.

"Does madame wish me to bring another service?" one asked.

"No!" said Amy. "You may go!"

The waiters eased themselves softly out of the room.

"I see you are about to have lunch," said Lee cheerily. "I've had mine. Go right ahead and I'll just sit here and watch you."

After another and briefer silence, Amy said sharply to Jack: "Well, aren't you going to invite him to leave?"

Jack's glance quailed. "He's a friend," he muttered.

"Friend nothing!" cried Amy. "He's had it in for us from the first! I saw it in his eye!" . . . She approached Lee with flashing eyes. "Get out!" she said.

Lee stood his ground. "Sorry you're taking it this way," he said. "I have a little business to transact with Jack—and with you!"

It was noticeable that neither of them asked what was the nature of the business.

"He's only bluffing!" said Amy. She was careful to restrain her tendency to scream when she was outside her own house. "He can't hang anything on you! It's impossible! Aren't you man enough to tell him to go?"

Jack succeeded in pulling himself together partly. "She's right, Mr. Mappin. Whatever you want, you've got no right to push yourself into a person's room unannounced and uninvited. Get out!" He pulled a gun from his back pocket.

Lee smiled. "That won't do you any good. The police have been notified and are on the way here. If they find another body, it won't improve your case any."

Jack's brief access of courage failed him. He turned the gun over in his hands, looking down at it with a sick desire. Lee could read the thought in his mind, and so could Amy. The woman was the quicker. Springing across the room, she snatched the gun out of Jack's hands and sent it spinning out of the open window. It was never recovered. The huge hotel has so many terraces and off-sets that it probably never reached the street.

"It would have been better," muttered Jack, looking after the gun.

"For God's sake, get a grip on yourself!" cried Amy. "Where's your manhood? Where's your courage?" The words tumbled out on each other. "This little meddler has no standing. He's just try-ing to trap you!"

Jack muttered to Lee, scowling: "What did you come here for?"

"Well," said Lee, "a free confession would save the state time and money."

"Not a word!" cried Amy.

"Not going to," muttered Jack.

"You see . . . you see," she went on. "He hasn't got a thing on you. He's only fishing for information."

"Don't try me too far," murmured Lee. "My business has brought me into contact with some pretty low characters, but of all the human swine I've ever known, this one . . ."

"You lie!" cried Amy. "If you won't leave this room, we will!"

Lee backed against the door.

Amy turned to Jack and whispered a word.

Lee, reading her lips, slowly shook his head. "No good," he said. He pointed to the telephone. "The alarm would be spread before you reached the bottom of the first flight of stairs."

They gaped at him.

"To try to escape would be an admission of guilt," said Lee.

There was a silence, followed by a sharp rapping on the door.

"And now it's too late," added Lee. He opened the door and stood aside.

Inspector Loasby entered with three of his detectives. Several people, who had recognized the police in spite of their plain clothes and had followed them into the elevator, tried to peer into the room from behind. Lee closed the door in their faces.

Lee said in his mild way: "You had better station a man at each window, Inspector, and one at the bathroom door. This man is quite capable of throwing himself out."

It was done. Jack Fentress' face was gray with fear, but the woman kept her chin up.

"What accusation do you bring against these people?" Loasby asked of Lee.

"This man," said Lee, "killed Mary Stannard by strangulation. This woman was his accomplice both before and after the fact."

"He lies!" screeched Amy.

"Must . . . must be out of his wits," stammered Jack.

"Mr. Mappin does not bring such charges lightly," said Loasby. "You must both consider yourselves under arrest. Do you wish to make a statement at this time? I must warn you, of course, that anything you say can be used against you later."

"Nothing to say," said Amy and Jack together.

Loasby looked at Lee. "I must have more to go on before I can take these people into custody."

"I'll tell you the whole story," said Lee. "Let us sit down."

Nobody sat but Lee himself.

"Does any man here write shorthand?" asked Lee. "If he can take down what I say, it will save me the fag of repeating it later."

"Watrous does," said Loasby, nodding toward the man by the bathroom door.

Watrous produced a notebook and pencil.

CHAPTER TWENTY-ONE

"I SUSPECTED JACK FENTRESS from the beginning," began Lee, "because his anger at being stood up at the altar, as he claimed, seemed to be tinged with anxiety. And more so on the following day, when it began to appear that Mary Stannard had been prevented from attending her wedding, there was fear mixed with his grief."

"Very interesting," said Loasby dryly. "We all know what a great psychologist Mr. Mappin is, but this is hardly evidence."

"Wait a minute," said Lee. "I haven't started yet. . . . The first time I interviewed Miss Dordress it was clear to me that she, like so many other women, had fallen in love with Jack Fentress—strange, isn't it?—and I inferred that she had offered him a handsome settlement if he married her.

"But, having progressed so far, I confess I was baffled for many days because I couldn't understand why, if Fentress wanted to marry Miss Dordress and her millions, he didn't just throw over Mary Stannard. It's done every day. It was not until yesterday that I discovered that Mary Stannard and Jack Fentress had been man and wife for more than a year. Then I saw the light. I got the entry from the register of the Reverend McCallum, in Elkton, Maryland."

"Pardon the interruption," said Loasby, "but with all the publicity about this case, why didn't the minister come forward and tell about this marriage?"

"Because they were married under different names: Mary Baker and Amasa Johnson. Mary Baker I recognized at once, because I knew that was my friend's real name. I have met some of her people.

She thought Mary Baker was too ordinary a name to win fame on the stage. Amasa Johnson meant nothing to me, but when I got back to New York, I went to the theatrical agency with whom Fentress does business, and the agent told me at once that it was he himself who had advised his client to change his name for professional reasons. Amasa Johnson would never do for a juvenile or leading man, he said. So he became John, or Jack Fentress."

"This was yesterday," said Loasby. "Why didn't you tell me at once?"

"Because, though I was then perfectly sure of the man's guilt, I lacked a piece of essential evidence. I found that only this morning. . . . Better let me tell the story in my own way, Inspector."

"Go ahead! Go ahead!" said Loasby hastily.

"I knew Mary Stannard quite well," said Lee. "She was an especially frank and candid girl. So I know she must have chafed under this secret marriage, especially when other men fell in love with her, thinking her free. So when her play closed recently and she saw a holiday ahead, she insisted on ending the anomalous situation and on being publicly married in a church."

"Why didn't Fentress just divorce her?" suggested Loasby, "if he had fallen in love with another girl?"

"Let's leave love out of it," said Lee dryly.

Amy Dordress touched a handkerchief to her perfectly dry eyes. "Do I have to sit here and submit to being insulted?" she whimpered.

"I can have you taken down to headquarters if you'd rather," said Loasby, "and let Mr. Mappin tell me his story in private."

She quickly changed her tune. "No, I want to hear it," she said, with a toss of her head. "It's so preposterous, it's funny!"

"I suppose Fentress could have divorced Mary," Lee resumed. "No doubt men can get divorces in Reno as well as women. But he's a public character, remember, and just consider how he would have appeared in the public eye. To throw over a girl like Mary Stannard for the Dordress millions. It would have made him out both a cur and a fool. It seemed better to him to put her out of the way and pose as a jilted bridegroom. Mary's insistence on a public marriage gave him just the opportunity he wanted, and of course he fell in with it."

"How could he have done such a thing?" murmured Loasby with a glance at Amy's ugly, twisted face.

"In order to live without working," answered Lee. "In a certain type of man, that is the strongest motive of all. . . ."

"He and his partner," Lee went on, "laid one of the most devilishly clever plots—on paper—that I have ever met with. It ought to have succeeded; it would have succeeded had it not been for a succession of accidents impossible to foresee. That, luckily for justice, is what prospective murderers so often overlook, the possibility of accidents beyond their control."

Amy affected a bored air. "The man is talking utter nonsense," she said, glancing out of the window.

"On the night arranged for the marriage," said Lee, "it was arranged between Jack and Mary that Jack should pick her up in his car in Fifty-first Street where she lived, and drive her to the church. But it was not to be directly in front of her house, because her grandfather, Major Dunphy, disliked Jack very much and they didn't want him to know their plans. Meanwhile, the plotters knew that earlier that Sunday evening Ewart Blanding was going to call on Mary to leave her some flowers, because it had been talked about at a party the night before.

"Here's where the first accident occurred. After Blanding had left Mary, and before it was quite time for Fentress to pick her up, Mary ran around the corner to pay a call on an old friend, George Restorick. It was purely an impulse of affection. Mary valued Restorick as a friend, though she had refused to marry him. She thought he was angry with her, and she wanted to square herself with her, if she could, before the ceremony. Knowing Restorick's character as she did, she believed that it would be the last time she would ever see him. She didn't tell anybody about this call, certainly not Jack Fentress, because the two men hated each other.

"She was probably a minute or two late in keeping her engagement with Fentress in Fifty-first Street. What they said to each other, of course I do not know. But I do know that she never left

Fentress' car alive. Fentress, in describing his movements that
night to me, said that he drove downtown by way of First Avenue,
and since it is my experience that a liar always works in as much
truth as he safely can, I assumed that he *had* driven down First
Avenue.

"There are many deserted little streets running from First Avenue
east to the river, and I assumed that the murder had taken place in
one of these. There is one street in particular that offered an ideal
situation for murder. It is East Fortieth Street. Fentress turned
into that street and stopped his car. What excuse he gave Mary for
this detour I don't know. Probably, like a modern Judas, he told her
he couldn't wait any longer for a kiss. At any rate, he strangled her
in that deserted street and, when life was extinct, he shoved her
body into the luggage compartment of his car and locked it."

"Wait a minute! Wait a minute!" interrupted Loasby. "What
proof have you that this took place in Fortieth Street?"

"That is the essential piece of evidence I just referred to," answered Lee. "You will remember that, when Mary's body was found,
the diamond in her ring was missing. You showed me the ring yourself. It was not robbery, because she was wearing a string of pearls
and a wrist watch worth many times the value of that little diamond. So it was obvious that it had fallen out. I often wondered
why Mary had such an affection for that ring. She always wore it,
even when she was in a position to buy much more expensive jewelry. When I looked inside the ring, I saw the legend A.J. to M.B.,
and Tiffany's mark. Of course, A.J. meant nothing to me then, but
now I know. It was Mary's engagement ring. She couldn't wear a
wedding ring, so all her affection was concentrated on this little
diamond.

"Well, Mary was strong for a woman, though of course no match
for Fentress. There was undoubtedly a struggle in the car when his
hands closed around her throat. During the struggle her hand
knocked against the outside of the door and the diamond was
thrown out of the ring. I found it this morning, hidden in the mud
of the gutter on Fortieth Street. At Tiffany's they told me it was of
the same weight and same style of cutting as that in the ring sold

to Amasa Johnson on such and such a date. When the ring is produced, their experts can testify positively whether or not it is the stone that came out of that ring."

"Well, I'm damned!" murmured Loasby.

"After he had locked the body in the luggage compartment," Lee went on, "Fentress proceeded to the church, and naturally put on a big show of anger and disappointment when his bride failed to show up. He is an actor, as you know, though not a very good one."

"Incredible!" murmured Loasby.

"A very cunning plan had been made for the disposal of the body," Lee resumed. "Ewart Blanding was deeply in love with Mary, and, as the plotters knew, he had called on her that Sunday night, so they assumed that it could be made to appear that he was the last person to see her alive. Ewart's orders from his mistress were precise for that evening. He was to fetch one of the entertainers to Miss Dordress' musicale and take her home again; then put the car up in the garage. Later in the evening, Fentress, who was provided with a key, was to drive to the Dordress garage and simply transfer the body from his car to the luggage compartment of the red convertible. Now note this well: *Ewart Blanding had been given permission to use the red convertible during the whole of the following day.* The plotters were confident that the crime would be discovered before the day was out.

"Here accident intervened to ruin their plans completely. Blanding did not obey his orders that night, but in a distracted state of mind started blindly driving north, and smashed the red convertible against a tree near Pelham. So Fentress was left with the body on his hands. He stayed that night with his friend, Jim Rutledge. He told me that he had driven over to his own place twice during the night to see if there was any message for him from the missing Mary. This was palpably a falsehood, because he had only to telephone to his own apartment house. What he *did* do, was to drive twice down to the Dordress garage to see if the red car had been returned.

"He was in a bad state of nerves when I saw him in the morning, but that was not surprising. At that stage of the case, I had some reason to suspect that George Restorick might be the guilty man, and Fentress offered to drive me up to Restorick's country place. Little did I suspect that the body of my poor friend drove with us in the luggage compartment behind. While we were looking over the ground at Black Maple, Fentress saw what looked like an ideal place of concealment under the floor of a little, unused pavilion in the grounds.

"After he had put me on the train at Bridgeport, he returned to Black Maple after dark, and, after removing a section of latticework, shoved the body under the floor of the pavilion and carefully covered the traces of his work. He did not know that this pavilion covered an old pit for the storage of ice, and he must have received a shock when he heard the body fall to the bottom of the pit.

"When Fentress returned to town that night, one may be sure there was a violent scene between the two confederates. The woman has a much better head on her than he has, and it would naturally anger her that he presumed to make so important a change in their plans without consulting her. Perhaps Fentress had foreseen she might even doubt that he had carried out his part of the job at all, and in order to prove it, he pinched off one of the blossoms of a spray of orchids that Mary was wearing, and gave it to her.

"Miss Dordress was even angrier, I am sure, when the facts of the smashing of the red car came out, and when it was unexpectedly revealed that Blanding had a woman with him who looked like Mary Stannard, who was lifted out of the car unconscious—or dead; and who subsequently vanished into thin air. Miss Dordress thereupon put the orchid I have referred to in the wreck of the red car, where it was certain to be found, and commanded Fentress to retrieve the body from the place where he had hidden it. Perhaps she accompanied him on that journey back to Black Maple. She is capable of it." Lee glanced at Amy. "No womanly weakness there!

"Fentress had the good fortune to find a piece of rope hanging in the garage at Black Maple. He opened the trap doors leading to the ice pit and, descending the ladder, fastened the rope around the body and drew it up to the surface. He failed to notice, however, that the balance of the spray of orchids had broken off and was left lying in the pit. I found it there. I also found bits of the rotten straw from that pit clinging to the clothes of the poor body when it was discovered. Also the clothes were wet to the skin, and the marks of the rope were still visible. The signs of the opening of the long-closed pit were very imperfectly hidden.

"I don't know whether the body was carried from Black Maple back to Pelham in the little farm truck or in Fentress' own car. It doesn't seem to matter much. It was probably Fentress' car, since there doesn't seem to be any object in doing all that extra driving. Anyhow, we know that the body was shoved through the cellar window of a vacant house opposite the hospital where Blanding had been seen carrying an unconscious woman in his arms.

"But fate—or perhaps we may say Providence—had finally intervened to bring all the plotting of the murderers to nothing. Unknown to them, when they moved the body, the woman who had been with Blanding that night came forward voluntarily to testify. Moreover, when Restorick told the story of Mary's visit to him that night, it was seen to be mathematically impossible for her to have been in Blanding's car when it crashed. Murder will out, they say. I wish I could believe that it was always so, but in this case, at least, the old proverb justified itself."

"Well, in this case fate—or Providence—had considerable assistance from Amos Lee Mappin," said Loasby generously.

Lee shrugged it off. "There's your case, Inspector. Of course I have only given you an outline. There are other bits of supporting evidence I haven't taken the time to mention. You will find that it was Jack Fentress who cried out: 'There goes Ewart Blanding' in Grand Central Concourse."

"There's only one question I'd like to put to you," said Loasby. "How do you account for Mary's wedding handkerchief that was found under the bush in Restorick's garden?"

"At that time," said Lee, "I had no evidence against Fentress, but only an ugly suspicion. And I didn't want to let him see that I was suspicious. I left him standing on the porch at Black Maple while I went in to search the house. I have no doubt that Fentress dropped the handkerchief in the garden himself, and afterwards made sure that I found it."

"Sure!"

Fentress covered his face with a groan.

"Get a grip on yourself!" said Amy Dordress sharply. "This story is only a tissue of speculations. A good lawyer could tear it to pieces in an hour."

"It's no use! It's no use!" groaned Fentress. "It all happened just as he says! There's no use trying to fight a man like that. He's not human! He's a devil!"

Loasby glanced at his man Watrous to make sure that he had taken down this voluntary confession. He had.

Amy Dordress cast a look of unspeakable contempt on the broken man. "The hell with it, then!" she said coolly. "They've got nothing on me!"

"You will both accompany me to headquarters," said Loasby crisply. He moved toward the telephone. "There must be a freight elevator somewhere in this fancy dump, so I can get you out without raising an uproar in the lobby."

It was so done.

As EVERYBODY NOW KNOWS, Amasa Johnson, alias Jack Fentress, was never brought to trial. The crowning touch to this sensational case was furnished when Fentress was found dead in his cell. He had swallowed cyanide of potassium. The plain inference was that Amy Dordress had furnished him with the means, but it could not be proved. Amy had money enough to corrupt almost anybody.

Amy did not kill herself. Not she! She was brought to trial, but in the absence of Fentress the evidence against her (as she had foreseen) was insufficient, and she had to be acquitted, though everybody in the courtroom, including the jury, probably knew in their hearts that she was as guilty as hell. She disappeared from New York and changed her name.

She was still drawing money from her estate, and by this means, some time later, an enterprising reporter succeeded in tracing her to San Francisco, where it was found that she had married a man who knew nothing of her antecedents. The story was a magnificent scoop for the reporter who ferreted it out. Amy's husband immediately divorced her. She changed her name and disappeared again. But, as she must continue to draw money from her agents, no doubt some day, when news is scanty, the episode will be repeated. So it cannot be said that she has escaped scot free for her share in the crime.

LEE MAPPIN MET GEORGE RESTORICK when he was released from custody and had the pleasure of driving him uptown.

"Let's stop at my office, so we can relieve Eversman's mind," said Restorick. "He's a tiresome old granny but he's a good egg. . . . While we're there, I'll have him write you a check."

"The hell with it!" grumbled Lee. "I didn't do this job for money, but for Mary's sake. I've got as much as I want."

"Then we'll give it to charity," said Restorick. "You shall choose the beneficiary."

"How about the Prisoners' Aid Society?" said Lee. "It's not a popular charity. A hundred grand would be a godsend."

"Okay," said Restorick.

"It would please Mary," murmured Lee. "Her kind heart always inclined toward the underdog."

EWART BLANDING, who had been attending law school (under some difficulties) while he worked as a chauffeur, was finally admitted to the bar, and Lee got him a small place with a good firm. Both Lee and Restorick were in a position to throw considerable business his way, and his rise in the firm was rapid.

COACHWHIP PUBLICATIONS

ALSO AVAILABLE

1

HULBERT FOOTNER
THE ADVENTURES OF
MADAME STOREY

ISBN 978-1-61646-236-9

COACHWHIP PUBLICATIONS

COACHWHIPBOOKS.COM

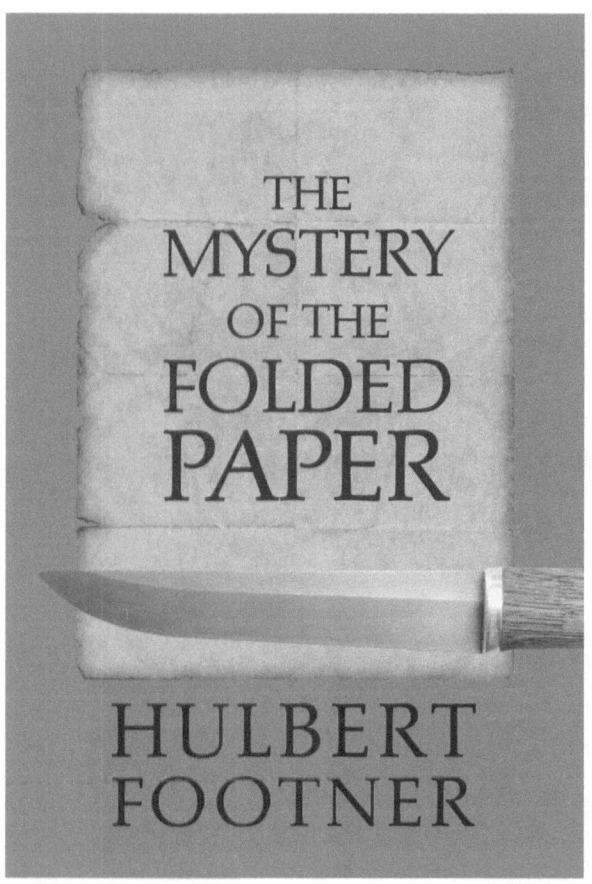

THE
MYSTERY
OF THE
FOLDED
PAPER

HULBERT
FOOTNER

ISBN 978-1-61646-255-8

COACHWHIP PUBLICATIONS

ALSO AVAILABLE

THE HOUSE WITH
THE BLUE DOOR
HULBERT FOOTNER

ISBN 978-1-61646-261-1

COACHWHIP PUBLICATIONS

COACHWHIPBOOKS.COM

WHO KILLED THE
HUSBAND?

HULBERT FOOTNER

ISBN 978-1-61646-256-6

THE MURDER
THAT HAD
EVERYTHING!

HULBURT
FOOTNER

ISBN 978-1-61646-258-2

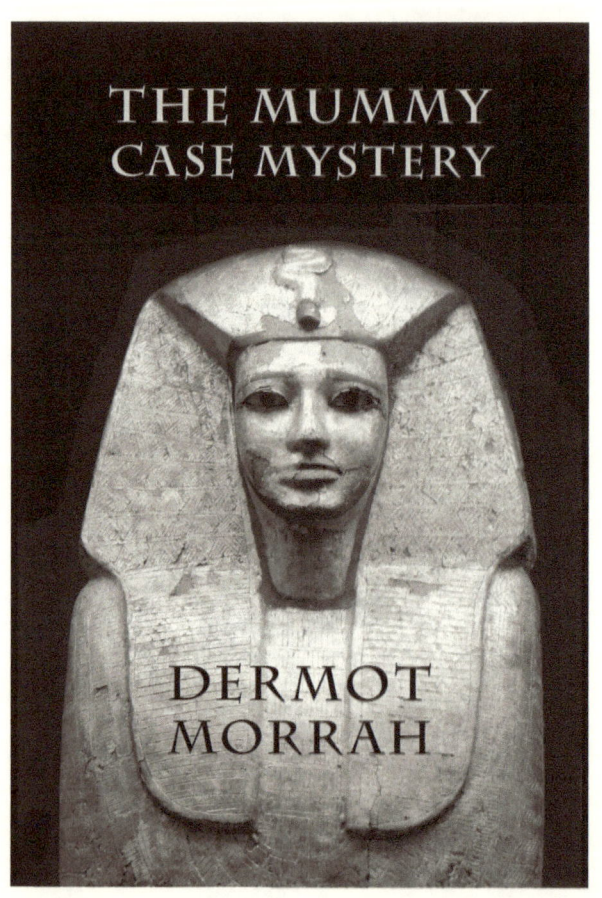

THE MUMMY
CASE MYSTERY

DERMOT
MORRAH

ISBN 978-1-61646-250-7

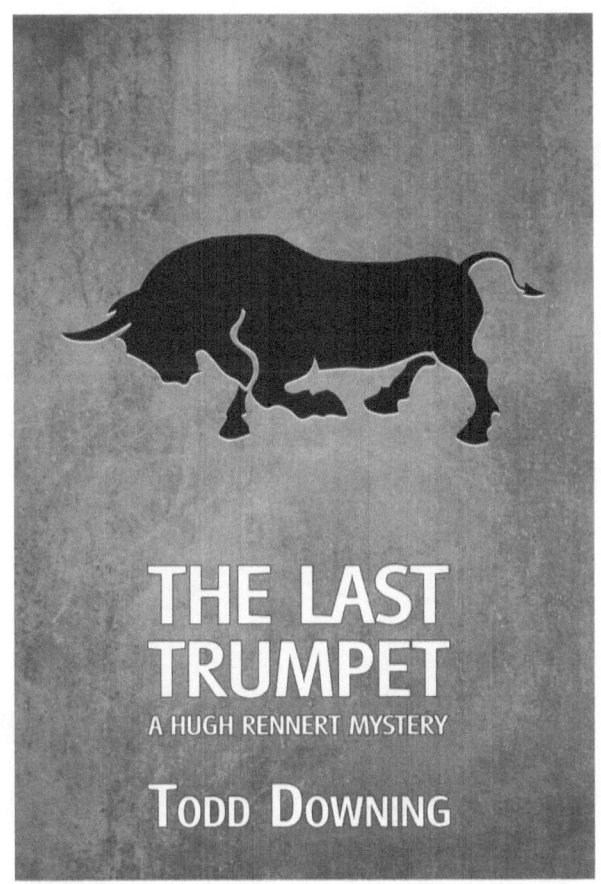

THE LAST
TRUMPET

A HUGH RENNERT MYSTERY

TODD DOWNING

ISBN 978-1-61646-152-2

THE STRAWSTACK
MURDER CASE
KIRKE
MECHEM

ISBN 978-1-61646-179-9

ISBN 978-1-61646-232-1

www.ingramcontent.com/pod-product-compliance
Lightning Source LLC
Chambersburg PA
CBHW031228260626
47169CB00007B/2204